A man's gotta do what a man's gotta do . . .

Using his powerful shoulder, Barlow shoved a big mule out of the way as he neared the Indian. But he was closer than he had realized, and in the next instant, he felt the cold slice of a knife blade tearing into the side of his abdomen, right under the lowest rib. Almost instinctively, he lashed out, smashing the young warrior—a Crow, he noted—in the face.

He reached into his coat to grab his pistol from his belt. He pulled it out and cocked it with the heel of his left palm and began turning toward his left. The other warrior was almost on him in the dim grayness of morning. He fired.

The ball thudded into the warrior's chest and dropped him right there. A couple of mules, made nervous by the gunfire, powder smoke, and all the commotion, shuffled nervously, trampling whatever life may have remained in the Crow.

Wildgun
The Novel

Jack Hanson

J

JOVE BOOKS, NEW YORK

This is a work of fiction. Names, characters, places, and incidents are either the products of the author's imagination or are used fictitiously, and any resemblance to actual persons, living or dead, business establishments, events or locales is entirely coincidental.

WILDGUN

A Jove Book / published by arrangement with
the author

PRINTING HISTORY
Jove edition / October 1999

The Penguin Putnam Inc. World Wide Web site address is
http://www.penguinputnam.com

ISBN: 0-515-12656-X

A JOVE BOOK®
Jove Books are published by The Berkley Publishing Group,
a division of Penguin Putnam Inc.,
375 Hudson Street, New York, New York 10014.
JOVE and the "J" design
are trademarks belonging to Penguin Putnam Inc.

PRINTED IN THE UNITED STATES OF AMERICA

10 9 8 7 6 5 4 3 2 1

Wildgun

The Novel

Prologue

"ANNA!" WILL BARLOW yelled, racing out of the still smoldering cabin. *"Anna!"*

He stopped, heart pounding in fear and rage as he waited to hear the voice of his almost three-year-old daughter. But only the soft sighing of the wind came to him in the otherwise peculiar silence. He knelt. "All right, Buffler," he said urgently to the huge black Newfoundland, "we've got to find our Anna. You git what I'm sayin' to you, dog? We got to find our little girl. Can you find her for me? Can you?"

Barlow didn't know whether the dog understood or not, but the Newfoundland turned and his nose checked out the air around them. Suddenly the huge dog trotted off around the side of the cabin and into the woods, with Barlow close behind.

The minutes dragged on, each one slower than the next, as Barlow and Buffalo had searched all around the cabin. More than once, Barlow was certain that the Newfoundland had picked up the scent of the fiendish devils who had destroyed his home. But each time he thought the dog had found the trail of the savages, it turned out to be a false one.

After some time of searching the bank on the cabin side of the stream, Barlow took the dog, his constant companion, to the other side and commenced a new search. He figured that the Indians who had committed the heinous acts back in the cabin had used the stream to cover their tracks. Thinking they might have ridden or walked in the water for some distance before coming out, Barlow and Buffalo worked the far bank for more than a mile in each direction. Barlow cursed himself for his lack of tracking skill. It was one ability he had never really been able to master, and it had never seemed important—until now.

But all the searching proved futile. He could find no trace of the beasts who had, in the span of less than an hour, he estimated, destroyed everything that he held dear on this earth. Sick at heart, he splashed woodenly across the stream, heading back toward the cabin.

The cabin was still smoldering, as it had been when he had thundered up the little rise and jerked his blowing mule to a halt not so long ago. The eerie silence lingered, too, broken only by an occasional hiss as a drop of old rain hit hot wood and evaporated. He stopped several feet from where the door had been. It had been torn loose and flung off to the side. He supposed he should be thankful that only a portion of the house had collapsed. The fire had not fully taken hold, something not at all unusual in this part of Oregon country, where it rained damn near every day. But the house meant nothing to him any more. Hadn't meant a damn thing since the moment an hour or so earlier when he had edged his way inside and saw the two brutalized bodies lying in still-fresh blood.

Whoever the raiders had been had taken their time, apparently secure in the knowledge that he was off on a hunt and wouldn't be back until close to dark. Barlow's stomach knotted again at the thought. He was loathe to go back in there, though he knew he had to. The thought of his wife, Sarah, and infant son, Will Junior, lying there in their butchered vulnerability heated the blood in his veins.

But little Anna could still be alive. And, unless she became too much of a burden, there was a damn good chance she would stay alive. Barlow figured Anna would be given to some family in the perpetrators' band to be raised as one of their own.

His shoulders straightened and his jawline hardened as the vow formed in his head: I will not let them keep her. And then the promise came out in words: "I'll find you, Anna," he bellowed to the sky. "I'll find you, girl, and bring you back!"

He looked down at the Newfoundland. His chest was still constricted with pain and loss, but he felt a little better now that he had a definite mission ahead—and a solemn promise to fulfill.

"C'mon, Buffler," he said, a sense of urgency suddenly gripping him, "we got work to do." He trotted to the corral, set his rifle down against the rickety log fence, and climbed inside. A minute later, he had two more mules tied to his string.

Then he steeled himself and walked purposefully inside the cabin. He grabbed a couple of the thick Hudson's Bay blankets he and his wife favored for sleeping, as well as for making into warm winter coats. He carefully wrapped Sarah's body in one, heedless of the sticky, coagulating blood he got on himself. He carried the blanket-wrapped corpse outside and tied it to one of the mules. Then he went back and did the same with Little Will's body, fighting back sobs all the while.

Barlow pulled himself onto his riding mule, an enormous, coarse-haired beast he called Beelzebub, and got moving. His face was grim and hard as his hate, rage, sorrow, and heart-sworn vow pushed him along. And God save the savages when he caught up with them, for he was devoid of mercy for the murderous, baby-stealing devils.

1

NINE YEARS EARLIER . . . Will Barlow wearily surveyed the carnage before him. Bodies were strewn across the glade, far more of them women, children, and old men than he had realized. He sighed, shifting his broad shoulders, juggling his long Henry rifle, which was resting across his shoulders, his wrists hooked over it, as if he were wearing a yoke.

"Ye all right, boy?" someone asked. "Ye seem a mite green."

Barlow swung his big head around to look into the sparkling, but yet somehow malevolent eyes of James Claycomb. "I'm fine, Jim," Barlow said quietly. "Can't say as this was what I had in mind when I come along on this here little venture, though." The sight sickened him. He had killed during this fighting, and before, and that did not bother him, but this—a massacre—was not why he had joined the militia.

"Hell, boy, they's just Injins, and ones that've been on the warpath," Claycomb said nonchalantly. "Y'all shouldn't go worryin' overly much about them critters."

Barlow stared at the mountain man, who had joined the militia while he was on a trip back to St. Louis from the

Rocky Mountains. He was a hard-edged man, with a rapier face and a temper to match. He seemed to have little liking for most people, though he could get along well enough with everyone when he set his mind to it. Barlow had liked Claycomb, and had enjoyed sitting and quietly listening to the mountain man's stories of the Rockies. But this put Claycomb in a new light.

"Still don't seem right somehow," Barlow said, shaking his head in sadness.

"I wonder if you got as much gumption as I thunk before, boy," Claycomb growled.

"You want to see gumption, you old sack of shit, you come on and try me," Barlow responded calmly. He was not afraid of Claycomb, no matter how much fighting the mountain man had done. Barlow knew he could take care of himself in any kind of scrap.

"Bah, ye ain't worth the time it'd take to whomp your ass, boy," Claycomb snapped.

"Figured you didn't have the stomach for comin' against me," Barlow said with a smirk.

Claycomb turned and stomped off, cursing quietly under his breath.

Barlow shook his head. He had no particular liking for Indians, though he had no strong dislike for them either. Still, when Black Hawk took his Sauk and Fox Indians on the warpath, Barlow thought it only right that he should join the fight against them. He was urged on by a sense of adventure, as much as a sense of right, though he would never admit that, even to himself. And, of course, there was the little matter of escaping the clutches of Emma Sue Longstreath.

Barlow was a wild young man, full of piss and vinegar. Had been that way since he was able to toddle out of his parents' cabin door. He was yet a child when the family moved from Ohio to Missouri, where he had grown up, on the fringes of civilization, which in part led to his boisterousness. He encountered all kinds of men in his backwoods home, from trappers and traders to the occasional gentleman passing through. He saw Indians, but neither feared,

liked, nor disliked them. They were, simply, just part of
the landscape to him. The men who impressed the boy the
most, however, were the rivermen. They were barbarous,
almost savage. They drank prodigious amounts of alcohol
and would fight anyone, anywhere at any time, including
their friends. Barlow admired them, and wanted to be one
of them.

This, of course, horrified his mother, though she had long
been a frontierswoman. She had hoped for more from her
son. But it was useless, she soon learned, to try to control
the reckless youth.

His father—a pious, hardworking man whose dreams
ended with trying only to feed and clothe his family and to
work his way to heaven—tried to beat such nonsense out
of young Will. But that had no more effect on the wayward
youngster than his mother's cajoling did.

Two older, wiser, and much calmer brothers managed to
keep the young Will in the region's primitive schoolhouse
long enough for him to learn numbers and a rudimentary
ability to read and write.

But he chafed under the enforced learning, and as often
as not he would slip off and head into St. Charles, where
he would cadge or steal liquor from patrons of the riverfront
saloons. And he would fight anyone who challenged him,
regardless of his foe's size or age. For some years, he
would regularly come out on the losing end in these battles,
but as he grew he began winning some, then more, then
most, until as a teenager he had a reputation as being one
of the toughest men along the Missouri River.

"You are a disgrace to this family, boy," his father,
William, told him on more than one occasion.

Young Will shrugged. "I ain't causin' no one no harm,"
he said. "Just havin' a little fun like most of the other
young men 'round here."

"Like most of the other rabble 'round here, boy," the
elder Barlow growled, his rigid Methodism rising to the
surface. Truth be told, this well of righteousness was never
far from the surface, especially where his son was concerned.

"We're just boys havin' a good time, Pa," Barlow said. "Didn't you ever do that when you were young?" He knew the answer to that—hell, he had heard it often enough, but he enjoyed teasing his sanctimonious father about it.

"By the time I was your age, boy," William thundered, "I was running my pa's farm and courtin' your ma."

Before Will could retort, his mother, Mary, spoke up. "It's nigh time you were lookin' for a nice girl and thinkin' about settlin' down, son," she said in her soft, seemingly perpetually sad voice.

"Ah, Ma," Barlow said, trying to keep the whining out of his voice, "there's plenty of time for sich things." He hated when she was like this. Not holier-than-thou like his father, but logical and . . . well, downright motherly.

"If you don't begin makin' something of yourself soon, Will," Mary continued, "you'll find decent young women scarcer than hen's teeth. Decent girls don't last long out here, son. As you would know if you paid any attention."

"I'll think on it, Ma," Barlow said, rising from the old wooden chair. He was eager to be out of his parents' presence. He needed some whiskey, he figured. "I surely will." He spun and hurried out the door.

He saddled up the only riding horse the family possessed, an old, weary, sort of sorrel mare that Barlow had named Beelzebub, as the animal had a devilish temperament and a demonic gate that left any rider praying for deliverance. Barlow had, on more than one occasion, threatened to take an ax to the horse and go buy a new one, but the lack of money—and poor aim with the ax when he was drunk— pretty much precluded that. With a weary sigh, Barlow climbed aboard the recalcitrant steed and got it moving in the general direction of town.

When he got to the Pig Iron tavern, he dismounted and rubbed his sore ass. "Goddamn unholy son of a bitch horse," he growled, swatting the horse on the head with his hat. He slapped the hat back on his head and thumped into the saloon. Nodding greetings to several friends, Barlow stopped at the bar and ordered a whiskey.

"You got the specie to pay, Will?" the bartender asked gruffly.

" 'Course I do, Smiley," Barlow said, trying to hide the sudden flaring up of anger. He pulled out two silver dollars and laid them on the bar. "Leave the bottle," he growled.

Smiley Watkins shrugged, scooped up the coins, and walked away, leaving the bottle on the bartop, alongside a glass. Barlow filled the glass and guzzled down half of it, then refilled the glass. As he lifted it for another refreshing swallow, someone pounded him once on the back, forcing him to spill a fair portion of his liquor.

In anger, Barlow started to spin, balling one hand into a fist, until he heard the bellowed, "How do, Will, ol' boy."

Barlow finished the turn, but he was smiling now. "Tom!" he exclaimed. "You ol' horse thief. Where you been hidin'?"

"Here and about," Tom Wallenbach said with a cryptic grin. Wallenbach and Barlow had been friends since they could remember. They drank together, fought together— both as partners and as adversaries—and raised a lot of Cain together.

"What the hell's that mean?" Barlow asked, not much surprised. His tall, thin loose-limbed friend was prone to giving such answers for no reason other than to annoy Barlow.

"You pour me a swaller of that firewater you got there and I just might tell ya," Wallenbach said with a lopsided grin.

"I ain't so sure your answer'll be worth a slug of such precious juice," Barlow smiled back. "But what the hell, if it'll stop you from being annoying for a tick or two, I suppose the trade-off ain't so bad." Barlow got another glass from the bartender, and poured his friend a drink before refilling his own. "There, you ol' reprobate," he said, sliding the drink to Wallenbach. "Now, tell me what . . ."

Before Barlow could finish the sentence, Wallenbach had swallowed his glassful of whiskey and was holding out the empty vessel, seeking more.

"Damn, if you ain't a troublesome son of a bitch," Barlow snapped, not entirely humorously. He refilled the glass. "Best be takin' this one a mite slower, damn you," he said, " 'cause you ain't gettin' another drop."

"Hell of a way to treat a friend," Wallenbach said, unable to hold back a grin. He took a sip of the cheap whiskey and then set the glass down. "To tell ye the truth, I been holed up with a certain lass." His grin spread until it threatened to split his cheeks.

Barlow's eyes widened. "Molly Rose Maguire?" he asked.

"None other." Wallenbach looked like he'd just been elected mayor—smug and wildly grinning.

"Well, I'll be goddamned," Barlow whispered, drawing the words out. "You wily ol' skunk you." He paused for a sip, then grew confused. "But what about her ma and pa? And all the rest of her kin?"

Wallenbach grinned all the wider, if that was possible. "Whole damn lot of 'em went to St. Louis. Molly Rose told 'em she had a heap too many chores to tend to for her to be traipsin' all the way out there just to go visitin' kinfolk she don't even know. Me and Molly Rose've been playin' married folk for the past five days."

"Goddamn, if you ain't somethin' else," Barlow said with a grin. He toasted his friend and they both had a small drink. Suddenly, a thought struck Barlow. "You ain't aimin' to make that a real arrangement are ya?"

"What? Up and actually wed Molly Rose?" Wallenbach said with a laugh. "Hell no! There's too many willin' young women around jist waitin' to be plucked by this hungry feller."

"Well, it's purely a relief knowin' that," Barlow said as he finished his glass of whiskey and refilled it. But he was a little put out, actually. He had wanted to be the one to spend such a spell with Molly Rose Maguire. Not that Wallenbach was the first to avail himself of Molly Rose's favors. But somehow he felt as if Wallenbach had somehow left him behind. Barlow had had some experience with women, plenty, he often told himself. In fact, until just now, he had probably outdone Wallenbach in that area. But now

Wallenbach had surpassed him, and that stuck in Barlow's craw more than a little bit.

"You ought to try sich adventurin' one of these days, my friend," Wallenbach said, apparently not noticing Barlow's annoyance.

"I reckon that would be right pleasurable," Barlow grumbled, "But it ain't likely to happen again just like it done to you."

"That's the truth, I suppose," Wallenbach said with a grin. His smugness grew. It wasn't that he wanted to belittle his friend, but Barlow had come out on top in most of the encounters they had had together, and now that he had won one, he couldn't help but gloat a little.

"Well, Molly Rose Maguire ain't the only willin' female in this here neck of the woods," Barlow said, his annoyance developing into anger. "And if you was any kind of man," he added, voice snapping, "you'd never have gone and opened up your big yap about what you been doin' with her."

"Now listen here, Will Barlow," Wallenbach said harshly. "I ain't about to listen to sich from the likes of you. If'n it was you who'd spent near a week with some woman—any woman—you'd be crowin' like a banty rooster in a new henhouse."

Barlow almost smiled at that. It was the truth, and anyone who knew him would know that. Still, he was used to finishing on top, and he was not happy that his friend wore such an air of victory. "Well, mayhap if you hadn't of cadged half a bottle of my whiskey off me just to give you the gumption to crow about conquering a strumpet like Molly Rose, well, maybe I wouldn't be so sore about it all."

"Ah, hell, Will, you're jist green-eyed with envy that I managed to have my way with her so easy, when she wouldn't even give you a tumble," Wallenbach said, his mood rapidly starting to go south.

"You're mad as a hatter, Tom," Barlow snapped. He just wanted his friend to go away and leave him in peace. At least for the time being. He would get over his annoyance, and soon he would find a woman willing to set up house—however temporarily—with him, and things would be back the way they should be.

"And you're just a sour ol' fart," Wallenbach answered in kind.

Barlow gave no warning. He just spun and struck, a ham-like fist pounding Wallenbach on the side of the face.

Wallenbach rolled backward along the bar, his vision blurred, his ears ringing. He finally came to a stop, clinging to the bartop for support. He shook his head, trying to clear the fog. He had been hit by Barlow before, but never this hard, and never so unexpectedly. Usually he could see that an attack was coming. But this assault was snakelike in its suddenness. Despite his befuddlement, Wallenbach knew he had to regain at least some of his faculties if he was to repel another attack by Barlow, which would be coming at any moment.

Barlow instantly regretted hitting his friend, but he knew that no apology would work at the moment. Disgusted with himself, Barlow swallowed the last of the whiskey in his glass, jammed the cork into the bottle, grabbed the bottle, and bulled his way through the crowded saloon. In the fresh air outside, he reluctantly climbed aboard Beelzebub and rode out of town, not sure of where he was going, and not really caring either.

2

LESS THAN A week later, Barlow had managed to concoct an arrangement similar to the one Wallenbach had made with Molly Rose Maguire. With the thought of the soon-to-be tryst in mind, Barlow was feeling considerably better about life as he impatiently waited for Emma Sue Longstreath's family to leave the farm.

On the appointed day, Barlow waited behind the fringe of trees across the plowed field from Emma Sue's cabin. After what seemed like hours, the entire Longstreath clan—minus Emma Sue, of course—pulled out. The young woman's father and two older brothers rode mules, while her ma and five sisters rode in the wagon. No sooner had the travelers cleared the near horizon, than Barlow sprinted across the field.

Emma Sue was waiting for him, and she jumped into his arms, eagerly kissing him hard on the mouth. He responded with equal ardor. Barlow appreciated the lush feel of her body against his. Even though he could not feel flesh, there was no doubt she was all woman under the thin dress. Emma Sue was short—her head barely reached his shoulders—and just a bit on the plump side. She had large, very round breasts and wide, well-pronounced hips. Her face

"But I . . ."

"You'll enjoy it a lot more if you listen to me."

"Yes'm," Barlow grumbled. He did as he was told and his hardness slid more slowly and deeply into her love canal. Concentration furrowed his brow as he strove to contain his rapidly rising explosion.

Emma Sue moaned and wriggled her ass until her pelvic movements matched his in a rhythmic churning of lust that escalated in speed and ferocity, still perfectly timed. Her moans intensified and grew more insistent, and her breathing turned ragged.

Barlow panted through gritted teeth, straining harder to hold back the anticipated flood.

"Faster Will!" Emma Sue suddenly shrieked. The yell turned into an extended moan as her buttocks beat a furious tattoo on the dusty straw tick mattress.

Suddenly Emma Sue's body spasmed, and she voiced her climax in an almost animal-like howl. Her body bucked and writhed as she raked her fingernails along Barlow's big back.

With a sense of relief, Barlow shot his manly fluid deep into the young woman. He groaned and grunted, and his back arched, pulling his neck muscles taut. At last he dropped down onto Emma Sue, sweat mingling on their heaving bodies. Then Barlow realized that he was likely to smother the young woman, and he pushed himself rather weakly up and over, until he was lying on his back next to her.

Emma Sue climbed onto him and grinned wickedly. "Too bad you're all used up," she said with glee. "I could use some more of that lovin'."

"You jist wait a few minutes, girl," Barlow said, still panting hard, "till I get my breath back. Then you'll have some more lovin'." He grinned back at her, but he was a little worried deep down. He wasn't at all sure he could recoup his reserves that quickly. He also wondered if she was insatiable or something. He had heard talk of such women, but he had thought it was just that—talk. Now he was not so sure.

• • •

Emma Sue wasn't all that interested in waiting too long, and less than twenty minutes later she was crawling all over Barlow, her mouth working wonders that surprised even him. He now suspected she had more experience in these activities than she had led him to believe. However, that thought—and all others—fled when her tender lips reached his reawakening manhood.

Within minutes, he was as rigid as a rifle barrel. With a saucy grin, Emma Sue climbed atop him and eased her wet womanhood down on his hardened shaft. A groan of pleasure escaped him as he was engulfed in her silken sheath, and she smiled, though a small shudder also racked her body.

Emma Sue began moving her robust hips slowly up and down, adding a little wriggle each time her bottom hit his groin—the point when he was as deep into her as he could get. Her breath quickly grew ragged and her pace increased as her hips and buttocks bounced with ever-growing energy.

Barlow was swept up in the passion, and his own groin moved in rhythm with Emma Sue's. The girl's big, round breasts danced enticingly before him, almost mesmerizing in their movements. He could not help himself. He reached up and grabbed a handful of each and squeezed, producing an excited squeal from Emma Sue. He shifted his hands a little and began to softly pinch both nipples.

That generated an even greater shriek of delight from the young woman. "Again," she hissed through clenched teeth. Her face was tight with concentration and lust, and a sheen of sweat covered her face and breasts. "Again!"

Barlow was quite willing to oblige. He squeezed her nipples harder, half worried that he would injure her and half elated that he felt such power.

"Ahhhhhhh," Emma Sue breathed roughly, pleasure shooting straight from her nipples to her crotch. Her shoulders shook a bit, and her back arched as her head lolled back. Joy rolled over her in small, compact waves.

Barlow began to feel his eruption building deep in his

loins, and he gritted his teeth to hold back the bursting of that dam. Emma Sue was moaning in ecstasy and seemingly no longer paying much attention to him as she bounded wildly up and down on Barlow's rigid shaft. Her breath came in short bursts punctuated by breathy little screams.

Barlow could hold off no longer. He released Emma Sue's tits and grabbed her broad, womanly hips. He rammed his pelvis up and down, matching her rhythm, pounding her hard, as if trying to get even deeper into her than was physically possible.

Emma Sue screamed, a long, ululating sound that tapered off just as he bellowed out his release. His hips bolted off the rickety bed, holding the woman up in the air as he spurted his essence into her. Then his ass plopped back on the bed, and she collapsed atop him, both struggling to catch their breath.

It was four days of utter bacchanalia for Barlow, and he enjoyed it immensely. But it had its price, too, which he found out soon after he left, and minutes before Emma Sue's family arrived back at the cabin. Word soon got back to him that Emma Sue was telling her friends and neighbors that she planned to marry Will Barlow soon.

"I never said nothin' about tyin' the knot with you, Emma Sue," Barlow snapped when he finally had a chance to get her alone again.

"But I just thought . . ."

"You ain't supposed to do no thinkin'. If I was figurin' to marry you, Emma Sue, I'd tell you about it first off."

"But didn't we have a fine time together, Will?" she asked, her face scrunched up in fear and worry.

"I cain't say as I've ever had a better time, Emma Sue," Barlow confessed.

"Then what's wrong?"

"Ain't nothin' wrong." He sighed, wondering how things could have turned out this way. "Just because we had us a fine time rollin' in the hay doesn't mean I aim to make you my wife."

"Why not?" Emma Sue was torn between anger and bitterness.

"I ain't so sure I want to git hitched just yet, Emma Sue," Barlow said. He liked Emma Sue Longstreath, so was reluctant to give her the real reason—that he could not be sure about her morality, after she had so easily given herself to him for such an extended period. Her quick acquiescence to his proposal to spend several days together, and her obvious knowledge of sexual techniques that he was barely acquainted with made him wary of her background.

"But we could have us such a great time together, Will," Emma Sue said, trying to sound excited. She had been used before by men and thought this time would be different. No one had been as eager to spend so much time with her as Will Barlow. So she had assumed—well, hoped—that he wanted this arrangement as a preliminary to proposing marriage.

"Well, I reckon we could," he responded, probing a tooth with his tongue. He was decidedly uncomfortable. "But . . . Well, there's still time, Emma Sue. We don't need to rush into anything."

"Well then, Mr. Will Barlow," Emma Sue huffed, "you best take some time and do some hard thinkin' about all this. I ain't about to wait around for you forever."

"You don't have to wait around at all," Barlow mumbled.

"What did you say?" Emma Sue asked, her annoyance rising.

"Nothin'," Barlow lied.

"Don't you make fun of me, Will Barlow," Emma Sue snapped. "There ain't many women 'round here willin' to take a chance on weddin' the likes of you."

"Don't bother me none knowin' that," Barlow said, trying to sound casual. "I ain't never told anyone I was in the market for a wife."

"But I gave myself to you," Emma Sue said, her anger growing.

"And to a heap of other fellers, I'm thinkin'," Barlow responded bluntly.

Emma Sue's normal paleness deepened. "How dare you say such a thing to me," she said harshly, fire burning in her eyes.

"Ain't it true?" Barlow countered. "I'd heard such was the truth but wasn't sure I should believe it. But I reckon now that enough of it is true that I ain't so certain I'd want to be hitched to you."

Emma Sue Longstreath spun on the heel of her high-top shoes and stormed off, vowing deep in her severely wounded heart that she would win Barlow over, somehow. She would do it now to pay him back for that cutting remark. That Barlow's statement was true, at least to some extent, did not matter. Emma Sue decided that a gentleman would not have thrown it in her face like that. So she vowed to win him over—and then reject him.

Barlow watched the woman walk away. He was shaking his head, wondering what possessed women to make them think a few sexual encounters somehow branded a man as hers for life. Well, he had no time to think of such nonsense now. He had told her that marrying her was out of the question. She would have to deal with it however she could.

3

BARLOW KNEW THE moment he walked in the door of his cabin that something was wrong. And, since he was usually to blame for that look on his mother's face, he figured he was in trouble again. Problem was, he couldn't for the life of him think of anything that he had done recently to put that expression on his mother's weather-worn countenance.

"So, young man, just what are you planning to do?" his mother asked harshly.

Barlow glanced from her to his father, but there was no clue on his stern visage. "Do about what, Ma?" he asked.

"About that unfortunate girl you despoiled."

"Who?" Barlow asked. He was startled, and the word had just popped out.

"Emma Sue Longstreath," Mary said through clenched teeth.

"What do you mean?" Barlow was still stretching for some time to come up with an explanation, or at least find out just how much his parents knew about the situation.

"She's with child," his mother said with a shudder of disgust, "and is saying that you are the father."

"She's a strumpet," Barlow snapped. "Half the boys in

St. Charles County have enjoyed her favors. Which she has always dispensed without much prudence.''

"May damnation befall you, boy!'' his father thundered. "You are an abomination to this family. You have soiled my good name, and you have ruined this family. So you will do the right thing by this family, by that girl, and by the community!'' William's Methodist hackles were raised, and he could see no other solution than to force his son to marry Emma Sue and then get out of his house forever.

Barlow slowly rose, face tight. "Your goddamned precious name is more important to you than the truth?'' he demanded harshly. "You have taken the word of a whore who would lay with any man in the county over that of your own son?'' He was every bit as angry as his father. "I don't believe she is with child, and even if she was, I don't believe I am the father.''

"A young woman has no reason to make up such accusations,'' William roared.

"Like hell, Pa,'' Barlow bellowed right back. "Cain't you see treachery when it arises?''

"All I see,'' William said, more quietly though still backed by the steel support of his piety, "is a young man—the seed of my loins—who is unwilling to face his responsibilities and do what is right and proper. A man so lacking in morals that he will insult a young woman—after defiling her—just to avoid doing what duty calls for.''

Barlow had had just about enough of his father's overbearing self-righteousness. While it was possible that Emma Sue was pregnant and just as possible that he was the father, he was not about to be forced into marrying the girl just to salve his father's misplaced sense of pride. He stepped toward William, fist raised.

"Don't you dare hit your pa,'' Mary said, stepping in between her husband and youngest son.

Barlow was mulling over a retort and trying to decide his next move when there was a knock on the door. No one moved for some time. Finally Barlow figured he'd answer it, since his mother would not leave him and his father alone, and his father was not about to get the door, considering it beneath him.

Barlow, still seething, yanked open the door. Tom Wallenbach and a stranger were standing there, each grinning a little. Barlow glared at them, not wanting an intrusion into this family squabble.

"Well, you gonna let us in or make us stand out here in the heat all day?" Wallenbach asked, trying to lighten things up some. He could see that Barlow was highly agitated and wondered what the problem was.

"Come on in," Barlow finally said. He stepped back to allow the two men to enter.

Both men greeted the elder Barlows, who had relaxed a bit now that the threat of violence had lessened. The visitors sat, and Mrs. Barlow scurried around, filling cups with coffee for the men and serving them pie.

"This here's James Claycomb," Wallenbach at last said, indicating the other visitor. "He's one of those mountaineer boys who trap beaver up in the Stony Mountains. He's back here on a visit."

Barlow nodded at Claycomb and the two shook hands. "So what brings you to our house, Mr. Claycomb?" Barlow asked.

"Your friend here suggested I come callin'," Claycomb said after slurping down some coffee. "Said you might be a man we could use."

"For what?"

"Injin fightin', boy," Claycomb said in his cackle of a voice.

There were several moments of silence as the others let that sink in. Then Barlow snorted in disgust. "Injin fightin'! Hell, mister, there ain't been no Injins to fight around here in years."

Claycomb's eyes narrowed in anger. "You thinkin' to call me a liar, boy?" he demanded, voice cracking and wobbling.

Barlow shrugged his big, humped shoulders. "I just spoke the truth is all," he noted.

"Well, I reckon that's true, there ain't been no Injins 'round here to fight. Till now."

Barlow's eyes widened.

Claycomb nodded. "Yep. Some Injins went on the warpath. Feller named Black Hawk has took his Sauk and Foxes to battle. He's been runnin' wild over parts of Illinois and Missouri and Iowa."

"So we're putting together a militia unit to run that son of a bitch to heel," Wallenbach said enthusiastically.

"That a fact?" Barlow said, not sure whether to believe his old friend.

"It is," Claycomb said firmly. "We can't let these red devils run wild like this, so we aim to cut him down afore too many more folks get hurt."

"And you want me to join this militia?" The thought intrigued Barlow, especially then.

Claycomb shrugged. "We're jist lookin' fer boys to fight. Your friend Tom here suggested you." He paused. "You look like a strappin' young man, full of piss and manly zest, and if your friend here is to be believed, you can handle yourself well in a fight. So, seems to me you'd be a plumb shinin' feller to have along with such a venture."

Barlow thought about it. The idea had a lot of appeal. He had always wanted to do something full of danger and excitement, and this would seem to fit the bill. Plus it would get him away from his father's pious sermons. And, most important right now, he could avoid Emma Sue and her accusations if he headed off to battle Indians. If he could stay out six months or a year, everything involving Emma Sue would likely have blown over by the time he returned. And he could live in peace then, free of his father's preaching, and out of the clutches of Emma Sue Longstreath. He could see no negative side to this adventure.

"I'm in," Barlow said quietly, glancing unconcernedly over at his father.

The elder Barlow looked frustrated.

"We'll teach them Innians a thing or two," Wallenbach crowed. "Won't we, Will?"

"Well, better that than the other way 'round," Barlow said with a laugh, the first in what seemed like a long time.

"That's a smart lad," Claycomb offered. He rose and held out his hand. As he shook Barlow's hand, he said, "We muster at Coughlin's farm over toward St. Louis day after tomorrow at dawn."

Barlow nodded. "Anything I need to bring?"

"Just yourself—and a horse, if you got one. The government will provide the rest."

Barlow nodded again, and saw the two men outside. He returned to the cabin, giving his father a look that warned him not to say anything. He finished off his coffee and then left the house. He returned late the next night, quietly packed a few things in a small canvas bag, grabbed his prized Henry rifle, saddled up Beelzebub, and rode out into the darkness. His only goodbye was a brief peck on the cheek he allowed his mother to give him.

He arrived at the mustering point several hours early and unsaddled the swaybacked horse. Using the saddle as a pillow of sorts, he leaned back and closed his eyes, sleeping until noise from other arriving volunteers woke him. Before long, a camp was built, and he took his place among the other men having coffee and a breakfast of bacon and biscuits.

By the end of the day, Barlow—and all the others—had been issued a flintlock musket, which Barlow refused in light of his superior rifle, matching pistol, powder, ball, lead, powder horn, patching material, a small shooting bag complete with tools for the weapons, a large belt knife, penknife, tin cup, fire-making kit, a small piece of canvas, a thin blanket, sea biscuits, and a handful of jerky.

Barlow and Wallenbach bunked next to each other that night and were up before the sun had risen, falling into place alongside scores of other men, most of them strangers. The two were assigned to Sergeant James Claycomb's unit. As the sun began to poke over the horizon, they were marching sloppily toward the northeast to a ferry across the Mississippi River.

A month later, Barlow's unit encountered Black Hawk's warriors in some meadow in southern Wisconsin. The fight was short, but for newcomers like Barlow and Wallenbach, fierce and frightening. It was unlike anything Barlow had ever encountered. Claycomb's men were chasing a small band of Indians and were getting close when they poured out of the trees into the meadow. They were about halfway across it, heading for the thick stands of trees to the west, when the Sauk and Foxes opened fire.

Several horses and a few men went down straight off, but Claycomb managed to get his men settled down and into defensive positions. They worked their way to the left, in unison, using covering fire to keep the Indians hiding behind trees, and finally made it without the loss of any-more human life, though two more horses had been killed.

Once in the trees, though, Claycomb changed. "Time to show them red bastards what it means to attack a bunch of us boys like that," he growled, face and demeanor hard, implacable.

"We goin' after 'em?" one man asked, excitedly.

"Yep," Claycomb responded flatly. "Leave your horses here, where they'll be safe, mostly. Stick with your partners and take the fight to them heathen, murderous bastards. We'll meet here again when our work is done." Then he turned and disappeared into the trees.

"I think that boy's gone mad," Barlow murmured.

"You may be right," Wallenbach agreed. "But we joined this here undertaking to fight Indians, and this is the first chance we've had to do so. And I aim to take advantage of it. So let's move out."

Barlow shrugged and followed his friend deeper into the woods. Minutes later, an Indian popped up from behind a thick bush and swung a war club at Wallenbach's head. Wallenbach managed to duck at the last moment, and the stone-headed weapon whistled harmlessly by his head.

Just behind him, Barlow fired his rifle, but missed in his excitement. As the Indian suddenly spun and charged him,

Barlow almost grinned. Though the warrior still carried the club, this was much like a barroom fight to Barlow. He brought his rifle up, catching the war club on it and flinging it away. Before the Sauk could draw a knife, Barlow had pounded him several times on the face and head with his hamlike fists, leaving the warrior in a bloody heap at his feet.

Barlow helped Wallenbach up, grinned, and said, "Well, let's move, boy, there's more fightin' to be done."

Wallenbach glanced down at the warrior and managed a weak grin. That flashing war club had been much too close, and his knees were trembling. But seeing his friend's broad, beaming face helped Wallenbach gain strength. He nodded and the two trotted off again.

In less than an hour, the two were back at the meeting place. They had encountered no other warriors. It was apparent as other men returned to the spot in the forest that few others had seen much in the way of battle this day.

Finally Claycomb showed up, the last to do so, which made Barlow wonder a little. "We scared those red skunks off a heap too soon, this ol' hoss is sayin'," he announced, "We should've been able to make wolf bait of a passel more of 'em before we sent 'em skedaddlin'." He almost sighed. "Well, boys, now we have to go chasin' 'em some more afore we send 'em all to the Happy Huntin' Ground."

The men grumbled a little. Claycomb let it run on for a bit, then said, "You boys got half an hour to bury them what's been rubbed out." He paused. "Anyone else hurt?" When no one admitted to being injured, Claycomb nodded. "We'll head out after 'em straight off after you get the dead buried." He slumped down against a tree trunk, pulled his battered hat down over his eyes, and moments later he was snoring.

Barlow and Wallenbach pitched in to help with burying the men of their unit who had been killed. The work was hot and sorrowful but went quickly. One of the men read a verse of scripture as each man was placed in the hole, and it was soon over.

As if he had planned it, Claycomb awoke just as the last

clump of earth was packed down. He nodded in satisfaction and then said, "Let's ride, boys. Time's a-wastin'."

They pushed on, always seeming to be just behind the fleeing Indians. Once in a while, the militia men would catch up with the Sauks and Foxes, and a battle would ensue. In those rare skirmishes, however, Barlow proved himself repeatedly as courageous, tenacious, and tough.

Because of those qualities, Claycomb took something of a shine to the broad-backed young man and would often regale Barlow with tales of the big mountains to the west and of the beaver trade. He would tell of fights with real Indians—warriors who were the best horsemen any of the mountaineers had ever seen—and about the joys of Indian women and how they could pleasure a man like no other woman.

Barlow took the stories to heart, wondering if all of them were true; indeed, there were times when he wondered if any of them were true. But he figured that most if not all the tales had at least a modicum of truth to them. Those stories had Barlow dreaming more often than not, of heading west when this Indian fighting was over. He quickly developed a severe hankering to see some of the places Claycomb had talked about and take part in some of the adventures the old mountaineer had mentioned.

4

LESS THAN FOUR months later, the "war" with Black Hawk's Sauk and Foxes was winding down. Militias from several concerned states had hounded and harassed the Indians, who stood and fought only on the rarest occasions. The Indians, burdened by women and children, hampered by lack of food, and thoroughly disillusioned, were no match for the militias of hardened frontiersmen and eager-to-win-glory boys from both country and city.

The militia scouts finally brought word that the Sauks and Foxes were heading for the Mississippi River in southwest Wisconsin. Everyone figured the Indians were planning to cross the river into Iowa and perhaps find succor, or at least a haven among other tribes there. Their bid to get back to their own homeland east of the river and live there peacefully had been disastrous, and it was clear to see that the routed Indians were simply trying to get to some sort of safety.

Not that such sentiments meant much to most of the militiamen. Black Hawk's people had caused trouble, the soldiers thought, and had to be run down and punished time and again until they unconditionally surrendered and ac-

cepted whatever handouts the white settlers and militia
would allow them.

In eagerness, the Missouri Militia turned and hurriedly
marched toward the Mississippi River. There they sat and
waited while their scouts probed the area around them,
watching for the arrival of the Indians. A few days later the
word came and the soldiers moved upriver a couple of
miles. Making camp, the men waited some more and fi-
nalized plans for their ambush.

Not that much planning was needed. Captain Littlefield
had passed down word that as soon as the Indians entered
the water the attack was to commence. Barlow didn't think
much of the idea, but he wasn't too concerned with it either.
This was war, and some brutal things would have to be
done. The sooner it was over the better.

Late the next morning, the militiamen heard the Indians
approaching from the Northwest. Before long, the Sauk and
Foxes rode into view. They were exhausted, ragged. Many
stopped and sat to rest, the women wearily tending to sad-
eyed children. Others, however, kept going and began edging into the cold, swiftly rushing Mississippi.

Barlow watched with a sense of detachment, so much so
that he was startled by the shout of "FIRE!" He snapped
into action on instinct, leveling his musket and firing. He
saw a warrior drop, and he nodded, then began reloading.
By the time he was ready to fire again, gun smoke had
obscured the battlefield. He drew a bead on a shadowy,
running figure and squeezed the trigger. The cloud of powder smoke blurred things even more, and he was not even
sure he had hit the Indian. He reloaded and fired repeatedly,
shooting at shapes that were barely discernible through the
choking cloud of smoke and dust.

The order to cease firing came just about two hours after
the battle had commenced. As the wind pushed away the
haze, Barlow stood and walked with a number of the other
men across the battlefield toward the water's edge. He was
disgusted with what he saw. He didn't mind killing warriors, and he knew that sometimes women got caught in the
salvos. But to him this seemed to be a slaughter. The bodies

of children, women, even old men were scattered all over.
He knew he had had trouble seeing when firing, but he
figured the captain must have known there were so many
noncombatants involved. There must have been something
they could have done to prevent the killing of so many
women and children. Barlow just prayed that he had not
been responsible for too many of those deaths.

He stood there a few moments, rifle across his shoulders,
looking out over the devastation. Then James Claycomb
strode up. After insulting Barlow a few times and wisely
deciding not to accept the young man's challenge, the
crusty old mountain man turned and walked off.

Barlow shook his head and then wondered where his
friend Tom Wallenbach was. They had gotten separated
during the battle when Wallenbach had wandered off to get
more powder and shot. That was the last Barlow had seen
of him. Not that he was worried, but he thought it curious
that he didn't see his friend around, as most of the militiamen were wandering around the battlefield. Some, like Barlow, seemed to be in a daze at the devastation; others were
poking Indians' bodies, stripping them of anything of value.
A few, like Claycomb, were actually scalping some of the
Indians, apparently relishing the devilish act.

Barlow began wandering, trying to avoid the more grisly
depredations being performed by his fellow soldiers, looking for Wallenbach. It didn't take long to find him. Wallenbach was sitting with his back against a tree, an arrow
sticking out of his shoulder. His face was pale, but he was
grinning.

"What the hell happened to you?" Barlow said, trying
to sound civil, but still repulsed by the carnage all around.

Wallenbach grinned. "Stuck my head up from behind
that there bush a mite sooner'n I should have," he said.
Despite the grin, his face showed the pain he was in. Still,
he was making a strong effort at appearing casual as he
waited for the militia's medical man to tend to him.

"I always told you that you was gonna git shot because
of your big fat head, boy," Barlow said, his mood lightening a bit as he realized that his friend would be all right.

"Wasn't my big fat head," Wallenbach groused. "It was my impetuous nature." He grinned again, but it turned into a grimace. "Always got to be in the lead in such things, jumpin' up and tryin' to raise hell before the next feller gits a chance to do so."

"Reckon you're right about that, ya damn fool." Realizing that Wallenbach was in pain, he asked, "You all right, Tom?"

"Yeah," Wallenbach said with another grimace. His face was pale and he was sweating heavily. "But I will say one thing, old friend, it hurts like all hell fire."

"I reckon it does." Barlow almost grinned. "Mayhap it'll teach you to keep some reins on your impetuousness."

"Jist might," Wallenbach said rather sheepishly.

The physician finally came over. "Best be on you way, son," he said to Barlow. "This man needs tendin' to."

Barlow ignored him for the moment. "You need anything, Tom?" he asked his friend.

"Nah. I'll be fine as soon as this ol' reprobate works his magic spells on me, Will." He tried to grin, but the pain had grown considerably, cutting off the smile.

Barlow nodded. "Treat him well, Doc," he said, a touch of worry in his voice. Then he turned and headed off. He wandered across the recent killing fields, not knowing why. It seemed there was really no place else for him to go. So few of his fellow soldiers had been killed that he would not be needed on a burial detail, the horses were well taken care of, and the camp was as set as it was ever going to be. So he roamed, trying to make sense of the bloodbath that had so recently taken place here.

He saw one of the militiamen grab something and raise it up. It took a moment for Barlow to realize that it was a dog of some sort. He instinctively turned and headed that way, picking up a little speed. He suspected the soldier had something devilish in mind, though he did not know why that thought had swept over him.

His concern was validated when he saw the soldier raise his knife, ready to plunge it into the dog's throat. "Murphy!" Barlow bellowed. "What're you doin' there?"

The startled soldier jerked around, dropping the dog. "It ain't none of your concern, Barlow," Murphy snapped, irritably.

Barlow stopped right in front of Murphy, who was somewhat taller but nowhere near as bulky. He had blood lust still in his dark brown eyes.

"You ain't had enough killin' for one day? Now you want to go butcherin' dogs?" Barlow asked harshly.

"Like I said, it ain't none of your affair," Murphy said stiffly. "But since you asked, the damn dog bit me. He's got rabies, like as not."

"You get rabies, it'll likely improve your disposition considerably," Barlow said flatly. "And if he did give 'em to you, there ain't gonna be no savin' you by killin' it. Hell, I'd bite you, too, was you to come around annoyin' the hell out of me."

"Go about your business, Barlow," Murphy warned.

"Or what?"

"Or you'll be sittin' over there with the wounded."

Barlow decided he had had enough of this arrogant son of a bitch. Besides, he was still bothered by all the killing today. The combination made him irritable and angry. So without a word, he just hauled off and lambasted Murphy in the face.

Murphy went down like a fresh-cut tree, eyes rolled back up into his head.

"Mayhap you'll watch your big yap in front of me, ya damn fool," Barlow muttered, looking down at Murphy. Shaking his head in disgust, he knelt and looked at the dog, which was a few feet away, snarling fiercely. "Why, you're jist a pup," he muttered. "Jist a damn little pup." He figured it couldn't be more than a month or so old. He came close to smiling. "Come on over here, little dog," he coaxed, holding out a hand, palm up.

The dog backed away a little bit.

Barlow looked around and saw that the body nearby had a pouch. He rummaged in the dead man's sack and found some pemmican. He turned back to face the puppy, a bit of the foodstuff on his outstretched palm. "C'mon, now, girl," he said quietly, voice even, "c'mon and get it now, I ain't gonna hurt you."

It took more than fifteen minutes of patient cajoling, but finally the puppy ambled up, nervous and jittery. It grabbed the bit of pemmican and darted off a few feet, where it ate while keeping a wary eye on everything around it.

Barlow put another piece of pemmican in his hand and held it out. The puppy returned, snatched the food and trotted off again, though not as far. Patiently, Barlow went through it three more times, and each time the dog went less far off. On the fifth time, Barlow grabbed the puppy by the scruff of the neck and rose, holding it close to him.

The animal yapped and bit and scratched, but caused Barlow no damage. Barlow continued to talk to the dog in calm, even tones, all the while petting the furry little creature. He looked the dog over, and could see no problems with the feisty female. Well, nothing that a few good meals wouldn't fix. He noted the relatively huge feet on the otherwise small dog and silently predicted it would grow into one hell of a big canine.

"That's a Newfoundland dog," someone said behind Barlow.

The soldier turned and gulped. "I didn't know, sir," he said quietly. "I jist thought to save her when one of the boys was about to kill her."

"She sure is a nice lookin' pup. Gonna be a big one, too, I reckon."

"Yes, sir, Captain Lincoln. I believe you're right."

"You aim to keep her?" Captain Abraham Lincoln asked, his sorrowful eyes serious.

"I reckon I jist might," Barlow said firmly. He had just made the decision, and it pleased him for some reason.

"That'd be a good thing," Lincoln remarked. He glanced around. "Lord knows, there's been more than enough death and killin' here for one day. Giving life to one of the Lord's creatures just might take a small bit of the glumness off this sad day."

"Yessir," Barlow said with a nod. He looked up at the

tall, lanky captain's unhandsome face. "You mind I ask you a question, Captain?"

"Reckon not, soldier."

"Do you condone what went on here today?" Barlow asked, wondering if he had gone too far.

"Do you think I would?" Lincoln asked solemnly, his voice deep and resonant.

"No, sir," Barlow said, meaning it.

"Well, as it turns out, I do not condone such things." He sighed. "I had my men still several miles up the river when this . . . attack . . . took place. Had I been here, this disgraceful event would never have taken place. As it is, I've been trying my damnedest to stop the heathen atrocities being performed by men who claim to be civilized."

"Yessir," Barlow said, realizing that being an officer might be even more onerous than being a regular soldier. At least at times.

"Speaking of which, I had better get back to those duties," Lincoln said. He smiled just a bit. "You take good care of that puppy, Private. I reckons he'll turn into a fine dog."

"Yessir." As Barlow watched Lincoln walk away, issuing orders quietly to an aide who had just arrived, Barlow realized that he felt marginally better about this day. He had saved a life, even if it was only a puppy's. And he thought Lincoln a fine man, one who could be trusted and believed. Unlike men such as Captain Littlefield and James Claycomb.

"Well, little feller, let's mosey on," Barlow said, scratching the puppy's head. As he moved toward camp, he stopped at some of the bodies and rooted through possible bags in search of food for the dog. By the time he got to the camp, he had a small sack full of pemmican and jerky, plus a few bits of fresh rabbit. He sat with his back against a fallen log and fed the puppy little bits at a time.

"Dinner?" someone asked.

Barlow looked up at Claycomb. "What's that, Sergeant?"

He pointed to the puppy. "I asked if that critter was dinner."

"Nope." Barlow shrugged.

Claycomb cackled a revolting little laugh. "Ye aim to name it?" he asked.

Barlow rubbed the dog's furry head and thought a moment. "Gonna call her Buffalo," he finally said with a firm nod. "She kinda looks like one. Might as well name her that."

5

WITH THE "WAR" over, the men were preparing to muster out right where they were. It was only two days since the battle, and Barlow sat there, wondering what he would do now. He had no great yearning to return home. There was nothing there for him anymore, and he had not been away long enough to have allowed the trouble with Emma Sue Longstreath to blow over. But he had few options, or so it seemed to him.

Making it worse, he had only a day more before he would have to decide on something, as the militia camp would be officially struck tomorrow, and he could either stay here, nearly penniless and with little in the way of supplies, or ride on to somewhere in the same condition.

As he sat there, playing with Buffalo, he made a concerted effort to ignore Jim Claycomb's expounding on his many adventures. Barlow had liked Claycomb at the start, but in the latter stages of the war against Black Hawk's people, his opinion of the crusty old mountain man had changed a lot. He now considered Claycomb a blowhard, a man so absorbed in his own perceived greatness that he was far more of an annoyance than a helpful companion.

Barlow was tired of Claycomb's boasts and long-winded

diatribes. The man was an insufferable fool, and Barlow usually tried to shut his mind off to the mountain man's babbling. He was still rankled by the man's casual attitude at the death of so many women and children in the so-called battle here where the Bad Axe River entered the Mississippi.

So intent was he on ignoring Claycomb that he was unaware that the man had strolled up until the man said, "Couple months and that pup'll be ready for the pot, boy. So you best feed her good."

"Ready for the pot?" Barlow asked dumbly, his mind still not focused. "You mean to say you figure I'm aimin' to eat this here pup?" He was disgusted at the very notion.

"Hell, roasted or boiled dog is a delicacy, boy," Claycomb said with a sneer.

"Not by me it ain't," Barlow said, trying to hold back his revulsion.

"Then you're a chicken-hearted little peckerwood."

"And, you, old man, are a walking bag of wind, always spoutin' off," Barlow snapped.

Claycomb laughed a little. "A heap of Injuns and many a mountaineer'll think you ain't much of a man if you don't cotton to roasted pup. Ye ought not to turn up your nose at sich doin's till you've done gone and tried it, boy."

"I don't need to go eatin' no puppy dogs to prove my courage to the likes of you, Claycomb. You like eatin' dog, go find your own. Or go steal one off the Indians over here. Just leave me and little Buffler here alone."

"I git a hankerin' for pup, and your precious Buffler is the only one around, she'll end up in the pot."

Barlow stopped rubbing the puppy's head, eliciting some weak whimpers and whines from the animal. Then Barlow stood. "You git within ten feet of this dog and I'll cut you a new asshole," Barlow said pointedly.

Claycomb cackled, then said in surly tones, "It'll take the help of a heap of these here militia fellers if you want to whup my hide, boy."

"Ain't gonna take no such thing," Barlow said quietly.

Just before he hauled off and pasted Claycomb a good shot in the face.

Claycomb's knees buckled and he went down right where he was, landing on his ass with a thump and a puff of dust. He looked dazed for a moment, then pushed himself to his feet, where he stood reeling a bit. "That weren't very neighborly of you, sonny boy," he mumbled, not quite sure his jaw would work the way it was supposed to.

Barlow shrugged, unconcerned. "You want neighborly, you might try actin' that way toward others." He put the dog down, just in case.

"I'll show ye neighborly, ye little snot!" Claymore charged, tackling Barlow with arms wrapped around his upper torso. They tumbled to the ground, falling over the log against which Barlow had been sitting minutes ago.

Barlow grunted with the impact of his back on the ground with the added weight of Claycomb half atop his chest, but a swift forearm to Claycomb's forehead swept the mountain man off him. He scrambled to his feet. Claycomb was still trying to stand. Barlow kicked him in the ribs, sending him rolling through the dust.

Barlow stood there, looking smug. "Ain't such a big man now, are ya, you ol' fart?" he crowed.

Claycomb pushed himself to his feet, glaring at Barlow. "This ain't done yet, boy," he growled. "This ol' hoss ain't about to let no pissant chil' like ye get away with sich doin's." He blew some bloody snot on the ground and then swiped the back of his hand across his face.

"Well, come on then," Barlow said mockingly.

Claycomb shuffled toward Barlow, looking defeated and weary despite the anger in his eyes. Then he suddenly darted forward, ramming his shoulder into Barlow's chest, slamming him down. Before Barlow's back landed hard in the dirt, Claycomb was pounding his face and head with quick, hard-knuckled fists.

It took only moments for Barlow to gather his wits about him. When he did, he silently cursed himself for having been so cocky. He should have finished off Claycomb when he had the chance instead of savoring his impending victory. If he had, he wouldn't be lying here getting the tar whaled out of him. He got an arm free and jabbed a thumb into one of Claycomb's eyes, eliciting a howl of pain and rage. But the hail of blows paused, allowing him to ram an elbow into Claycomb's sides a couple of times. Claycomb fell off him.

Barlow rolled the other way and started to get up. At the last moment, he spied Claycomb's moccasined foot coming toward his head. He snapped his hands up, caught the foot and twisted hard. Claycomb went down, raising a small dust cloud. Barlow released the man's limb and stood, breathing heavily. He ran a hand over his face, and it came away bloody from his nose and a cut over one eye. It didn't seem bad, and Barlow had had worse wounds from any of scores of bar fights.

Barlow stalked forward and kicked a reeling Claycomb in one knee. The mountain man sank down on that side, and Barlow then hammered a huge fist into the side of Claycomb's face. Claycomb dropped like a spine-shot buffalo. Barlow bent over, grabbing Claycomb's greasy buckskins at the collar and rump. He lifted, pulling the mountain man to his feet, more or less, still bent over. Then he ran him forward before suddenly stopping and launching Claymore with a powerful shove. Claymore half stumbled, half flew over the riverbank and landed with a splash in the Bad Axe River. Claycomb sputtered and flapped his arms wildly.

"I do believe he don't know how to swim, Will," one of the soldiers said. He was disinterestedly watching Claycomb's effort to keep his head above water.

Barlow nodded. "Reckon he'll learn quick, Bill," he noted. "Or mayhap not."

"Get that man out of the water!" someone else suddenly bellowed.

Barlow turned and looked at Captain Littlefield. "What fer?"

"Just do what I said, Barlow," the officer bellowed.

"Beggin' your pardon, Cap'n, but you got no sway over me no more. I was mustered out this mornin'. You want that skunk saved, y'all can do it your own self.''

Littlefield's face reddened, and he sputtered, but there was nothing he could really do, and he knew it, which is what really angered him.

''You really want that crusty old fart to die, Will?'' Bill Coffelt asked.

''Don't make me no never mind. Son of a bitch has been nothin' but trouble for me. He tells the tales all the time about surviving Indian attacks and stampedin' buffler and all. I reckon if there was any truth to those yarns, he can figure out a way to survive a dunkin' in a river.''

Coffelt grinned. ''He might even see it as the road to salvation,'' he noted with glee. ''I bet he ain't ever been full-immersed baptized afore. Maybe you should go into the preachin' business, Will.''

''Now that'd be somethin' to see, wouldn't it? Me preachin'!'' He roared with laughter.

Claycomb finally managed to flap and fight his way to the far bank of the river and stand up. Angrily he clambered up the bank and glared across the river at the still laughing Will Barlow and Bill Coffelt.

''Quit your yappin', you ol' fool,'' Barlow finally yelled across to Claymore. ''Just saddle your damn horse and ride on out of here. We've all had enough of your nonsense and troublemakin'.''

That drew a smattering of applause from the gathered soldiers. Grinning, Barlow turned and walked back to where a confused Newfoundland pup was whimpering a little. The dog calmed down as soon as Barlow picked it up and held it close to his chest, murmuring softly to it.

By morning, the time had come to make a decision, but Barlow was still not sure of what to do. All he knew for certain was that he could not stay here; did not want to stay here. Not with the specter of the massacre still so fresh in his mind. Barlow still craved adventure, having found very little of it during the Indian ''fighting.'' But he had nowhere to go that he knew of.

He wandered over to where Tom Wallenbach was resting with the other wounded soldiers.

Wallenbach was doing well, and smiled when he saw his friend. "You about ready to pull out, Will?" Wallenbach asked.

"Reckon so."

"I get to ride back on a wagon," Wallenbach said with a laugh. "Damn if Ma and Pa ain't gonna be surprised when they see that!"

"Reckon they will at that," Barlow said with a smile. "And I reckon Molly Rose Maguire will take a shine to you somethin' fierce." His smile widened. "Hell, she'll probably latch on to you and not let go. You'll be a wedded man by the time fall arrives, my friend."

Wallenbach tried to look sad but couldn't manage it. "I suppose you could be right. You'll stand with me at the wedding, though, won't you? If there is a wedding."

"Don't seem likely, Tom," Barlow said, suddenly growing serious.

"Something wrong?"

Barlow shrugged, and looked out across the meadow. While the bodies were gone—buried over the past few days by the soldiers and what Indians who had been captured—it still did not look good if one examined it too closely. "Not sure what I'm gonna do, Tom," he finally allowed.

"You're not headin' back to St. Charles?" Wallenbach asked, rather shocked.

"Reckon not." Barlow shrugged again. "Ain't nothin' back there for me."

"What about Emma Sue?"

"She's half the reason I ain't goin' back," Barlow said with a rueful smile. "I ain't aimin' to marry her. Never could cotton to her *that* much. And I don't much like the way she went about things just before we left out with the militia. I don't expect that things've blown over in the few months we've been gone."

Wallenbach mulled that over for a few moments, then nodded. "I understand, Will. Sure is gonna be a different place without you there, though."

"Reckon that's a fact," Barlow said with something that almost resembled a chuckle. "Mayhap you can go into the Pig Iron for once without gettin' into a fight if I ain't there."

"That'd be somethin' new and interesting." Wallenbach almost allowed himself to smile. "So, where will you go, old friend?"

Barlow shrugged once more. "Haven't figured that out yet. Reckon I'll just mosey around a bit till somethin' strikes my fancy." He stood. "You be good to Molly Rose, boy, or I'll come back and thump ya."

"That day'll never get here," Wallenbach said, struggling to his feet. "But I suppose if Molly Rose'll have me, I'll be happy to treat her well."

Barlow nodded. "Look in on my folks when you get back and tell 'em I'm fine and out seekin' my fortune."

"Sure, Will. Sure, I'll do that." He paused, still mystified at his friend's decision. "You take care of yourself now, y'hear?"

"You, too, Tom."

They shook hands, and Barlow wandered off. A few minutes later, still decidedly unsettled about his future, Barlow saddled up old Beelzebub after eating his final Army-supplied meal. With Buffalo tucked into his shirt and his rifle slung across his back, he rode out, having no idea of where he was going.

One afternoon some weeks later, still just wandering, looking for a campsite for the night, he came across a small camp of traders—mountain men who had given up trapping for the relatively easier and more profitable job of supplying the mountaineers.

"Stay with us the night, boy," the group's leader, Andrew Branigan invited.

"You sure it won't put you out none?" Barlow asked.

"Nope. There's plenty of meat on the fire, and we could use some new company."

Barlow nodded and unsaddled Beelzebub. He let little Buffalo, now up to fifteen pounds or so, run around and do her business. The dog was a hit with the other men, and found herself enjoying hunks of meat at every turn.

"Where you boys headed?" Barlow asked when he had taken a seat at one of the fires and was gnawing on some half-raw buffalo meat.

"Independence," Branigan said. "Got us a load of furs from rendezvous. We'll sell 'em there and then make arrangements for our supplies for next year. We'll meet the rest of our boys back in the mountains come spring."

"Them mountains as scary as I've heard tell they are?" Barlow asked, tossing away a scrap of gristle and pouring himself a mug of coffee.

"I reckon some folks find 'em so," John Myles offered. He stretched out long legs. "But they ain't so scary to most folks. Of course, some of those red devils out there can put the fear of God in any man who's got hisself at least a lick of sense."

"I just fought in the war against Black Hawk and his Sauks," Barlow allowed. "Those Injins didn't seem all that scary to me."

"You ain't fought no Injins," Branigan said. "You want to fight real warriors, you need to go agin the Crows or the Blackfoot. Now *them* is Injins, boy. Tough, mean, best horsemen you'll ary see."

"Sounds like you respect 'em," Barlow said, rather surprised.

"That I do," Branigan said. "We don't like most of 'em all that much, especially the Blackfeet, but they're deservin' of our respect."

Barlow nodded. He wasn't sure he understood, but he accepted it for now. He thought about the tales that Claymore told of the mountains, and as the men talked, he heard many of the same things coming from these men. He decided there must be at least a fair amount of truth in what they were saying, and he began to think this might be the type of venture he could really take a shine to. That thought strengthened as he asked questions and listened intently to the answers.

In the morning, Barlow sat at Branigan's fire again, pouring himself some coffee, which he sipped while Buffalo bounded about, cadging food.

"You seem interested in our endeavor, Mr. Barlow," Branigan said over coffee.

"Reckon I am," Barlow acknowledged.

"How'd you like to join our little band here?"

"Really?" Barlow asked, heart suddenly pounding with excitement.

"Yep. Ye can go back to Independence with us. We'll wait out the winter there. Once we figure there's enough grass for the animals in the spring, you can head back to the mountains with us when we haul supplies out there for rendezvous. 'Course, we don't trap no more, and you'll just be a camp helper or laborer for us, but it'll get you to the mountains."

Barlow didn't have to think about it. He simply nodded, beaming.

6

THEY ARRIVED IN Independence within several days, and Barlow was left on his own. The traders he had hired on with didn't have enough work to keep everyone employed through the fall and winter, though they occasionally had use for the services of a strong back and willing hands. Barlow did whatever they asked of him, wanting to ingratiate himself and earn their respect. But work with the supplies was not nearly enough to keep him occupied all the time.

After a week or so in town, he decided he needed some kind of steadier employment, since he needed a place to stay, food to eat, and he had a frequent and powerful desire for whiskey and women. He walked around the waterfront, inquiring about jobs. He found nothing permanent, but he did find enough places willing to pay him a day's wage for a day's work through various odd jobs. None of it was particularly decent work—mucking stables, cleaning out rancid saloons in the few hours they were closed, and other such joyful tasks—but they gave him enough money to subsist on.

He spent some of his free time with the suppliers who had hired him, but considerably more in the company of mountain men, trying to learn something useful for survival in the mountains. He listened without talking, at least for a while, but the more he listened, the more he felt that some of these men were the biggest blowhards he had ever encountered. Their tales of Indian battles and buffalo hunting and glass mountains, of starvin' times and places where the ground bubbled with boiling mud were too outlandish for any man with common sense to take for real. He allowed them some room for exaggeration, but there were tales so preposterous that he finally felt he had to speak up. When one of the mountain men talked of a river running uphill, Barlow could no longer contain himself.

"There ain't no sich thing," he argued, slapping his mug on a big wooden table in one foul saloon.

The others looked at him, some smiling, others with wonder. He had been associating with this bunch of men for more than a month, and they all knew him well enough to respect him just a little. Still, he had to earn their full respect, and since he was not out in the mountains where he could do it with his work and courage, they saw this situation as an attempt to establish a place in their tight little group. None had any argument with that, but they would wait to see how he handled himself before passing judgment.

"You callin' me a liar, boy?" Sim Rutledge said, challenge strong in his voice.

Barlow debated that for a moment. He was, indeed, calling Rutledge a liar, but he wasn't sure he wanted it to sound that strong. He was not afraid of Rutledge—a tall, broad-shouldered thuggish-looking fellow—but he did not want to seem too insolent. He knew he did not have more than a tenuous spot among these men, and he wanted to solidify his position among them, not be shunned by them.

"Well, now, I wouldn't say I was exactly calling you a liar, you understand," he finally ventured. "I reckon I might just be questionin' your recollection of events is all." Barlow hoped that explanation would suffice.

"Sounded to me like you was flat out callin' me a liar," Rutledge retorted. He was not nearly as angry as he appeared to be. He simply wanted to goad Barlow into a fight to test the young man's mettle.

"Maybe your recollection ain't the only thing that's suffered from your years in the mountains," Barlow muttered. "Mayhap your hearin' has faltered some, too."

"Last chil' who said such a thing to me is in the Happy Huntin' Ground now, boy," Rutledge growled.

Barlow shrugged. He was getting a bit steamed. "So, you had some friends make wolf bait of him for you. Ain't much to concern myself about, far's I can see."

That brought a few chuckles and sniggers from the other men and a slight smile to Barlow's lips. Barlow thought he was doing well here, holding his own against an older man with a lot more experience in life.

Barlow never did figure out how Rutledge moved so fast. One moment he was sitting there glaring at Barlow, the next, he was across the table with his hands on Barlow's throat, choking him even as the chair toppled backward. Worried, and frightened for the first time that he could remember, Barlow lashed out wildly with fists, elbows, and knees, frantically fighting for his life.

He finally managed to break Rutledge's grip on his throat and roll out of the way. He staggered to his feet, breath raspy in his throat, chest heaving as he tried to make up for the loss of oxygen. He wondered if he hadn't made a big mistake here. Rutledge didn't look all that big or tough to him, and he had expected the mountain man to be like Jim Claycomb—more talk than actual action. But Barlow could still feel Rutledge's hands around his neck, choking the life out of him, and he was more than a little worried that he had tackled someone who could easily kill him without working too hard at it.

Barlow made a conscious effort to force the fear back. If he couldn't, he knew he was likely to die. If he could conquer the fear, however, he stood a fair chance with this rough and tumble mountain man—for he would not be taken by surprise again.

"Still think you'd like to call me a liar, boy?" Rutledge asked harshly.

"If you're gonna keep spoutin' sich booshwa as you had been, yep, I still say you're a lyin' sack of shit," Barlow responded, pretty certain he had not let any fear creep into his voice.

"Ah, then ye need some more teachin' in mannerly doin's around your betters, boy," Rutledge noted evenly.

"I'm mannerly enough around my betters," Barlow responded cockily. "It's them that ain't my betters that I don't figure I have to be congenial around."

That drew some hoots from the other mountain men, many of whom shouted for Rutledge to attack Barlow. Others jeered Rutledge, or Barlow, as was their wont. And then some bets were being made.

Rutledge did charge, ramming into Barlow's chest and driving the young man back, until Barlow's back hit the bar and he stopped. Rutledge tried to knee Barlow in the groin, but the young man blocked it with a thigh. As Rutledge brought his torso up, raising his fist at the same time, Barlow popped him on both ears with cupped hands.

Rutledge howled and staggered back a few steps, then righted himself and shook his head to clear the ringing in his ears. He realized that this young farm boy was no newcomer at close-in fighting. He silently cursed himself for having been less then cautious. He had assumed that despite his size, Barlow was not a very accomplished fighter. Such assumptions could get one gravely hurt, even killed. While he was not in this to battle to the death, he did not want to end up seriously injured or worse because he had underestimated his opponent.

Barlow moved away from the bar a couple of steps to give himself some room. As he did, he caught a movement out of the corner of his eye. He spun, dropping to one knee as he did so. Another of the mountain men was charging at him. Barlow surged upward as the startled mountain man arrived, grabbed him around the calves, and then dumped him over his head onto the bar. With a shove, Barlow pushed the man off the bar, behind it. Then he spun, expecting that Rutledge would be attacking.

But Rutledge was still waiting, trying to catch his breath.

He had figured his friend's assault would take care of Barlow for him. Since it hadn't, his admiration for his bull-necked opponent grew.

"If you need more help, ye fractious ol' fart, best send 'em at me," Barlow snarled. "Or if you're done catchin' your wind, you can make another run at me. Whichever you decide, friend, jist get to it. I'm gettin' thirsty and tired of standin' here."

Rutledge's face suddenly split into a huge grin. "Ye got sand in ye, boy," he said. "Ye plumb do. Waugh! Ye showed this ol' chil' a thing or two, boy, or I wouldn't say so." He sifted his eyes a little. "Hey, Caleb," he called, "come on out from behind that bar, boy. This ain't no time for sleepin'."

Caleb Simon pulled himself up behind the bar. He looked rather dazed. He shook his head a few times, and some life returned to his still somewhat glassy eyes. "It over?" he asked.

"Yep," Rutledge said with a laugh. "That ol' hoss done hisself well agin us, Caleb. I, fer one, ain't aimin' to tangle with him again—at least fer a long spell."

Simon nodded. "I reckon that's a wise thing," he agreed. "I got me a powerful dry that needs to be fixed anyway."

Barlow stood there dumbfounded. These two men had been trying to kill him moments ago, now they were bantering about—and with—him. He suspected it was a trick, so he was wary, but he still turned to help Simon climb over the bar. He tensed when Rutledge strolled up, but relaxed when the big mountain man threw an arm around his shoulders.

"Looks like me and Caleb owe you a drink, son," Rutledge said with a grin.

Barlow looked cautiously from one to the other and back. "You boys mind explainin' jist what's goin' on here?" he said softly.

Rutledge shrugged, but retained his grin. "You been loiterin' with us boys for more than a moon now, son. Ye been good, nary openin' your mouth too much. Jist listenin' like a green no-nothin' should. Me and the other boys was startin' to wonder if you had any gumption whatsoever. When you piped up and give me guff about my yarns, it was the first real sign ye had some grit. We decided to see jist how much backbone ye really did have.''

''And ye showed us somethin', too, boy,'' Simon threw in. ''Damn, but you like to snapped my spine there. Damn, if you ain't somethin'.''

''And now we know you got the hair of the bear on ye, boy,'' Rutledge added, ''we'd be mighty agreeable to havin' ye join us at our table whenever ye like. Ye even got the right to speak—some.''

Barlow shook his head in amazement. He was still vigilant, but was pretty sure these men were telling him the truth. If they had wanted to attack him again, they would have done so right away, he figured. They didn't need to lull him this much just to gain an advantage of him. Besides, he had seen the likes before. Some fellows were like that—had to test a newcomer before allowing him into their inner circle. He was just glad that none of them had gotten hurt in this initiation.

''You sure this ain't some kind of trick?'' he asked, still a little dubious.

''We're speakin' true, my friend,'' Rutledge said, suddenly serious.

Barlow grinned tentatively. ''Then I'd be happy to share a jug with you boys,'' he said.

The whole group was feeling full of piss and vinegar that night when they descended on one of the odious brothels that littered the banks of the Missouri River. The men were roaring drunk, but the staff didn't mind. The women—of varied hues, sizes, and ethnicity—knew they would get more cash and foofaraw out of this loud, wild bunch of men in one night than they would normally make in a month. In return, they showed their appreciation in most enjoyable ways.

It became a regular event for the eight mountain men and the newcomer. They would often gather at some saloon, eat and drink prodigiously, and then visit a whore-house, where they would fornicate with the same enthu-siastic spirit.

Even winter settling in over the land did not lessen the debauchery the men took part in, though a few of the men who were a little older tended to beg off now and again. By February, though, even the young Will Barlow was feel-ing the effects of so many sprees, and he began to look forward to the time he and the traders would head west. He was excited about the adventure he expected to find out in the mountains, but he also just wanted to get away from the confines of the town.

As winter began winding down, Barlow was in for a surprise, too. Buffalo had been acting rather odd for a cou-ple of months, but Barlow had not thought much about it. However, the dog's strained whining woke him one night. Barlow got up and turned the lantern up so that he could see. Buffalo was lying in a corner of the shabby room, whimpering, almost howling.

"What the hell's wrong with you, dog?" Barlow mut-tered as he knelt beside the animal. Then, "Lord A'mighty." There was a newborn puppy lying there and another partially out.

Minutes later, the second one was completely born. Buf-falo looked around, eyes sad, and tried to get up to take care of her puppies, but she didn't have the strength for it. She whined a few more times, as Barlow petted her, not knowing what else to do. There was an awful lot of blood around, a lot more than there should have been, Barlow thought.

Then, with a final whimper, Buffalo died.

"Goddamn son of a bitch," Barlow breathed. The dog was only seven months old or a little more. He shook his head, saddened by it. Adding to his sorrow, he noticed that one of the pups also seemed to be dead. The other was alive, squirming a little. Barlow lifted the pup. It was so small that it fit comfortably in his one hand. He cleaned the newborn up some and then stuck it inside his shirt. After sadly getting rid of Buffalo and the stillborn pup, he went to a general store and managed to get some milk and a way to dispense it to feed it to the brand-new puppy.

For the next two weeks, he spent most of the time in his room, tending to the little puppy. By then the dog's eyes were open and he began feeding the animal meat broth. Barlow was amazed at how much the puppy resembled its mother, as far as breed went. But he recalled seeing several Newfoundlands running around the area where he had roomed in Independence.

By the time Barlow said farewell to the mountain men led by Sim Rutledge and left Independence with Andrew Branigan's small band of traders, the puppy—a male he decided to also call Buffalo—was just over a month old and, though still on the runtish side, healthy.

Which is more than Barlow could say about himself. He was feeling incredibly poorly, after having filled his gut with cheap whiskey the night before. As always, he had overdone the liquor, the food, and his time with a delightful quadroon from one of the bordellos. Now his head throbbed, his manhood felt rubbed raw, and his stomach roiled as if he had swallowed a whirlpool. Beelzebub's bone-rattling gait did nothing to improve his humor or the way he felt. Only Buffalo's comforting warmth in his shirt and the familiar little whines and growls kept him going during that first morning. By afternoon, his youthful constitution had recovered enough to where he only felt half dead.

The night meal was a hurried affair, in which Barlow gobbled down bolts of meat and swallowed hot, thick coffee, which settled his stomach. He turned in right after eating and was asleep within moments.

He tore into breakfast like a starving man and polished off an astounding amount of food—something he had learned over the fall and winter that was a common occurrence among the men who made their living in the mountain country. With that, he was in much better shape, and he was even fairly nice to Beelzebub when he saddled the rickety old horse.

Since he was the camp helper, he had more than enough

duties to do, including most of the cooking, tending fires, gathering firewood, helping load and unload the trade goods, and dozens of other menial tasks. It was hot, hard, and often boring work, and at first Barlow was annoyed with it. But he soon realized that the others were the leaders of this venture, and he had willingly hired on as a camp helper—nothing more. It didn't make the work any less tedious, but with a better attitude about it, he did not resent the chores as much, which made the days flow along smoothly.

But there was some excitement in the buffalo hunts that began only days after they left Independence. He found he loved them and proved to be a better hunter than he or the others had thought.

And just over a week out from the town, the men set up their night's camp not far from a Pawnee village. Barlow had trouble sleeping that night, caught up in the excitement of soon getting to see a real Indian village, with real Indians, rather than those disheartened people whom the militias had hunted down.

7

LEAVING TWO MEN behind to guard the horses and supplies, the others rode slowly into the village the next morning. Barlow was thrilled to be among them. He had figured that as the camp helper and lowest man in the camp at the time, that he would be left behind on guard duty. Then he had learned that the men would not leave such an inexperienced man behind. It was not that they did not trust him—they did—it was just that he had no experience in such matters, and if some Indians had come along looking to cause some trouble, Barlow would not have known how to handle it. Andrew Branigan and John Myles—the leaders of the trading group—also wanted to give the newcomer a chance to meet real Indians. He would meet a lot of Indians between the Settlements and the Rocky Mountains and in the mountains, so he had to start learning how to deal with them, some of their customs and ways.

As Barlow clopped into the village, he was too awed and amazed by all that he saw to be embarrassed by the old horse he rode, though more than one Pawnee pointed to the swaybacked nag and laughed. Barlow was oblivious to it all. He just stared, trying not to gape.

The Pawnee lodges were made of earth. They were fairly

large and sturdy looking. Some were mostly freestanding, while others were built into small humps of grass-covered earth. Racks of weapons stood in front of many of the lodges, and a few horses were tethered here and there. Racks of drying buffalo and antelope meat were scattered around the village between the lodges. Though everyone had stopped what they were doing to watch the white men riding in, Barlow could tell that many of the women had been busy at scraping and curing hides. One woman still stood with a mixture of buffalo brains—used for curing the hides—dripping from her hands. Some warriors sat in the sunshine outside their lodges, staring at the visitors curiously, their work temporarily forgotten.

Some children had paused in their games to give the newcomers the once-over, but many soon lost interest and went back to playing, giving the village a colorful, noisy air—much like a town, Barlow thought.

Because the days were still rather cool, most of the Indians wore blankets wrapped around their torsos, either at the shoulder or waist. A few had forgone the garments, preferring to warm their bones in the still-feeble sunshine.

Barlow began to realize that these people looked proud and comfortable in their place in the world. They were not the downtrodden beggars who sometimes wandered the streets of frontier cities like St. Louis, St. Charles, and Independence. No, they were people much like any others Barlow knew—some fiercely proud, some almost vacant, some friendly, some vicious, some curious, others disinterested, some happy, others sad.

Something nagged at Barlow's brain, and it took him some time to realize what it was—there were few young women here. He wondered about that. He looked around more closely and thought he saw some of them peering out from the entryways of lodges. He nodded a little. It was wise, he decided, that the Pawnees hide their young women when a bunch of unknown white men were around. He would have done the same thing had he been in their position. Of course, he disliked it seeing as how he was one of those white men, and the thought that the Pawnees would hide their women from him was annoying, even insulting. Besides, he wanted a good look at the young women. The older ones he saw were not particularly attractive, but he suspected that the younger ones were much better looking, as they were in his own world.

They stopped in front of one lodge outside of which stood an impressive array of Pawnee men. Barlow figured they were chiefs. Three of the five men had the strip of hair that ran from the back to the front of their heads, greased and roached, built up into an impressive scalplock. The sides of their head were shaved. The other two wore war bonnets of eagle feathers. All looked composed, almost arrogant.

Andrew Branigan held out his right hand in greeting and then spoke for some minutes in Pawnee. One Indian, who Barlow assumed to be the head chief, responded in his own language, the words sounding solemn.

Branigan finally nodded and dismounted.

"Let's go, boy," John Myles said to Barlow.

"What's going on, John?" Barlow asked, a little concerned.

"Parley with Two Sticks," Myles said, dismounting. He nodded toward the Indian who had spoken. "He's the closest thing to a top chief these Pawnees have."

"He peaceable?" Barlow asked, climbing off his horse. It hadn't occurred to him till just now that the Pawnees were anything but peaceful. Now he realized that they could be very warlike, and that was not a thought he wanted to contemplate for very long.

"Yep. He ain't above tryin' to chisel us whenever he thinks he can get away with it, though."

"That don't seem right," Barlow said as he dropped the reins to his old horse.

"You ain't ever met a white man who'd do such?" Myles responded with a small smile.

Barlow grinned and nodded. "Reckon I have at that. Just never thought of an Injin doing it."

"There's many a man out in the mountains who'll tell you that all Injins are notional critters, that they'll be your

friend one minute and attack you the next. And there are a
many who will do such a thing. What most of those boys
don't want to admit to anyone is that white men ain't no
different. They're just as notional. Befriend you one minute, club you on the head and take your money the next.''

Barlow thought that one over as he entered the Pawnee
lodge. He could see where white men would do this, and
he decided it wasn't all that strange that Indians would do
the same thing. Too many men thought only of their own
gain and too little of others. He sat between Ed Hunnicutt
and Myles and looked around. A fire in the center of the
lodge spread a dim light. Barlow could make out sleeping
robes and storage areas, but he couldn't see much else very
clearly. He began to sweat in the close confines of the warm
earth lodge, unwilling to acknowledge that he was suddenly
frightened for no real reason. Even Myles's assuring words
were of little comfort at the moment.

A pipe was lit, and Two Sticks smoked from it for a
moment before passing it to Branigan. The trader took it
and solemnly puffed, blowing smoke in various directions,
then nodded and passed it to Hunnicutt.

Myles leaned over and whispered to Barlow. ''You're
next, boy. You take a puff and blow it to the north, one to
the south, then to the east and west—the four directions.
Then a puff toward Mother Earth and Father Sky. Understand?''

Barlow nodded worriedly as he took the proffered pipe.
He did as he was instructed, hoping he got it right. Then
with a sigh of relief he handed it to Myles, who without
hesitation puffed and passed the pipe on.

When Myles had done so, he nodded at Barlow. ''You
did well,'' he said quietly. ''These Injin—all Injins—think
this is powerful medicine. Whether you believe it or not
don't matter. If you're going to deal with Injins, you have
to do some things their way or you won't get nowhere.''

Barlow nodded.

Soon after, the pipe had finished making the round of
white men and Pawnees. It was put aside reverentially, and
as Branigan and Two Sticks began conversing in Pawnee,

three women began handing out bowls of stew and tin mugs of harsh, foul coffee.

Barlow glanced up to nod thanks when a bowl was thrust in front of his face and was struck by the beauty of the young woman who was serving him. He almost gasped but managed to contain it. He took the bowl and nodded thanks, not sure whether he should acknowledge her in any other way. Then she was gone, and all Barlow could do was sit there and listen to the heavy thumping of his heart.

Barlow was startled when Buffalo rustled inside his shirt. The puppy had slept through everything so far, but Barlow figured the smell of food had woken the dog. He smiled to himself and opened his shirt enough so that Buffalo could poke his head out. Barlow fished a piece of meat out of the stew bowl and fed it to the pup, not realizing that the Pawnees were astonished at the sight of the dog popping out of Barlow's garment. He did become aware of the Indians when he glanced up and saw them all staring at him. He froze, another piece of meat in his hand, looking from one dark face to another. "Something wrong?" he asked.

There was some conversation in Pawnee between Branigan and the warriors, then Branigan looked at Barlow. "Two Sticks wants to know how you make a puppy grow out of your belly." He was trying to hold back his laughter.

"You lyin' sack of shit," Barlow said in irritation. "He didn't ask no such thing."

"He sure as hell did, boy," Branigan countered, still trying to mask his amusement. "These boys are some superstitious. And now they think you have great magic or something."

"They must be mad as hatters," Barlow muttered. He looked at the Indians and set the bowl of stew down. Then he opened the shirt some more and pulled Buffalo out and set him down. The dog piddled right there, much to everyone's amusement, and then went straight to the bowl and started lapping up the liquid.

Barlow had the sudden gut-wrenching thought that this might be dog stew. He tried to push that out of his mind. He pulled open his shirt. "See," he said slowly, "nothing there. I just keep my dog there for safety and warmth." He looked at Branigan, who translated.

The trader also translated Two Sticks' reply: "You have strong medicine, Dog Carrier—that's his name for you now, boy—and you'll have a rich life."

"Thank you," Barlow said.

"Now he wants to know what you'll take for the dog," Branigan said seriously.

"What?" Barlow glared at Two Sticks a moment, then looked angrily at Branigan.

"He wants to buy the dog from you, boy. You can strike a good bargain with him for it, I reckon."

"You tell him the only way he's gonna git his hands on this dog is if he puts me under," Barlow snapped.

"That's a damn fool thing, boy," Branigan hissed. "You could ruin everything for the sake of that damn animal."

Barlow shrugged. "Ruin everything my ass, Cap'n," he said evenly. "You said yourself this here is nothing more than a courtesy. You don't need to do no tradin' here. And he ain't gonna treat us none too poorly lest word get back to the Settlements. If that was to happen, ol' Two Sticks there would be one sorry son of a bitch. Hell, them boys back in Independence're likely to come out here and raze this whole damn village. At best, Two Sticks'll never get another trader to stop by here, and his people won't like it none when they can't get no goods."

Branigan looked at him in surprise, shocked that the young man, scared at being in an Indian village for the first time, could deduce that so quickly. "You might be too smart for your own damn good, son," he said, a touch of admiration in his voice.

Barlow shrugged.

Branigan turned to Two Sticks and said in Pawnee, "My friend says he can't give up his dog. It was a gift from his grandfather, a man much revered in his land." He stopped and waited, ignoring the sweat that had begun to trickle down his face. He knew the Pawnees, like most other Indians, highly respected courage. He wasn't sure, though, that this wouldn't be seen as defiance, not courage.

Two Sticks talked with his warriors quietly for a few moments, then he nodded at Barlow. "I understand," he said solemnly, which Branigan translated with a great deal of relief.

Then Two Sticks said in terrible, but mostly understandable English, "Fatten him up, he'll make a hell of a stew!" He laughed, joined immediately by his fellow tribesmen, and moments later by the white visitors.

With the tension broken, the men began talking of general matters. Barlow picked up his bowl and the horn spoon and began to gulp down the stew, still trying not to think of what it might be made of. He hoped it wasn't dog, as it was delicious, and he would hate to have turned his puppy into a cannibal. He continued to pick out little pieces of meat and hand-feed them to the dog, who wandered around the group from time to time, nuzzling at the men, both red and white, looking for handouts. He received plenty.

Barlow worried for a while when the dog began to wander off, and tried to stop him, but finally gave it up. He worried that one of the Indians might just choose to brain the dog and throw it in the pot despite Barlow's objections. But he realized he could not keep the dog inside his shirt forever, and that he had to trust the Indians' word that he would not be harmed. It didn't make him feel any more comfortable, but after a bit he began to relax when he saw that the Pawnees were getting as much enjoyment out of feeding the puppy as his friends were.

He turned when a soft, melodious voice said, "More?" in his ear. He smiled at the beautiful young Pawnee woman. "Please," he said with a nod, handing her the bowl. He didn't know if it was impolite or not, but he could not stop himself from watching her.

She was short and somewhat thinner than he had expected, almost delicate in some ways. Her hair was long, loose, pitch black, probably made shiny with a liberal coating of bear grease. He had gotten only a glance at her face, but it was indelibly burned into Barlow's mind—high, very prominent cheekbones, fairly epicanthic eyelids, smooth, very dark skin, deep, almost black eyes, full lips, rounded chin.

He watched until she had returned with another full bowl of stew, plus a refilled mug of coffee. He could see now that she had a womanly figure even if she was still very young—he judged her to be perhaps fifteen. He nodded his thanks again and began spooning in stew, but still managed to watch her walk away. He did not know who she was or what her place in this lodge was, but he vowed to himself then and there that if she were not married, he would have her. He would figure out some way to get to her. Barlow smiled, turning back to look at Buffalo as the puppy bumped his hand with his wet nose, looking for some more food. "Greedy little cuss, ain't you, boy?" he whispered, grinning.

8

BARLOW QUICKLY GOT bored with sitting there. He could understand virtually nothing of what was being said, as Branigan had little time—or inclination—to translate the fast-moving conversation. After what he estimated to be an hour or so, Barlow leaned over and asked Myles in a whisper, "You think it'd cause any consternation if I was to get out of this lodge and wander around the village some?"

"I reckon not, but you better let me check first," Myles replied. A few minutes later, he caught Branigan's attention and posed Barlow's question to him.

Branigan talked to Two Sticks in Pawnee for several moments, then turned to Barlow. "You can go. Jist mind your manners, boy. You understand?"

"Yep."

"Good." Branigan winked and then nodded toward the young Indian woman. He had seen the way Barlow had looked at her, and he knew what was going through his friend's mind. "Jist go easy," he added, nodding slightly toward the young woman again.

Barlow's eyes widened in surprise, but he caught himself and regained control. "I will," he vowed. He stood, lifting Buffalo with him as he did. Then he strolled outside, trying to look nonchalant. Out in the sunshine, however, he realized that his heart was pounding with a beat like a horse galloping across a wood bridge. He had a powerful hankering for that young Pawnee woman. He was also scared to death now that he was alone in the middle of a Pawnee village. He half expected some warrior to come and club him over the head for some perceived slight, leaving him to die on the dusty ground.

He started walking slowly, holding Buffalo tightly, as if that offered him some protection. But no one seemed inclined to bother him. After a few minutes he began to relax a little. And as he did, his thoughts returned to the young woman. He had never wanted a woman as bad as he wanted this one. He didn't care that the desire was fueled by her seeming inaccessibility. And that was the problem—how could he get close enough to her to let her know he craved her?

Branigan had implied that it was possible for him to meet her, but as he strolled, Barlow couldn't think of any way that he could. And if he couldn't meet her, he certainly couldn't have her. Filled with lust, he wandered aimlessly and soon found himself at a broad patch of clear land along the Republican River. He stood there a bit, letting Buffalo run around, drink from the river, and even venture into the water a little way, where the river pooled serenely.

He heard a noise behind him and he spun, suddenly worried again. Then his heart skipped a beat and his manhood stirred as he saw that it was the woman he craved. He stood there, not sure what he should do, if anything. If she were a white woman, he would have no trouble with such a decision. But she was a Pawnee and they were in her village. He did not know the rules here. Hell, he wasn't even sure she would want him. And if she didn't, and he made a move for her, the whole village was likely to come down on his head.

She moved tentatively toward him, and he smiled hesitantly at her. Both were encouraged, and she stepped a bit more firmly in his direction. His smile strengthened and grew. In moments, she was standing in front of him. He was unsure of himself, almost worried. He knew *what* to do. He just wasn't sure of *how* to go about it. Hell, as far as he knew, she didn't even speak English, which wasn't absolutely necessary, he guessed, but might make the going a little easier.

He smiled. If she didn't speak English, she would at least understand the gesture. His confidence rose when she smiled back. Encouraged, he asked, "What's your name?"

"Plenty Robes," she said in passable English.

"You speak my language?" he asked, surprised.

Plenty Robes nodded. "Speak good."

He smiled at the woman again. Throwing caution to the wind, he asked, "You know what I want?"

"Of course," Plenty Robes said with a giggle.

"And that's all right by you?"

"Yes. I want, too. It's big fun!"

"You do?" Barlow was shocked. The only women he had ever met who claimed to want—and to enjoy—sexual activity were prostitutes, whom he suspected said that more to please their customers than because of any real desire for it.

"Much. You a goddamn big fella. Maybe good. I hope."

Barlow was dumbfounded. But he'd be damned if he'd pass this chance up. "There someplace to go?" he asked, his mouth suddenly dry.

"Yep. Come with me." Plenty Robes took his hand and led him off through the brush along the river.

A quarter of a mile later, she stopped at a small clearing that Barlow suspected she had used before for this type of activity. It didn't matter to him. He was not aimin' to marry her, just share her favors and then leave when Branigan gave the word.

Plenty Robes spread her blanket on the ground and turned to face him. He smiled and pulled Buffalo out of his shirt and put the puppy on the ground. "Now don't you go and get yourself lost, you damn fool," he mumbled at the dog. *Or worse*, he thought, *get put in the cooking pot!* When he turned back around, Plenty Robes had dropped her dress and stood there unashamedly naked, wearing only her moccasins.

"Oh, my," Barlow breathed, taking in the sight. She was unlike any woman he had ever seen before. Her breasts were firm and rode high and proud. Her skin was a uniform dusky color, like a well-worn copper penny. The tips of her breasts were dark, almost black, and small nipples were folded into the surrounding dark flesh. Her belly was gently rounded and directed his attention to the tangle of curly, pitch-black hair at the juncture of her legs. Her hips flared out slightly and flowed smoothly to short, well-formed legs.

"You like?" she asked coyly.

"Goddamn, yes!" Barlow whispered, afraid that his real voice would make this vision go away.

"Goddamn good." She grinned, then lay down on the blanket. "Come here now," she said evenly. "Let's see if you're a big fella all over," she added pointedly.

Hoping he would meet with her approval, Barlow squatted and yanked off his shoes and socks, then stood, tugged his equipment over his head, followed by his shirt. Without hesitation, he shucked his pants, glad that his manhood stood out proudly, ready for action. He knelt at her side and kissed her hard on the mouth, his tongue flicking hers roughly, taking control. She played back with great enthusiasm.

He shifted backward a little and let his mouth trail down over her chin and across her throat and then in the canyon formed by her breasts. He did not stop until he got to her navel, into which he buried his tongue. He worked his way back upward, tongue, lips, and teeth blazing a hot trail that elicited soft moans from Plenty Robes. He grabbed one breast in his hand, and under the pressure of his thumb and forefinger, the nipple began to blossom. He replaced his fingers with his mouth, nipping at the little bud, sucking it and much of the breast flesh behind it into his mouth and then withdrawing slowly, until the button popped out from his teeth. He repeated the process on the other breast, taking as much time as he had with the first.

Plenty Robes was breathing raggedly now and moaning.

Her hips wriggled and her entire body seemed to be on fire. Barlow sensed she could feel the beginnings of an orgasm rearing up inside her and wanted release.

As if he could read her mind, Barlow retraced his path down her belly, but this time did not stop at any one place. He paused briefly so he could move between her legs. He lifted her and tossed her thighs over his shoulders and held her suspended in air by her ass as he clamped his mouth to her soaking womanhood. His tongue worked into the slit, burrowing deep inside her, and she let loose a long gasp of pleasure. His lips sucked her lower lips into his mouth and he tongued the soft, spongy flesh. He released them and sent his tongue darting time and again over her pleasure button.

Within moments, her body arched and spasmed with a strength he did not know she possessed. He did not stop his ministrations, however, until he was sure she was finished with this climax. Even then, his gentle teeth, persistent tongue and hungry lips made love to her, slowly building her back up to another earth-shattering explosion. Then he placed her buttocks back on the blanket and grinned at her.

"You like?" he asked, not mocking her.

"Goddamn yes!" Plenty Robes said, breathlessly. "Goddamn yes! Yes, yes!"

He squiggled up between her legs until the tip of his manhood brushed her vulva. Taking himself in hand, he positioned himself at the entrance to her love tunnel and then plunged hard into the soft, velvety wetness, all the way in. She gasped, he moaned.

Barlow grinned down at her and was rewarded with a dazzling smile in return. Then he began moving his hips, withdrawing almost all the way from her and plunging home to the hilt again. He set a slow, enticing pace, and within moments, Plenty Robes was matching his movements, her groin rotating against his as she found the rhythm.

The pace picked up and kept moving faster. Suddenly Plenty Robes threw her arms around Barlow's neck and hooked the back of her heels on the backs of Barlow's thighs. Her buttocks came off the blanket, as she smashed her pelvis against his. She gasped and screeched softly, face stretched in passion.

Then she went limp, but she smiled brightly, and her eyes sparkled. "You goddamn good!" she panted, her breasts still heaving.

Barlow grinned almost arrogantly. "You're damn right, woman," he said. "And I ain't nowhere near done yet."

"Not done?" A mischievous look appeared in Plenty Robes's eyes.

"Nope." Barlow rolled, bringing Plenty Robes with him until he was flat on his back and she was on top of him.

Plenty Robes eased herself upward, his manhood sliding agonizingly slowly out of her silken sheath, until only the tip remained in her. She paused, hovering there, a wicked grin splashed across her burnt copper face. Then she slipped back down, even more slowly.

Barlow sucked in a breath as pleasure roared from her hot womanhood, through his manhood, and coursed through his body as if part of his bloodstream. He groaned when she went through the movement again, the pleasure exquisite. He felt as if he would explode any second. He wanted to fill her with his juices *now*!

But she was not about to allow that. Not yet anyway. She sank down onto him and then rocked back and forth, not milking him, but managing to rub her pleasure bud against the lower part of his engorged shaft. He relaxed a bit and grabbed hold of Plenty Robes's breasts. He squeezed and fondled them, pulling the nipples as hard and as far as he thought he could without hurting her. He rolled the nipples between thumbs and forefingers, too, each deft pinch bringing a shiver of delight from the Indian woman.

She screamed and bounced up and down on him in a frenzy of lust and pleasure. He let go of her breasts and grabbed her flaring hips, holding on desperately to make sure she didn't go flying off him and land in the bushes somewhere. Finally she shuddered so violently that for a moment Barlow thought she would hurt herself. Then she stiffened, sucking in a huge breath, and finally crumpled onto his big, broad chest. She was barely able to breathe.

"You all right, Plenty Robes?" Barlow asked with a touch of worry.

Plenty Robes nodded, unable to speak.

They lay that way for a while, until Plenty Robes's breathing returned almost to normal. Barlow stroked the woman's back and buttocks, reveling in the feel of her soft, but firm flesh under his callused hands. Every time she moved even minutely, her vagina would contract, grabbing at his manhood inside her. It kept him hard and eager to continue their lovemaking, but he was being as patient as he possibly could be.

Still, he could not wait forever, and he almost unconsciously began moving his pelvis, creating some friction between their sexual organs. It was not much, but it was highly pleasurable, and it seemed to be stoking the fires of her lust again.

Minutes later, she pushed her upper torso off of him, until she was sitting on his erectness again. "Not done, right?" she queried with a grin.

"Not done," he agreed.

"Then we take care of your goddamn big fella."

"I'd sure like that," Barlow acknowledged with a grin.

She began sliding up and down on his swollen member again, moving slowly, teasingly. But he was getting close now and was in no mood to wait. He grabbed her hips again and began working her on his manhood, faster and faster, his brawny arms working frantically. Her tits bobbled in front of his face, exciting him all the more.

She smiled at him, seemingly enjoying the pleasure of having a big, powerful man working her so well. And it looked to him as if another orgasm had begun to make its presence known in her innermost core of femininity. She began wriggling her bottom, stoking herself some more, but apparently waiting for him to reach his climax. He had been good to her, and it was obvious to Barlow that she wanted to make this as good for him as she possibly could.

Suddenly he bellowed like a buffalo bull in rut, and he bucked her furiously while pounding his hips up and down into her. Her scream of delight mingling with his animal-like grunts made a song of love and lust that the whole village could hear. Had they known, neither of the participants would have cared.

The explosion of passion lasted longer than either Barlow or Plenty Robes had thought possible, but finally it came to an end, and they slumped breathlessly together in a sweaty pile on the blanket.

About the same time that they regained their breath somewhat, little Buffalo bounded up and licked at their perspiration-slicked bodies. He made mock little growls, before curling up between the two people. In moments, all three were asleep.

9

WHEN BARLOW RODE out of the Pawnee village two days later with the group of traders, he was in high spirits. Yes, it was true that he was drained, but his spirits rode in the clouds. He still could not believe he had spent virtually two entire days in the company of a naked, incredibly lusty, very beautiful Indian woman doing nothing but fornicating and feeding.

They had spent the rest of that first day in their little glade along the river. Getting hungry, Plenty Robes finally got dressed and wandered off. Barlow had sat there, feeling rather self-conscious about his nudity. Within minutes, he, too, had gotten dressed. He relaxed some, though he was considerably worried that the woman would not be back.

But Plenty Robes was not gone long. She returned with roasted meat wrapped in a piece of buckskin. He refused to ask what kind of meat it was when he dug into it a few minutes later, but he did think it was quite tasty. She also brought a gourd of water and a small basket of early blueberries. They ate and made love again. Then, at Plenty Robes's urging, and with a lack of enthusiasm from Barlow, they took a dip in the small pool of the river. Barlow was against bathing, thinking it unhealthy, but he had to admit the dunk in the river was refreshing.

They stayed there that night, sleeping comfortably on one blanket, covered by another, under the stars, enjoying the light breeze that ruffled the surrounding brush and the rippling serenity of the river.

Buffalo had wandered in and out of the little haven through most of the day, but came back to stay just before nightfall. The pup curled up next to Barlow after insisting on a good petting and went to sleep. He was still there when Barlow and Plenty Robes awoke in the morning. The dog roused himself and stretched, watched for a moment as the humans began making love again, and then left, almost as if wondering just what in the hell these silly people were doing.

A couple of hours later, Barlow decided he had better go see what Branigan and the others were up to, or at least let them know he was still alive. With Buffalo wandering along at his side, Barlow strolled to where the others had left their horses the day before. None was there, not even Beelzebub. Panic flooded through him, and the early spring sun suddenly gained a couple dozen degrees of heat. He stood, alarmed and wondering what to do.

He breathed deeply with relief moments later when he heard a small commotion and turned to watch Branigan and the other traders riding into the village.

Branigan stopped next to him. "Have a pleasant evening?" Branigan asked. There was no expression in his face.

Barlow disliked that he could not read Branigan's face some of the time. But he had learned that when Branigan was blankly stoical of face like now, he was usually joshing. "That I did, Cap'n." He grinned widely. "A grandly pleasant night." He suddenly looked confused. "Jist wish I knew where my ol' horse was."

Branigan finally broke into a smile. "I reckon you do at that," he said. "That old nag of yours is back in our camp. We took it back last night with us. Weren't sure just what you were up to"—which drew some sniggers from the other traders—"so we didn't bring it back now."

Barlow nodded, relieved. "When are we pullin' out for good?" he asked. He hoped it wasn't right away. He didn't want to walk back to his camp. More important, he wanted more time—as much as he could manage—with Plenty Robes.

"I expect we'll leave out sometime tomorrow, maybe the next morning. Depends on how much more tradin' the Pawnees are ready for."

Barlow nodded. "Need me fer anything, Mr. Branigan?" he asked. He didn't know what he'd do if Branigan had some chores for him. He was eager to find Plenty Robes again, lest she think he wasn't interested in her any more.

Branigan almost smiled. "Reckon not. You go on and find that leetle Injin gal again."

"Yessir." Barlow spun and loped off, Buffalo bounding happily alongside him.

Barlow was surprised but pleased to see that Plenty Robes was in their little hideaway. She had brought a metal pot of stew—again, Barlow didn't really want to know what it was made of—as well as more roasted meat, some berries, and more water.

"Did you miss me while I was gone?" he asked, trying to mask his relief with bravado.

"Yes. Much," Plenty Robes said. She was serious.

"Afraid I wouldn't come back?" he asked, startled again.

"Yes. Maybe you had enough of me." She seemed a little concerned, though it appeared to be lessening since he was there.

He sat and dug into the stew, which was still hot, he found a piece of gristle and tossed it to the dog. "Well, Plenty Robes, I ain't had near enough of you, girl." He grinned reassuringly. "You know, I thought mayhap you wouldn't be here when I came back." He smiled again. "Mayhap you had enough of this big ol' boy."

"I like big boy," Plenty Robes said with a wide smile. "I like big boy's big boy, too!" She reached over and grabbed his crotch and gave it a quick squeeze before sitting back again.

Startled, Barlow ended up spitting out a mouthful of stew. It took him a moment to calm down. "Well," he said, having taken three attempts to get the word out of a suddenly dry throat, "Big boy and the other big boy like you, too, Plenty Robes."

"Both big boys ready to play again?" Plenty Robes asked, no sense of false modesty in her words.

"That we are, girl."

A moment later, they were rolling naked around on the blankets again.

Later that day, as the heat rose a little, they picked up their belongings and Barlow followed Plenty Robes into one of the earthen lodges. In the cool dimness they put their things down and made love again. When they were done, something dawned on Barlow.

"You sure this is all right?" he asked a little nervously.

"Yes. Good."

"Your folks won't mind?"

"No. They think you give me plenty foofaraw for this."

A stab of fear pierced Barlow. "I ain't got no foofaraw to give you, Plenty Robes," he said, concerned.

"No need. I don't want none. I just tell 'em that."

"You sure?"

"Sure. Don't need no foofaraw. Just want more big boy!" She giggled, and rolled herself on top of Barlow.

His uneasiness faded with time, and he soon learned that her parents really didn't seem to mind him there. He didn't understand that, but he was not about to worry about it now. In fact, her father seemed to be an affable man, and they chatted pleasantly when Iron Arm was around—with Plenty Robes translating.

Barlow didn't know where his stamina with Plenty Robes came from, but he was not going to question it. He just hoped it continued. Which it did, much to his amazement.

But finally it had to come to an end, and Barlow was

waiting with heavy heart when Andrew Branigan and two
of his men rode in with Barlow's horse in tow. Barlow
tossed Buffalo over his shoulder and pulled himself up onto
Beelzebub, then laid the dog across the saddle in front of
him. He patted the puppy's head. "A few more weeks,
boy," he said quietly, "and you're gonna have to start
walkin' all the time. You're gettin' too big for this poor
old horse."

Beelzebub neighed and wagged his shaggy head in
agreement.

As they rode out of the village, Barlow had to look back.
Relieved, but hurting in his heart at the same time, he spotted Plenty Robes standing in an open spot watching him.
He tipped his hat a little at her, afraid to do anything more.
She half waved and then turned and walked quickly away.
Barlow watched for a minute, wondering, hoping, if she
had done it because she was going to miss him as much as
he was going to miss her. Sadly, he faced front again and
rode on.

The work for Barlow was grindingly, relentlessly monotonous. He realized within minutes of riding out of the Pawnee village that Branigan had given him considerable
leeway so that he could have plenty of time with Plenty
Robes, and now he would have to make up for it. Some of
the other traders resented the fact that Barlow had had such
a fine time with such an astounding beauty in the village,
while they had had to perform the tedious camp work that
Barlow was supposed to be doing.

Barlow took it stoically, though not without considerable
frustration. He had always been the kind to fight at the drop
of a hat when someone caused him even a little bit of trouble or annoyance. But the war against Black Hawk, such
as it was, had taught him that such an uncontrollable temper
was more of a flaw than a mark of manly pride. Not that
he wouldn't fight anyone, anywhere, anytime if the situation warranted it, but starting a ruckus just because his
bosses were being hard on him was downright foolish. If
he did it just once, they would leave him out here, alone

and without supplies. So he accepted the abuse the men dished out, mentally noting that it really wasn't nearly as bad as it could be.

But making it all the worse, was the fact that he missed Plenty Robes considerably. He had never met a woman like her, and he was dead certain he would never find her equal again. More than once, between the abuse of the traders and his thoughts of the vivacious Indian woman, he considered saddling Beelzebub and riding like hell back to the Pawnee village. He could live with Plenty Robes quite happily. If they couldn't do so in Two Stick's village, he would take her back to one of the frontier towns. It wasn't all that unlikely to see a white man with an Indian woman in such places. He could find work somewhere, doing something. The thought was sometimes sweet, but with every mile west he rode, he knew it was less and less likely. And in his more rational moments, he was certain he could never make it work—not getting though Indian country by himself, nor trying to explain it to the Pawnees even if he got that far.

He gave up the thought after a while, though when times were particularly hard, he would sometimes dream of what might have been. And, as the days on the trail turned into week and he performed the excruciatingly mundane chores efficiently and without complaint, the traders eased up on him. Eventually, he was allowed to go on the buffalo hunts again. The excitement of those times, as well as the prospect of fresh buffalo meat in his belly made the days pass considerably easier and helped his thoughts of Plenty Robes to begin to fade somewhat.

Before long, summer bore down on them, making the going even tougher. Water got scarce, though they generally managed to find enough. Still, riding through thick clouds of dust day after day was wearisome, trying all the men's patience. It was only by dint of his desire to get to the mountains that Barlow refrained from pounding on one or another of the traders at some point.

The only one who seemed close to impervious to the hardships of the daily drudgery was Andrew Branigan. He almost always appeared cool and in control. He did the best he could, too, in trying to keep all his men subdued. Branigan had come to like Barlow considerably, in large part because he, too, seemed to keep a tight rein on himself, for which he was thankful. He had heard some talk back in the Settlements of what a wild man Barlow could be. He hadn't believed it, since he had seen no evidence of it. Still, he had noticed the anger simmering in the young man's eyes on occasion, and he half expected Barlow to explode in fury at any moment.

Barlow had considered tearing into one or more of the men almost on a daily basis. After a month on the trail, he was tired, hot, dusty, and cranky virtually all the time. One in particular—Ev Dinsmore—was especially vexatious to Barlow. His complaints and demands were a constant thorn in Barlow's side. So much so that Barlow finally followed him out into the darkness beyond the ring of firelight one night at camp. Barlow waited patiently at a respectful distance while Dinsmore took care of his personal business. As Dinsmore was returning to the camp, Barlow lambasted him on the side of the head but hoped he hadn't hit him hard enough to knock him out. He didn't want that.

Waiting a moment, Barlow knelt at Dinsmore's side. "That's a warning, Mr. Dinsmore," he said quietly. "You've vexed me more than enough. Any more complainin' from you and this here thump I just give you will seem like the tap of a foundlin' babe."

"I'll have you left out in this godforsaken land to die, you son of a bitch," Dinsmore hissed, hoping the words were clear. He wasn't sure because of the ringing in his ears.

"One word of this to anyone and you won't live long enough to see me left to die out here, you goddamn pig. I didn't hire on with this here outfit to be your slave, boy. I hired on to be the camp keeper for Mr. Branigan and you others, and I do my work well. To everyone's likin' but yours, anyhow. You got a complaint on how I do my chores, you set down with me and Mr. Branigan, and we'll set things to right. You don't jist up and piss and moan about things without offerin' anything constructive. You understand me?''

"You'll never work for this company again, damn you, Barlow," Dinsmore snapped, trying to mask his fear.

"That'll be up to Mr. Branigan," Barlow responded evenly. "Unless you buy him out, in which case I wouldn't stay on anyway. I'd as soon fornicate with a rabid skunk as hire on to the likes of you." He rose. "You just remember what I said, boy. Treat me like a slave again, and I'll whomp you so bad you'll wish you were dead." He walked off.

He worried a little that he might have gone too far, but Dinsmore did mind his manners around him from then on. The other men, too, appeared to back off some on their whining. Barlow also noticed that Branigan seemed to have put a little distance between himself and Dinsmore and was acting slightly more friendly toward Barlow.

A little more than two months after leaving the Pawnee village, Branigan and his brigade arrived at the prearranged spot where the rendezvous was to be held that year. They pulled up in the large triangle-shaped piece of land where Horse Creek entered the Green River. They were yet a month or so early, so they picked what seemed to be the best spot for their camp and made themselves comfortable. They hunted buffalo and elk and antelope, keeping themselves well fed as they waited.

Before long, men—both white and red—started trickling into the area, and the place was soon roaring with excitement.

10

THE RENDEZVOUS WAS almost as eye-opening and awe-inspiring as the visit to the Pawnee village had been for Barlow. It was the wildest thing he had ever seen. Once things really got started, it was a scene from a dream. Barlow was stuck quite a bit of the time tending to the traders' animals, packing and unpacking supplies, manning the counter where his bosses were doing their trading, packing the thick, plush beaver pelts that were bought into trade for supplies, and much more. It chafed at him, since he wanted to take part in the wide variety of licentious activities.

He slipped away whenever he could, and while he felt somewhat intimidated by the wild men of the mountains, he was big enough, strong enough, and cocky enough to take his place among them in many of the activities—after he watched for a while, getting a feel for things.

After about a week, the trading pretty much ground to a halt, and Barlow at last found himself free to roam the rendezvous. There were, really, three camps of white men involved in the rendezvous, strung out over several miles. Barlow wandered through all three at times, mostly watching and listening, learning, sometimes taking part. He was not much for throwing knives or tomahawks, but he put his

Henry rifle to good use, finding that he was as good a shot as many of the vaunted mountain men.

He mostly kept away from the card games and such. He didn't trust these men to not cheat. He had played plenty of poker of various kinds back in St. Charles, but these men were a different breed from the men back there, and he wasn't sure he wanted to get mixed up in trying to determine whether they were cheating or not. Of course, there was always the little problem of not having any real money or other goods to use for wagering.

But the drinking and fighting! Now these were things he not only knew well, but enjoyed and was good at. The rotgut that passed for whiskey out here was no worse, really, than the foul beverages he imbibed back in the Settlements, and he was still young enough to have an iron constitution. He could drink with the best of them, and when he was in his cups, he was as touchy as the next man out here, which meant regular fights. Fortunately, those fights never got to the point where knives or any other kinds of deadly weapons came into play. Because of that, Barlow held his own and won most of the fights he was involved in.

He also discovered early on the Indian camps nearby. Not so much the camps, but what they offered—women. With warm thoughts of Plenty Robes still roiling in his brain, he learned he could pay a visit to some young Indian maids and for a bit of foofaraw, could sport with her. He scrounged up a few handfuls of beads and headed for a Shoshoni camp. He had heard from some of the men that this camp had the best women.

He waited his turn among a line of other men, most of whom were drunk and argumentative. The day was hot, and the entire area rank with the odors of sweaty, unbathed men, piles of horse manure, burnt food and grease, blood, human waste, and more. But Barlow, who had yet to have anything to drink that afternoon, controlled himself, and only got into two fights in the line. Both times he cold-cocked the men and stepped over them, moving closer to the front of the line.

His turn finally came, and he slipped into the dim, relative coolness of the buffalo-hide lodge. Three Shoshoni girls, each about fifteen or sixteen lay naked on buffalo robes scattered around the tipi. Two were lying there with grunting men flopping around atop them. One was unoccupied. With a shake of the head, wondering if he had made a mistake in coming here, Barlow went to the girl who was alone. He handed her the beads, which she tossed into a hardened buckskin box beside her ''bed.''

''Hurry,'' she said, the single English word heavily accented.

She was not a bad looking young woman, kind of sweet of face, with beautiful breasts and a curly mop of black hair at the conjuncture of her legs that seemed to beckon him. He felt himself responding. Because of that, he unbuttoned his pants, freeing his erectness. If he had not been so hard and desirous of a woman right now, he likely would have walked out, considering the disinterest the woman showed.

Sighing, Barlow knelt between the woman's legs. Without preliminary, he thrust himself into her. He pumped for several minutes, before the explosion shot her full of his essence. He held himself up off her with his arms and knees, not wanting to crush her with his bulk, as he tried to regain his breath. It didn't take long. He stood, stuffed himself back into his pants and buttoned them up.

Still shaking his head, he walked back out into the hot sunshine. He was sated physically, but disgusted with what had just happened. Not that he had expected the young woman to fall in love with him, but thoughts of Plenty Robes swirled in his brain, and he could not help but wish this Shoshoni had at least shown some interest and perhaps had managed a little bit of movement under him. He headed for Branigan's trading tent and grabbed a bottle of whiskey. With Buffalo at his side, he wandered off, toward Horse Creek. He found a quiet, solitary spot and sat, his back against a tree. He petted Buffalo's head with his right hand and used his left hand to bring the bottle to his mouth with frequent regularity.

•   •   •

He awoke with a raging hangover. Pouring a quart or so of bad whiskey into his empty stomach was not the best idea, he realized almost immediately after wakening. He crawled to the edge of the creek and stuck his head under the water for a few moments. He pulled back, shaking his head, which was a huge mistake, he decided. Then he tried to drink the creek dry in a vain attempt to quell the raging wildfire in his stomach. That had no more effect than anything else he had done. He moaned as he crawled back up toward the tree. If he had been capable of it, he might have laughed at the curious expression with which Buffalo was watching him.

Barlow lay flat on his back next to the puppy. He absentmindedly petted the animal. "Damn, and they say dogs're dumb. Lord a'mighty, ain't no animal I know is so dumb as to get himself feelin' this way of his own doin'."

He wasn't sure how long he lay there, but finally he decided he had to get up. While the thought of food sickened him even more, he knew it would help him a little. Before he braved such a move as getting to his feet, though, he felt around until his hand came into contact with the bottle. There was nothing left in it. "Damn," he muttered, setting off a thrashing in his head that threatened to make him black out again. He gritted his teeth and sucked in air as best he could, until the worst of the new pounding subsided some.

"Well, boy," he finally mumbled, "you ain't gettin' nowhere layin' here like this." He rolled onto his belly and pushed himself up to hands and knees. He remained there a few minutes, letting the new pains abate and gathering his strength and courage. Sucking in a great, huge breath to settle himself, he suddenly shoved upward. He reeled, halfway to his feet, and blindly flailed around until his hands grabbed the tree trunk, and then a couple of branches. With that support, he managed to get into a standing position. To thank the tree for its invaluable help, he spewed the trunk with vomit, while he hung there wanting nothing more than to just collapse and die.

After what seemed like forever, he weakly turned and

leaned back against the tree, heedless of his own, still fresh vomit there. At least this way he could stand and not have to rely on his arms to hold him up. Another eternity passed before Barlow garnered the fortitude to shove away from the tree. He staggered, the slightly sloped bank sending him wobbling toward the creek. He managed to stop himself before he hit the water. Slowly, painstakingly, with pain roaring through his head, he turned and lurched back up the little bank, and kept going.

Barlow did not bother to call to Buffalo. He figured the animal was smart enough to follow him at this point. If not, he would worry about him later. Right now all Barlow wanted was to get something to ease his pain and suffering.

He reached Branigan's trading tent, and leaned heavily on the makeshift counter, panting.

"What the hell's ailin' you?" asked Joe Havens, one of Branigan's traders.

Barlow looked at him in bleary-eyed annoyance. "Jist git me a jug of whiskey," he ordered.

"You sure?"

Barlow's look would have given pause to a rampaging buffalo. Havens's eyes widened, and he looked frightened for a moment. Then he grinned and picked up a bottle of whiskey.

Barlow grabbed it, jerked out the cork, and tilted the bottle to his mouth. The brutal liquid roared down his throat like hot lava and splashed into his stomach with a comforting explosion. He put the bottle down on the counter and breathed deep. A sense of warm contentment and peace settled over him. "Damn, that's better," he mumbled.

He headed out, leaving the bottle behind. While a good, healthy sized swallow would serve to calm and settle his stomach—which it was doing already to some extent—more than that would only make things worse.

Back at his camp, Ev Dinsmore snapped, "There you are, Barlow. Where the hell have you been? We had to make our own meal this morn . . ." He skidded to a halt when he saw the bleary fierceness in Barlow's eyes.

Branigan came out of his tent and knew immediately

what was wrong with Barlow. He grinned. He was disappointed in the young man, but on the other hand, he had done the same thing with some frequency when he was that age. "C'mon, Will," he said rather cheerily, "set by the fire. There's meat roasted and almost fresh coffee."

"I reckon both would do me well, Mr. Branigan," Barlow said gratefully. He had not thought about it until a few moments ago, but he had suddenly realized that there was a very good chance that Branigan would be furious at him. He was quite relieved to find out that was not the case.

He squatted at the fire and poured himself a tin mug of coffee. He gulped some of it down, though it was almost scalding hot. It was not nearly as good as his, he knew, much too thin, but it was hot and it helped. He drained the cup and refilled it. Then he grabbed a piece of meat that was dangling over the embers of the fire. He tore into it, bolting down chunks of it, hoping they would stay down.

Buffalo, frisking around nearby, ate heartily of the scraps Barlow tossed him.

After two more cups of the weak coffee and several more hunks of meat, Barlow ignored everyone else and curled up right there and went to sleep. When he awoke this time, he felt considerably better. He eased himself up into a sitting position and poured himself some coffee. That got him feeling pretty much human again, and so he grabbed more meat—someone had put on fresh antelope while he had slept—and gobbled it down.

"Feelin' better?"

Barlow craned his neck. Branigan was standing behind him, his face blank of expression. "Yessir, Mr. Branigan. Considerably."

"That's a good thing, son. You got a heap of duties to be catchin' up on around here."

Barlow nodded, thankful that it did not set off a blast of pain. "I reckon I do at that." He paused, then asked, "You ain't put out with me, are you, Mr. Branigan?"

"Furious," the trader said, but he winked.

"Anything you need done tonight?" Barlow asked, relieved.

"Most of your chores can wait till the morrow, but I suppose you best make sure there's enough wood and water. And see that the horses are doin' well."

"Yessir. Soon's I pour a little more of this damn coffee in me."

Branigan nodded and went back into his tent.

It took Barlow less than an hour to accomplish what he had to, as well as a few other tasks he came up with. Then he allowed himself two small swallows of whiskey before turning in for the night.

He was his normal self in the morning, up before everyone else, with decent, thick coffee brewing and fresh meat cooking. After the meal, he cleaned up around the camp, tended the horses, went out hunting, returning with two antelope, which he skinned and butchered, then packed several more parcels of beaver pelts.

Finally he headed to Branigan's tent, where the company leader was marking figures in his ledger. "You got any more chores for me, Mr. Branigan?" he asked.

"Can't say as I do, Will. You go on and enjoy yourself."

"Thankee, sir." Barlow turned to leave but stopped and turned back when Branigan called to him.

"Plannin' on another spree, Will?" Branigan asked, his blank expression masking his glee.

Barlow laughed. "Not this boy, sir. Not a drinkin' spree anyway. Not to say that I won't ever do sich again, but I think I need to put me a little distance between the last one and the next one."

"Wise thinking, son. Very wise."

"Yessir." Barlow scooted out the door. He didn't know why, but somewhere in the past minute, he decided to head to the rendezvous camp a couple of miles northwest of this one. He hurried out and saddled Beelzebub. With Buffalo— now four months old and weighing more than thirty pounds—roaming around the horse, from one side to the other, he headed out.

He slowly rode through the different camp, where some man named Bonneville had constructed a small wooden fort. He found out quickly that most of the boys called it

Fort Nonsense, as it was in a most unlikely place from which to trade or worse, trap.

Except for that fort, though, this camp was pretty much like the one where Barlow was staying. Contests were going on all over, men argued and shouted, fights broke out with monotonous regularity, Indians raced through, showing off their horsemanship, and more.

At one point, Barlow thought he heard a voice he recognized. He stopped, listening hard, but he couldn't hear it again. Not with the din around him. He could not place the voice, but he knew it was familiar. Since it would have had to have been very close for him to have heard it, he turned his horse and walked toward a small camp along the river. Then he heard the voice again, and he grinned. He rode into the little camp and dismounted.

A man at the fire looked up, seemingly annoyed. Then his face broke into a smile. "Will," the man said. "Will Barlow!" He rose and extended his hand.

"Mr. Rutledge," Barlow said with a big grin. "Fancy meetin' you here. Where's the other boys?"

"Out and about." Rutledge laughed. "I rassled with a bit too much awardenty last night, and I ain't as young as I used to be fer sich doin's. So's I decided to jist rest my lazy, ailin' bones right here fer the day."

11

"WELL, BOYS, LOOK who's here," Caleb Simon said, strolling into camp with several of the other men who worked with Sim Rutledge. "Damn if it ain't young Will Barlow." He sounded faintly drunk. "How've you been farin', boy?"

Barlow and Rutledge were sitting near the fire, sipping thick black coffee heavily dosed with sugar, and desultorily chewing on some buffalo meat. They'd been there for an hour or more, neither seeing any urgency to do much of anything else.

"Passable," Barlow said. "Come out here with Andrew Branigan, like I'd planned. Mr. Branigan ain't so bad a man to work for, though I can't say the same about some of his partners," he added with a laugh.

"Don't know the others so well, but ol' Andrew is a decent enough ol' hoss, I expect," Simon said, as he and the others took places around the fire—which was little more than embers now. They filled cups with coffee, some liberally dosing it with whiskey, and grabbed meat.

"Only real pain in the ass was Ev Dinsmore."

Simon shrugged, not knowing who the man was. "You have any troubles on the way out?" Simon asked.

"None to speak of," Barlow answered with a shrug. These were men who would not want to hear about minor traveling woes like long stretches without water or flooded rivers at other places. Or the mosquitoes or snakes or anything else that was common. Only something special, out of the ordinary, would merit mentioning.

The others nodded, liking the fact that Barlow knew enough not to mention the mundane dangers they all faced every day.

"Well, ye made it out here alive, and that's something," Rutledge said. "One of our boys, Ed Brown, didn't. He was put under in a fracas with the Rees on the way out."

"Sorry to hear that," Barlow said. He spent a moment trying to picture Brown a thin man of medium height with a face like a ferret. But he had been good natured and generous with whiskey when he had the money.

"He was a good ol' hoss, Ed was," Simon said.

An idea struck Rutledge, and he sat up a little straighter. "You plannin' on headin' back to the Settlements with Branigan and all, Will?" he asked.

"Hadn't really thunk on it," Barlow said. The question surprised him a little, since he really hadn't thought about it. He had more or less assumed he would go back east with the traders. As far as he knew he had no other options.

'Would doin' so suit ye, boy?"

Barlow shrugged. "I don't know as if it'd suit me, Mr. Rutledge, but then I ain't so sure that I have much choice."

Rutledge was silent for a while, then said, "Well, mayhap ye got a choice, boy." He paused, then added, "How'd you like to throw in with this ol' hoss and my *compañeros* here?"

Barlow's eyes widened. It was almost too great an offer to comprehend. "You mean it?"

"Hell, yes. I don't make such offers lightly, boy."

"Why ask me?" Barlow questioned, still somewhat dumbfounded. He looked around the ragged circle of hard faces. "There must be scores of other boys here who're experienced. Why not ask one of them?"

"Most of 'em're under contract to one company or another."

"What company do you boys work for?" Barlow asked quietly, still trying to digest what he had heard.

"Company?" Rutledge snorted, accompanied by hoots and jeers from the other men. "We're free trappers, boy. Beholden to no one." Pride oozed from his voice.

Barlow nodded. "Still, cain't all of 'em be contracted out," he went on.

"Reckon that's true," Rutledge acknowledged. Then he shrugged. "Look, boy, we can ask any of a number of fellers, but what the hell, many of the boys've been out here a spell are set in their ways. You're a newcomer and can mayhap adapt to our ways of doin' things a little more readily. Besides, we all saw back in the Settlements that you got sand in ye, boy. And that's a trait that means somethin' out here."

"So what say, boy?" Simon threw in. "Ye with us or not?" He grinned, joyful as always.

He was happy, proudly happy. But worried, too. "What about you others?" he asked with more than a little uneasiness. "You boys mind?"

Most muttered that it was all right with them. One or two said nothing, giving tacit approval.

"We may be free trappers, boy," Rutledge said, "but I was elected cap'n. And what I says goes. Ain't a matter of whether my *amigos* like it or not." His voice was flat, matter-of-fact. "Something like this goes against their grain, they're free to leave on their own—or vote fer a new cap'n."

Barlow was taken a little aback, but he could see on the other men's faces that this was a fact of life. And not a one of them thought this was out of line. They all knew Barlow, knew he could fight, and that he had no give-up in him, so they didn't mind. Some might prefer that a fr'end of theirs was chosen, but this was not a decision any of them thought worth arguing over.

"Well," Barlow started, ready to accept, overwhelmed with pride that they would ask him to join their group, when another thought intruded and soured his disposition. "Well," he began again, "I'd sure as hell like to go along with you all, but . . ." He paused, embarrassed. "Well, dammit, I got nothin' 'cept that damn ol' horse and Buffalo here," he added, patting the dog's head, "and my rifle. I got no supplies, no traps, almost no powder and shot. And, worse, I ain't got the wherewithal to git what I'd need."

"Well, now, I don't know as if that's an insurmountable problem," Rutledge said easily. "Hell, ye can have ol' Ed's possibles. All his plunder is paid for and he cain't use it no more. You might's well make use of it."

Barlow's eyes rode wide again, surprised. "You'd do that?"

"Sure," Simon said. "He ain't got no kinfolk that we know of, so no need to sell his things off and send the money back east. We was just gonna divide it up amongst ourselves. But hell, if we can get another man for the outfit from it, that shines with this ol' hoss."

Small nods from the rest of the men supported Simon's statement.

"So what's it gonna be, boy?" Rutledge asked. He was half grinning.

"Jist one more thing I can think of that might put a hitch in this plan. Supposin' Mr. Branigan thinks my contract with him don't run out till I get back to Independence?"

"Nary thought of that," Rutledge said, rubbing his stubbled chin. "But I don't reckon he'll kick up much of a fuss." His grin widened. "If he does, me and the boys'll have a leetle talk with him."

"That'd do it." Barlow didn't really think Branigan would fret about his leaving.

"Before ye answer though, boy, here's a small warning," Rutledge said, the grin gone. "You sign up with us, you'll be expected to do your full share of work in addition to your own trappin' and such. That means helpin' with the communal supplies, carin' for the pack animals, tendin' fires, gatherin' firewood, everything else. Everybody has to do his part."

"I have no quarrel with any of that," Barlow said seriously.

"Good. Because if ye start slackin' off on this, me and the boys'll leave your ass out there in the wilderness to fend for yourself."

"I wouldn't expect no less."

Rutledge nodded once, sharply. "Now, jist one more thing. I tol' ye jist a bit ago that these boys elected me their cap'n. You will be expected to do as I say. I will brook no arguments from anybody, least of all a greenhorn. Caleb is second in command. You're to obey him as you would me."

Barlow nodded.

"Then welcome to our little band, Mr. Barlow," Rutledge said, face lightening.

"Waugh!" Simon shouted. "This here calls for a drink. Charlie, fetch us up a jug pronto!"

Looking not put out at all, Charlie Watters rose and strode to a stack of supplies. In a moment, he was back at the fire, two jugs in hand. Both were opened and began making the rounds. Before long, the men were in a festive, albeit feisty, mood. Arguments started, escalated, and then died just as quickly. Bets were made on turns of a card, and an impromptu knife throwing contest cropped up a couple of times.

By nightfall, the men were roaring drunk, and the arguments that began over any little thing that came to mind grew more heated, and instead of fizzling out, led to fighting, which the others would try to break up. That, in turn, would lead to another bout between others in the small group.

Being just as drunk and rowdy as any of the others, plus being the new man, meant Barlow had more than his share of altercations with the others. But he held his own with them and even managed to get over pretty easily the insults slung at him. And he was quite proud of Buffalo. The Newfoundland puppy had growled in puppy ferocity, seemingly trying to protect him more than once when he clashed with one of the mountain men.

The men, one by one, dropped off to sleep where they were sitting or where they fell. Before long, the little camp resounded with drunken snores and other bodily noises.

And it was one silent and rank crew that staggered to the fire one by one in the morning. Most growled or groaned—or both—as they poured souplike coffee into their abused bodies. More than once one of them trotted off to the bushes to vomit or contend with bowels loosened by too much drink.

Barlow drank three large tin mugs full of coffee and managed to wolf down some of last night's roasted buffalo meat—and keep it down. But he did not feel like moving. After his breakfast and a dose of the hair of the dog, he laid away from the fire, in the shade of a willow, with his head on an old log. He pulled his well-worn, wide-brimmed hat down over his eyes. With Buffalo's head on his chest, Barlow fell asleep, grateful to be able to blot out the cacophony of the rendezvous even if only for a short while.

Being the youngest of the group, Barlow recovered more quickly than the others. He almost laughed at the sight of the men still looking so wretched. But he kept the humor inside. Most of the men looked as if they would take a tomahawk to him if he so much as opened his mouth.

He quietly saddled Beelzebub and rode out, Buffalo trotting alongside, and headed back to his own camp. As usual, Branigan was in his tent working on his ledger books. Barlow called inside, asking for permission to enter. He walked in when it was granted.

"You look like you've got somethin' on your mind, Will," Branigan said.

"Reckon I do, Mr. Branigan." He paused, not sure how to say the words. He had decided on the ride over there that he would talk to Branigan right away and get it settled as soon as possible. Now that he was there, though, he was suddenly uncomfortable, almost ashamed. It seemed to him that he was breaking his word by asking out of his contract, and that galled him.

"Well, best just say it, son," Branigan said quietly.

Barlow nodded. "I was hopin' you might . . . Well, sir,

I wanted to know if you could see your way clear to . . .''

"Out with it, Will," Branigan commanded, face blank.

Barlow sucked in a deep breath and blew it slowly out. "I was hopin' you'd let me out of my contract, Mr. Branigan," he said flatly, twirling his hat uncomfortably in his hands.

"And why would you request this of me?" Branigan asked sternly.

"I got a chance to head into the mountains with Sim Rutledge and his free trappers," Barlow said, unsuccessfully trying to keep the excitement and wonder out of his voice.

"Free trappers? They're the worst of the lot," Branigan said.

Barlow was not sure if his boss was serious. "I wouldn't know about that, sir," he said uneasily.

"How did this turn of events come about?"

"I ran into their camp yesterday up the creek a little ways. We got to be talkin', and, well, sir, one of their men was killed on the way out here and they asked me if I'd like to take his place."

"And you agreed?"

"Well, yessir," Barlow said. "But only if I could get out of my contract with you," he added, hoping the lie wasn't evident on his face.

"What're you going to do about supplies and such?" Branigan demanded. He had already made up his mind to let Barlow go, but he wanted to make the young man sweat a little first. After all, he didn't want to seem like too easy a touch.

"It's all took care of, Mr. Branigan."

Branigan nodded. "And I expect you figure to get your whole salary, even though you'd be ending your work for me some months early?" He looked almost angry.

"No, sir," Barlow said flatly. "I'd like the money and all, but I ain't the kind to ask for somethin' that ain't mine. I trust you, Mr. Branigan. I know you'll pay me what you think is fair for the time I've spent in your employ and the amount of work I've done for you."

Branigan was glad to see that his belief in Barlow had not been misplaced. He stood there, pretending to be pondering the idea. Finally he nodded. "All right, Will," he said. "When would you like your service to me to end?"

"Whenever you think you can do without me, sir," Barlow said, trying mightily to hold back the excitement that bubbled within him. "Jist as long as it's before Mr. Rutledge and his men pull out. I'm not sure when that'll be for certain, but I expect we have a few days, in which I could work in whatever you had for me to do."

"Well, there's not that much left to do till we leave, but I expect there are a few chores you could help with. Let's say that your employ will officially end at dusk the day after tomorrow."

"Very generous, Mr. Branigan."

"We'll settle up what I owe you then."

"That's more than fair, sir." A moment later, Barlow raced outside, his heart pounding with excitement.

12

BARLOW DECIDED IT was only right that he move out of Branigan's camp and into Rutledge's once his employment with Branigan ended. He had little, really, to pack, and that was done quickly. He left Beelzebub saddled and tied to a tree, and with Buffalo in tow, headed for Branigan's tent. He wanted to collect his wages and to bid farewell to his boss. He was only a little worried as he called for entrance. He thought highly of Branigan and did not really believe the traders would try to cheat him on wages, but that thought did intrude on his consciousness just a bit.

"All ready to go, Will?" Branigan asked, smiling.

"Yessir," Barlow said softly. He suddenly felt lousy. Andrew Branigan had treated him more than well, and he suspected that the trader had bigger plans for him. In many ways, he did not want to leave. On the other hand, he could not let this chance pass by. He would never forgive himself if he did.

"Well, I'm sure going to miss your services, Will," Branigan said. "But you have your heart set on this, and I can certainly understand that. I had eyes for much the same kind of adventuring when I was your age."

"Did you act on them?" Barlow asked, sort of surprised.

Branigan didn't seem the kind who would have held dreams of finding adventure in any aspect of life.

"Of course," Branigan said, laughing heartily. "Hell, I was in the mountains near a decade ago. Those were shinin' days, boy. That they were. But I got tired of standin' halfway up to my ass in freezin' water hopin' some goddamn beaver was dumb enough to take my bait." His laughter flowed more smoothly. "And I figured out after a couple seasons that I could make a heap more money—well, maybe not more, but at least steadier—by supplying the mountaineers than in trappin' beaver. Too much risk involved with trappin', Will. Just keep that to mind."

"Risk?"

"Hell, yes, son. Hostile Injins, wild griz, stampedin' buffalo, the weather. Hell, any of them things and more can send you to an early grave. Or, if you survive, have you pullin' into rendezvous with no plews and no money to outfit yourself for the next season. With tradin' the way I do, there ain't half the risks." He grinned and said conspiratorially, "But I'll tell you this, son, I wouldn't have traded those years in the mountains for nothin'. There jist ain't nothin' to compare, even with all the starvin' times and freezin' times and Injin fights and all."

Barlow was impressed.

"Well, let's get us settled up here," Branigan said. He handed Barlow a small buckskin bag of coins. "I think you'll find that's accurate," he said. Seeing Barlow's hesitation, he added with a grin, "You can check it, son. In fact you should. You won't offend me by doin' so."

Barlow smiled in embarrassment but opened the bag and poured the gold coins into one hand. He counted them, putting them back in the sack as he did. When he was done, he looked up, ashen faced. "You made a serious mistake, Mr. Branigan," he said.

"Oh?" Branigan's face suddenly went blank.

"There's too much specie in there. More than I'm owed." He could use the extra money, he thought, but he could not steal from Branigan—which is how he saw taking this money—not after the trader had treated him so well.

"I was certain I had the right amount," Branigan said evenly. He took the sack, counted the money, looked in his ledger book, counted the money again, did some computating on a piece of paper torn from the ledger and then handed Barlow the bag again. "It's correct, Will," he said. "Everything figures out just the way it should."

Barlow watched Branigan's face and saw the smile in his eyes. "You're sure?" he asked.

"You watched me figure it all out, didn't you? Well, if I say it's right, who's to argue with me?"

"Not me, for damn sure," Barlow said, suddenly breaking into nervous laughter.

"It's been a pleasure havin' you in my employ, Will," Branigan said, holding out his hand.

Barlow shook with Branigan. "And I'm in your debt for all you've done for me, Mr. Branigan." He hefted the sack of money. "This means a lot to me."

Branigan grinned a little. "Just remember when you're out there, son, to keep your eyes open."

"I'll do that, Mr. Branigan." Not having anything else to say, Barlow turned and walked out, his sense of loss mingled with exhilaration about the new future he had mapped out for himself. He pulled himself into the saddle, and got Beelzebub into motion.

Minutes later, he lit into Rutledge's camp. "I'm at your service, Cap'n," he said, a slight touch of fear kicking up inside him again.

"Not yet you ain't, boy," Rutledge said with a laugh. "This here's still rendezvous, and it's time for more spreein'! Once we leave here, then you'll be in my service, boy." He made it sound almost like a threat.

"Then this boy's gonna go spree some more," Barlow said with a grin.

"That's the spirit, boy," Caleb Simon said, walking up. "We're all headin' on over to see about some women here directly. Why don't ye come along?"

"Well, I'd like to, but . . ."

Simon's eyes widened. "There ain't somethin' wrong with ye, is there, boy?" he questioned suspiciously.

"Hell, no," Barlow said with a laugh. "It's jist that . . . Well, I did that the other day, and I got to say, it didn't shine whatsoever." He flushed. "I've always been the kind who likes a woman who takes part in sich activities, if you catch my drift. This one here laid there like a sack of grain, and was about as pleasin'. From what I saw of the others, they weren't no better."

Simon and Rutledge laughed.

"We're goin' over to see about gettin' us some permanent women, boy, not just some slut who's out fer a handful of foofaraw for two minutes of fornicatin'. That's about as fulfillin' as humpin' a watermelon," Simon said.

"We gonna take these women with us to the wilds?" Barlow asked, suddenly interested.

Simon nodded. "Got to have us women along. Hell, we need 'em fer cookin' and fer curing them plews, if nothin' else. Doin' shit work like that don't shine with this ol' cuss. And, of course, havin' some sweet Injin lass to warm yer bed in the winter is one hell of an extra, this chil' thinks."

"I expect that's true," Barlow said with a laugh. "I'm all saddled and ready to go when you boys are."

Half an hour later, all eight men of Rutledge's band of free trappers trotted out of their camp. Soon after, they rode into an Indian encampment.

"What're these people?" Barlow asked Charlie Watters. In the past couple of days, Barlow had found Watters to be one of the friendliest men in the bunch. He was only a couple of years older than Barlow, and the two seemed to get along pretty well.

"Nez Perce," Watters responded. "Damn good Injins, the Nez Perce. Always friendly to whites. Handsome people. Good fighters when they need to be, though they ain't nearly as warlike as some others. The women are quiet, industrious, chaste to a certain extent, but still shinin' in the robes."

Barlow laughed a little. "How can they be chaste yet still good in the robes?" he asked.

"Well, they ain't like some Injin women," Watters said

with a grin. "Some're little more than sluts that'll fornicate with anything that gits hard fer 'em. These Nez Perce, though, they'll stay with a man, and won't be humpin' with no others when you're lookin' the other way."

Watters was nothing if not rather crude, in word as well as behavior.

"Faithfulness is a good thing in a woman, I think," Barlow offered. "Red or white."

"That's a fact."

"What else can you tell me about the Nez Perce?"

Watters shrugged. He was not much good at explaining things. "Hell, I don't know. The womenfolk do fine decoratin' on clothes. And the men raise horses called Appaloosas. Damn if they ain't some fine horses. Plumb shine, they do." He pointed. "There's a couple of 'em now."

Barlow nodded. The horses were indeed nice looking and sturdy, but he had spotted a couple of young women and was far more interested in watching them than he was in looking at horses. The two young women, perhaps fourteen or fifteen years old, were half hiding behind a meat rack. They would pop out, spy on the white men and then giggle and hide their faces again. From what Barlow could see of them, both were beautiful, slim, and playful. Barlow's thoughts turned immediately to Plenty Robes, but those memories faded quickly in light of the attractiveness and vivaciousness of these two Nez Perce.

"All the Nez Perce girls that good looking?" he asked, pointing.

Watters grinned. "Hell, not all of 'em, but as a whole the Nez Perce girls are a heap more pleasin' of face and figure than most other Injin women."

"That's good to hear," Barlow said, laughing.

The men sat there on their horses as Rutledge and Simon stopped in front of a large tipi and went inside. It was hot out in the sun, and the virtually constant wind kicked up dust from the camp and blew it about. Sitting there was not all that pleasant, Barlow thought, especially when the two girls left.

The two leaders finally came out of the lodge, along with

some Nez Perce warriors. They talked another minute, and then the two whites mounted their horses. Rutledge looked his men over. "Ol' Fat Lance says we're to come back tomorrow," he said sourly.

"What's the trouble?" one of the men asked. "We usually jist ride on in here and take our pick of the ones ain't married, hand him over some foofaraw, and be done with it."

The others, except for Barlow, grumbled in assent.

Simon answered with a big grin. "The ol' buzzard got hisself roaring, stinkin' drunk last night, and ain't really up to hagglin' over women and foofaraw jist yet."

The men were mostly mollified by that, knowing the feeling well. Still, they had had their sights set on riding back to their camp that afternoon with Indian women at their sides. But the glumness couldn't last too long. Not when there was so much going on at the rendezvous.

During the ride and the rest of the afternoon, Barlow could not keep his thoughts from returning time and again to the enticing sight of the two beautiful, copper-colored Indian woman who giggled wildly as they played peek-a-boo from behind strips of drying meat. His mind told him that there was almost no chance of either of those girls being offered as wives for the white men. He also knew that even if that came to pass, he would have no chance of being one of the lucky men to win one of them over. But that did not keep him from pondering the possibilities— and the likely delights were his dream to come true.

Sleep did not come easy that night for Barlow, as thoughts of the two women kept flickering through his mind. But he refused to resort to whiskey to help bring his whirling mind under control. He wanted to have all his wits about him when they went to Fat Lance's village.

He was tired but excited in the morning as he stoked up the fire and made coffee. Having arisen before everyone else, those chores naturally fell to him. As the other men began rising, Barlow found other tasks to do away from them. They all appeared to be bored or hungover, and he did not want any of them to see his almost childish excitement at the possibilities the day carried. Finally, they all mounted up and rode out.

Barlow never knew exactly how it was all accomplished. Like the day before he and most of the other men sat outside on their horses while Rutledge and Simon went into a lodge. The minutes dragged by as the temperature continued to creep upward. There was a breeze, but it offered no relief, serving only to blow hot dust all over them. Grumbling began after half an hour or so, and rose in pitch and intensity until Simon poked his head out of the lodge and told everyone to quiet down.

Finally several Nez Perce men came out of the lodge with Simon and walked to where the white men's extra horses and mules stood, guarded by Barlow and Watters. They spent some time looking at all the animals before heading back inside. Minutes later, the Nez Perce came back out and took all the horses and mules but two. When the animals had been led away, Simon motioned for his men to join him in the lodge.

Barlow entered next to last, his heart thumping, wondering just what awaited him on the inside. Once his eyes adjusted to the gloom, he saw with a leap of his heart that both the girls he had noticed yesterday were there. His hopes soared.

"Deal's done, boys," Rutledge said with a grin. "Go pick out a wife."

The men stood for some moments, eyeing the women, trying to make their decision. It was evident that Rutledge and Simon had already made their choices. Barlow wanted to charge over to either—or, hell, both—the two beauties he hankered for, but was afraid to move, being a new member of this group and all. But he never took his eyes from them, particularly the one who was slightly shorter, a bit darker skinned, and a tad heavier.

The men began moving. With a silent curse, Barlow watched as Bill Nottingsworth and Bob Francher headed for the two women he wanted. He didn't know what to do—stand there and wait till the others had made their picks, or just charge ahead and take the one he wanted.

Barlow was more than a little amazed as the preferred one of the two girls stepped around Nottingsworth and headed straight for him. She stopped right in front of him and looked up, though not directly into his eyes. "I take you," she said and then giggled.

"I like that," he responded, grinning like a fool.

"That's my woman there, boy," Nottingsworth snapped, trying to tug her away. "I seen her first and I'm takin' her."

Barlow was about to paste him one in the mouth when Rutledge said, "Let her go, Bill. She's made her choice, and it ain't your greasy hide she wants."

Nottingsworth glowered at the captain for a moment, then turned and shuffled angrily away.

Barlow was too filled with joy to worry or even wonder if Nottingsworth would continue to give him a hard time.

13

HER NAME WAS Mountain Calf, and she was just fifteen winters old. Her face was as pretty as a sunset. When she disrobed late that afternoon, Barlow could have sworn that her dusky copper skin glowed even in the gathering dusk. Long, pitch black hair hung straight down her back, glistening with grease and natural shininess. A high, smooth forehead sloped down to slight eyebrows over two of the deepest, darkest eyes Barlow had ever seen. High, soft cheekbones framed a short, slightly squat nose over a small, full-lipped mouth.

Barlow was entranced, and the more he looked, the better the view got. Her dark skin gleamed with a warm inviting sheen, and her small breasts rode high and proud, their tips enhanced by tiny nipples the color of burnt sienna. He walked a slow circle around her, eyes hungrily devouring every inch—the smooth, strong back, plump buttocks, and the finely formed legs that ended in a sparse patch of black pubic hair.

Mountain Calf stood, totally unembarrassed and completely relaxed as Barlow completed his circuit. She glanced at his pelvis as he moved in front of her again, and she smiled a little. It was very obvious that Barlow liked what he saw. And, judging by the bulge in his wool pants, she was sure she was going to like what she saw very shortly, too. That wasn't too much of a surprise to her. She had sensed that he would be big in all ways. That and the something she had seen in his bright eyes had attracted her, and when she saw that ugly wretch of a man coming toward her, she knew she had to get away from him. Choosing Barlow at that point had not been all that difficult.

Barlow stopped in front of her, and licked his dry lips. He suddenly scooped her up in his arms, and then knelt to lay her gently down on the bed of buffalo robes. Then he stood and began shedding his clothes. He was not entirely comfortable, considering that all the other men with their new Indian wives were barely yards away, and none of them was using a shelter of any kind other than whatever cover they could find from the vegetation in the area.

Barlow stretched out beside Mountain Calf and pulled her into the hard-muscled cocoon of his arms. She seemed to melt against him, her soft skin exciting him as it rubbed against his own. One of his hands began slowly, gently stroking the flesh of her arm, side, and part of her leg that he could reach. Then he moved the hand up to cup a small, firm breast, and his thumb worked light circles on the nipple.

Mountain Calf murmured and began to shift from side to side a little, as if she were trying to burrow deeper into his body. Goosebumps appeared on her skin, and her womanhood dampened. She rolled a bit toward him, and grasped his rigid manhood lightly, then slid her hand smoothly along its length.

Barlow sucked in a breath as fire flared straight from his shaft to his brain. The touch of her small hand was so exquisite that it forced him to forgo toying with her breast for a few moments, as Mountain Calf's hand gently brushed his scrotum.

"No stop," Mountain Calf commanded in a gentle, but insistent voice.

"Ah, right," Barlow muttered, restarting his tender manipulation of her breast and nipple.

She moved up a little and kissed him, then her small teeth nipped at his lips in between her tongue's darting assaults on his. He shoved his other hand between her thighs, reaching until he felt the tangle of hair at her groin. In a moment, one thick finger had found her pleasure button and was rubbing it gently but persistently. His finger slid inside her damp tunnel. Mountain Calf moaned loudly and her hand squeezed his cock hard.

With lips still locked, Barlow continued to play with her breast and small, pebble-hard nipple with one hand while his other hand slid in and out of her womanhood, pausing now and again to flick over her love button. Within moments, Mountain Calf was wriggling, her hand on his shaft not moving. It was as if she were hanging onto the solid object to keep her balance.

Mouth occupied, she could breathe only through her nose, and she was struggling a bit to get enough air into her. When suddenly she jerked her face away from Barlow's and let out a piercing shriek as her vaginal walls clamped down on his finger and her thighs locked his hand in place. She shuddered as the release of her passion flooded through her.

Mountain Calf finally went limp, but that did not last long. Between the feel of Barlow's throbbing manhood in her hand and the continuing movement of his finger in and out of her sopping love tunnel, she quickly found herself rejuvenated and hungry for more.

With a quick lick of his lips, she raised her hips high and threw one leg over him. She closed her eyes in ecstasy as she lowered herself onto his shaft. The fit was tight and it took some pleasant work before she was able to slide all the way down until her buttocks were sitting on Barlow's pelvis. A delicious shiver wormed up her spine from the incomparable pleasure of having him buried so deep in her. He filled her completely, stretching her in a most pleasurable way. She sat where she was for some moments, not really moving, just reveling in the feel of his thickness stuffing her.

Mountain Calf leaned forward, holding herself up with a

hand on each side of Barlow's head. Her tits dangled just over his face, and with a smile, he lifted his head and tongued one tiny nipple, then the other, back and forth. Mountain Calf began pumping her hips slowly on his erection, while at the same time shifting her pelvis a little back and forth, stimulating her love bud.

Barlow slapped his huge hands onto her buttocks and kneaded them gently. Her ass muscles worked smoothly under his palms, adding another dimension to his enjoyment.

Pleasure rushed up and outward from Mountain Calf's groin, blossoming like a flower, until it permeated her entire body, making her quiver and whimper. Small eruptions began in her groin, and she rocked faster and pumped harder atop him. The explosions grew in number and magnitude, building on each other, expanding, uniting, until a shockwave thundered through her, shaking her violently. Her back arched inward, and her breasts bobbled wildly; her womanhood clutched and grasped at his erect member.

The intensity of her climax suddenly brought Barlow's essence boiling forward, shooting deep into her. His hips rose as he hammered himself into her, surprised at the abruptness and force of his ejaculation. Strange guttural sounds poured from his mouth, mingling with Mountain Calf's high-pitched shrieks.

Then they collapsed into a sweaty heap of flesh and spent desire. Within moments, Barlow was asleep. Mountain Calf considered rising and doing some chores, but she liked the feel of his shrinking member still inside her, and she was content to just lie there. Before long, she, too, had nodded off.

Barlow's eyes snapped open, but he did not move. Something was happening, and he wasn't sure what it was. Pleasure filled him, and he wondered if he were really awake or whether he was having a most pleasing dream. Then, amid the chattering of birds and the sounds of the rendezvous all around him, he heard soft, slurping sounds. He lifted his head and looked straight down. A smile of utter joy spread across his face as he watched Mountain Calf's mouth working up and down on his rapidly growing shaft.

She stopped for a moment, suddenly aware that he was watching her, and asked, "Good?"

"Very good," he said with a sigh.

Mountain Calf nodded and went back to licking and sucking on him.

Barlow lay back and savored the unaccustomed attention. Few of the women he had been with were very willing to do such a thing, and not a one of them had done it so well nor seemed to ever have nearly as much fun doing it as Mountain Calf appeared to be having.

Mountain Calf's mouth and tongue were soft, gentle, and knowing. Barlow moaned blissfully, and allowed his head to fall back on the buffalo robe. Delectable sensations flowed from his hardness and swept through his body, splendidly titillating all of his nerves every bit as wonderfully as Mountain Calf was doing to his manhood.

Barlow soon felt himself rushing toward his climax. He was torn, wanting her to continue her efforts until he was done, but also wanting to take her in a more traditional fashion. The glorious sensations flooding through him made the decision for him. He reached out and grabbed Mountain Calf's long hair in both hands. He tried not to force her head down on him any farther than it was, not wanting to choke or hurt her. It was difficult, but he managed.

Mountain Calf could sense Barlow's impending climax, and her mouth picked up a bit of speed as she increased her suction. One hand grabbed the base of his shaft and slid gently, rapidly up and down. Her other hand lightly stroked his scrotum.

Barlow suddenly bucked his hips up hard. Snorting grunts emanated through flared nostrils as his juices shot forth in a series of powerful, body-wracking spurts.

Mountain Calf took it all in stride, swallowing quickly and steadily until Barlow was done. Then she took a breather and smiled up at him. She squeezed his slowly shrinking manhood, coaxing out more of his sap, and licking it away. Until it seemed there would be no more. She slithered up his body and kissed him lightly on the lips. "I do good?" she asked, grinning at him.

Barlow smiled wearily, contentedly back. "You done goddamn terrific, woman," he said. Shivers of euphoria still shot through his body. He had never felt anything so powerful, so utterly ecstatic in all his life.

Mountain Calf smiled and slid off him to the side. He slipped an arm under her neck, and she curled up into his body, quite pleased with herself. She had not been sure that becoming the bride of a white man would be a good thing when they had approached her about it. She knew that she would be far richer than her friends who stayed in the village, but she also knew that many of the white trappers thought little of their Indian women, often leaving them miles from home or trading them off to someone even worse. But Mountain Calf had always had a streak of adventurous nonconformity in her, so she had gone along with the idea. She had picked out Will Barlow because he looked like a halfway decent fellow. When she had first seen him nude—and hard for her—she was thrilled. He was big all over, and she liked that. Her positive thoughts had increased when they had first made love, as he had proven himself to be a good man in the robes. She had decided as he had slept earlier that she wanted him and wanted to keep him.

The group of free trappers and their Nez Perce wives pulled out two days later. They left with a whoop and a holler, accompanied by a volley of rifle fire from the men still left at the rendezvous, which was fast winding down.

It was an impressive group despite its small size—eight white men and eight Nez Perce women, all mounted, and twenty-five or so horses and mules, many loaded with supplies.

They rode slowly and stopped early that first day, not wanting to tax themselves or the animals after several weeks' layoff for the rendezvous. But starting the next morning, they began to adjust to life on the trail again. They moved northwest and in a few days were at the Tetons, which they crossed the next day, into Pierre's Hole. There they built a camp.

"We'll set about hunting buffalo in the mornin'," Rutledge said.

"Damn, that shines," Barlow muttered, smiling.

"We ain't gonna run 'em, ye goddamn fool," Nottingsworth snapped, knowing what Barlow was thinking. He was still mighty riled that Barlow had gotten Mountain Calf, and he made that no secret in the days since they had left the rendezvous. "We need to make meat and gather us up skins fer makin' lodges of. We ain't got time for chasin' goddamn buffalo all over the goddamn countryside." He shook his head. "Goddamn, ye be one dumb goddamn chil', boy," he said, a sneer sneaking into his voice.

Barlow flushed in embarrassment, as well as anger. He knew now that his thought was stupid, but he also knew that Nottingsworth could have been a little more circumspect in the way he had mentioned it. He could have accepted it, even spoken in that derisive tone, from some of the other men in the group. But he was especially touchy around Nottingsworth. "Reckon that makes sense," he said tightly.

"Course it does, ye idiot," Nottingsworth pressed. "Any goddamn fool with a lick of sense would have thunk of it."

Barlow seethed, and it took all his will to keep from exploding. He sucked in a few breaths, and let them out slowly. "Then it's really a wonder that you were able to figure it out." He smiled ingratiatingly at his foe. "After all, everybody knows you ain't got the sense the good Lord give a duck's ass." He felt better now that he had given Nottingsworth a shot back.

"Why you goddamn fractious son of a bitch," Nottingsworth snarled. He started to rise, going for his knife at the same time.

"Sit down, Bill," Rutledge said quietly but with a strong edge to his voice. When Nottingsworth hesitated, the trappers' leader repeated his command, with more authority.

Nottingsworth flopped back down. He glowered at Barlow. "You ain't gonna have ol' Sim there to protect your ass all the time, boy. One of these days, he ain't gonna be standin' there, and I'm gonna carve you a new asshole.''

Barlow smiled with no humor. "You best git several others to help you, boy," he said evenly. He was thoroughly disgusted with Nottingsworth's contemptible demeanor and felt like just pounding the offensive trapper into submission. But he figured that Rutledge would not be pleased at such a development. With only eight of them, they could not afford to lose one of the men, Barlow reasoned, even one of Nottingsworth's repulsive character.

"I ain't gonna need no help with the likes of you," Nottingsworth snarled.

"I'm all a-tremble now, you clap-ridden old sot," Barlow said with a hollow laugh. He still boiled with anger, but he was trying not to show it. He did not want Nottingsworth to know he had angered him so much.

Before Nottingsworth could retort, Rutledge barked, "It's robe time fer this chil'. I advise you boys to leave off your jawin' and turn in, too. He was tired of listening to the two of them insult each other.

"Reckon you're right, Cap'n," Barlow said, rising. "Mornin' does have a way of sneakin' up on a man." He spun and walked away, leaving a fuming Nottingsworth sitting there.

14

IT WAS THE bloodiest thing Barlow had ever been involved in. The men sat there, relatively comfortable, no more than a hundred fifty yards from the herd of buffalo. Using care, they dropped nearly two dozen buffalo without scaring off the rest of the herd. Finally Rutledge called a halt to the shooting, which had lasted less than half an hour. With that, he took a purposefully badly aimed shot that spooked the animals, which took off with a rumble, and within minutes were gone, leaving only their dead fellows and a cloud of dust.

The men and women headed out to begin skinning and butchering the huge buffalo. Barlow had, of course, done so on the journey out there, but not quite like this. When he or the others hunted for the traders, they usually killed only two buffalo at most. They would cut out what meat they would need for a day or so, and leave the rest, including the hide, lying there. But the mountain men needed hides for lodges and enormous amounts of meat to carry them through the winter. So the work was methodical and dull, quite unlike the almost joyous work of butchering for the group of traders.

The men did most of the skinning and butchering. The

hides were slit up the belly and legs, and then ropes were
tied to the skin. Using a horse or mule, they would pull the
hide free with a great sucking, tearing sound. The hide
would be towed to the carcass and flipped over, so the hair
side was down. Then the butchering would begin. Large
chunks of meat and fat were tossed onto the bloody buffalo
skin. The tongues, livers, and a few other choice cuts were
put aside to be eaten over the next few days.

Within minutes of starting, Barlow found himself covered in blood from head to foot. He glanced around and
noticed that everyone else was in the same condition. It
could not be helped. There was no prettiness in this work.
It was hack out meat with knife or tomahawk, toss the
hunks onto the hide, and go back for more, as often as not
having to crawl inside the still steaming carcass to cull out
whatever meat they could.

If that wasn't bad enough, the heat rose soon after the
butchering started. Though it was not unknown to get a
freak snowstorm or something in these parts in August, this
was not one of those times. The temperature soared and
stayed there, goaded to worrisome heights by the ominous
orb of the sun.

As the hides became covered with meat, a couple of the
women would come along with mules and tie the skins to
the mules and drag them back to the camp, then return with
the empty hides to be filled again. Barlow did not want to
ask where they were storing the meat.

In the camp, the other women worked industriously at
slicing the meat and hanging it on every conceivable place
so that it could dry in the sun and heat.

It took the better part of the day for the men to finish
their work, and by the time they were done, they were rank,
smelling highly of blood, grease, sweat, and entrails. They
finally left the butchered carcasses for the wolves and vul-
tures. While none of the men was particularly fond of bathing, not a one refused to head to the river when they were
done. There they stripped down and washed themselves and
their clothes as best they could, using one of the few cakes
of lye soap they had brought along.

Afterward they headed to camp, where some of the set-aside special cuts of fresh buffalo meat were sizzling over several small fires. Each man grabbed a prize piece of meat for himself and sat. Except for Rutledge, who wandered off. He returned quickly, carrying two bottles of whiskey.

"Reckon you boys are about half froze to cut your dry," Rutledge said with a grin. "After all them hard doin's of today." He opened one bottle, took a long, almost painful swallow, and then handed the bottle to Caleb Simon. He handed the second to Charlie Watters. Then he grabbed some food and took a seat, leaning against his saddle.

The men were quiet as they ate and passed the whiskey around. None paid much heed to the women still working diligently all around them. They had done their toil for the day. The rest was women's work.

"Whar away ye thinkin' to head this year, Sim?" Bob Francher asked. They were pretty well full of meat now and relaxed from the whiskey flowing through their systems.

Rutledge shrugged. "Up toward the Missouri somewhere, I expect. Maybe the Three Forks area."

"Damn, ye jist aim to have us a run-in with Bug's Boys, don't ye?" Nottingsworth said. He did not sound concerned.

"Growing scairdy in your ol' age, boy?" Rutledge asked with a grin.

"That I be," Nottingsworth said with his usual honking laugh. "Right fearful that there ain't gonna be no more Blackfoot left fer me to raise hair on."

"Has been a spell, ain't it?" Watters added.

"That it has," Simon threw in. "Them boys even laid low last season." He looked thoughtful for a moment, then asked, "You boys think somethin's happened to them red devils?"

"Like what?" Nottingsworth asked, not quite as scornful as usual. He didn't want to irk Simon, who was bigger, stronger, and, despite his usual good nature, as fierce as any Blackfoot when angered.

Simon shrugged. "Hell if I know. Fire, flood, famine." He began to laugh.

"I heard down to rendezvous that the free trappers and Rocky Mountain Fur boys roughed the Blackfoot up last year just after the rendezvous," Francher said. "Right here in Pierre's Hole, if ol' Bill Sublette was tellin' true. And I ain't ever knowed him not to speak straight."

"Figures," Simon said with a chuckle. "First time we head to the Settlements in God knows how long, and we miss the chance to give those fractious Blackfoot a right good thumpin'."

"Those Blackfeet as fearsome as I've heard?" Barlow asked.

"Damn right they are, ye cowardly sot," Nottingsworth said scornfully.

Barlow waited several beats, trying to force back the sudden flare-up of anger. "Are you always this damn foolish, boy?" he finally snapped. "Or is this somethin' you do just to amuse me?"

Nottingsworth wasn't sure what to say. He was certain that no matter what he answered, he would come out looking like a fool, so he kept his mouth shut, but he stewed.

When Barlow realized that Nottingsworth was not going to respond, he said tightly, "Now, would one of you boys with some sense be so kind as to answer my simple little question?"

Simon grinned at the young man's audacity. But he was serious when he said, "They're the meanest goddamn critters you'll ary come across. Ride like they're part of the damn pony, fight like devils, ain't afeared of no one, and hate us Americans somethin' powerful."

"What've they got against us?" Barlow asked, surprised.

"Don't nobody really know," Watters said. "Some folks say it was started when some expedition of Americans come through here thirty year ago or so. Others say it had something to do with one of the men in that venture came back out here a few years later. One or the other of 'em tangled with the Blackfeet and killed one of 'em. Them red devils ain't nary forget it."

"Don't seem reasonable," Barlow commented.

"Ain't no Injins can be considered reasonable, boy," Francher said. "They all of 'em has their own ways, which don't make a heap of sense to folks like us."

"Can you trust any of 'em?" Barlow asked, fascinated but rather surprised by the information.

"A few," Simon said. He swigged some whiskey, burped loudly, and passed the bottle on. "The Nez Perce ain't ever gone against a white man far's anybody's ever seen or heard. Same with the Flatheads. The Shoshonis're pretty dependable. Ain't many others I'd put my full trust in."

"It pays to be mindful of your surroundings at all times, boy," Watters added.

"I reckon it does," Barlow agreed. He grew quiet then, thinking about all that had been said and detachedly listening to the others quietly talking. It was still on his mind when he turned in not long after, but he soon forgot about it in the arms of Mountain Calf, who was as hungry for him as ever. She was as fresh smelling as could be, and no one would ever have known that only half an hour before she was blood and grease splattered from working the entire day with freshly killed buffalo.

They spent ten days in Pierre's Hole, and when they left, they had more than enough meat to last out a reasonably long winter. Each couple also had a lodge made, though none planned to use it unless the weather suddenly turned bad.

Rutledge led them east, back over the Tetons, and then north into a land that had Barlow scared down to the soles of his moccasins. Stinking spumes of water and mud boiled and shot high into the air. The ground and air reeked of sulfur, giving it the aura of hell. Even the horses and mules were spooked, and they picked their way carefully along ground that was sometimes crusted with reeking crystals. The animals were often reluctant to move forward, and the men had to curse and whistle at them, and often quirt them to get them to proceed. It was an eerie couple of days, and

Barlow, at least, was mighty glad when they had made their way out of the hellish landscape.

That night, as Barlow was unsaddling his horse, he suddenly smiled. "Damn, Beelzebub," he said, "mayhap it was you who brought me through that godawful place. Or mayhap it was you who brought me *to* it. Hmmm, that so? Mayhap that's why you were so balky back there. Mayhap you wanted to stay there with your namesake, ol' Scratch hisself?" He laughed at his foolishness. But he did admit silently that he was powerfully relieved to be out of that grotesque place.

"Always knowed you was a real coward, boy," Nottingsworth said from nearby. He never missed an opportunity to insult Barlow.

Barlow cursed, wishing that Nottingsworth had not heard him, but knowing it was far too late for such sentiments. "Well," he said evenly, "traipsin' through such a peculiar place did strike a note of concern within this ol' boy. But that's mayhap because I got sense, which is somethin' you cain't lay claim to. And a man without sense ain't afeared of anything, I reckon, either in this world or in the next."

A burst of laughter rippled out from the trees, and Barlow smiled, silently thanking Simon.

"If you ain't got anything more to say—or anything of importance, you best go on about your business," Barlow said. "There's more'n enough chores to be done."

Nottingsworth spit at Barlow, but missed his mark by a wide margin. He turned and stalked off.

Caleb Simon drifted over toward Barlow, stopping on the other side of the young man's horse. "You and that ol' chil' are gonna have to tangle one of these here days and settle these troubles between you, boy. You know that, don't ye?"

Barlow nodded. "Reckon I do. Cain't say as I'm lookin' forward to it, though."

"Scared of him?" Simon asked.

Barlow shook his head. "Nope. I've fought bigger men than him." He paused, trying to find the right words to explain. "It's more like I expect that Mr. Rutledge would be mighty disappointed in me was I to take on one of his longtime friends and partners. So I aim to try'n keep a rein on my temper." He grinned a little. "Which, if truth be told, is a lot damn harder than most anything else I could do."

Simon nodded. "Them're noble reasonin's, boy, but I still think you'll have to go agin that chil' afore long."

"If it comes to that, Caleb, I'll be ready for it." Barlow thought about the problem for a while as he tended his horse. The insults and digs at his character were tough enough to take for him, what with his hot temper, but all the worse was Nottingsworth's desire for Mountain Calf. Nothing overt had occurred, but Barlow had caught Nottingsworth staring lustfully at the Nez Perce woman on more than one occasion. Barlow didn't like it, but since Nottingsworth had not actually made any kind of move, Barlow knew there was nothing he could do about it. Yet.

In the weeks since they had been brought together, Barlow had come to care for Mountain Calf considerably. He wasn't sure it was love, but there was more there than just the sex. He was comfortable with her and could see no problem in spending a good long time with her.

He hoped she felt the same. She certainly seemed to, if her actions and the delight in her eyes when she was with him were any indication. And that made him feel pretty damn good. It also kept him from worrying too much about Bill Nottingsworth's obvious lust for her. He figured that Nottingsworth would not make an overt move to take Mountain Calf, and if Nottingsworth knew she was unwilling to be with him, Barlow thought there would be little problem. Still, he vowed to keep on the alert.

He finished tending to Beelzebub, and then headed off to help unload the mules. This was, he had decided shortly after the group had left Pierre's Hole, as bad as traveling with the traders. There he had had to unload all the supplies pretty much every night. Now the loads of meat and hides had to be unloaded each night, but at least now he didn't have to do it alone. Still, it was an onerous task, and it often seemed never ending. He sometimes thought that he finished unloading the mules just in time to begin loading them up again in the morning.

Done with that, he headed off to find Mountain Calf. Buffalo perked his head up when he saw Barlow. The dog was growing rapidly and was already becoming quite protective of Barlow. And of Mountain Calf. The woman took good care of the puppy and appeared to enjoy having the animal around. At times, Barlow wondered if she were just being nice to the dog as she waited for it to fatten up for the pot. He often thought he should mention that such was not to be Buffalo's fate, but in his heart he could not believe she was planning such a devilish end to his pet. At least he seriously hoped not.

Barlow grabbed Mountain Calf and kissed her hard, while lifting her and twirling her around in his strong arms. That earned him a small growl from the Newfoundland puppy. "Ah, you jist hush your trap, dog," he snarled back in mock ferocity. "This here's my woman and I can do sich things with her."

Mountain Calf pulled his mouth down to hers again, agreeing in principal, if not in words, with Barlow's comment. He forgot about the dog. And moments later, they were tangled together, panting and hungry, rolling on the buffalo robes they used as a bed.

15

THE SMALL GROUP, well-supplied and ever-alert, rode slowly. They were in no rush, and with the pack animals loaded as much as they were, they did not want to run the risk of losing any. But they did not linger at any one place. The weather was still too warm for the beaver to be bearing prime fur, so they had no reason to tarry anywhere to trap. At least not for a few more weeks. So they kept up a steady, slow pace, falling into the monotonous drudgery of the trail.

Days turned into weeks, which became a month, then two. Cold, harsh weather swept over the mountains, and the men started staying in a spot for several days at a time—long enough to pull a reasonable catch of beaver out of the streams and ponds of the area. Then they would head on, moving relatively quickly to the next spot that looked like it had plentiful beaver.

The men generally worked in pairs for their trapping. It was safer and far more efficient that way. Dan Parker had been Ed Brown's partner, and it fell to Parker to take up trapping up with Barlow now, but he balked at the idea.

"I got nothin' agin you, boy," he had growled in his phlegm-thickened voice, looking at Barlow. He didn't seem much concerned about how Barlow felt about his words—

or his attitude. "Ye got to unnerstand 'at. But it don't shine with this ol' hoss to be paired up with some green chil' what don't know his pecker from a moose turd."

Barlow was embarrassed, hurt, and steamed all at the same time. But he had learned a while ago not to show such things to others. He forced himself to smile. "I understand," he said with a nod. "It ain't in my nature to force myself in where I ain't wanted." He ignored the almost inaudible snort from Nottingsworth. "I reckon I can see to my traps and sich by myself. Ain't no one needs to be put out none."

"No," Rutledge said flatly. "I ain't havin' no men out on their lines by hisself when we got the numbers to make sure we all got someone to watch our backs." He paused. "Thar anybody here you'd find acceptable as a partner, Dan?"

"Well, me'n ol' Bob there, we git along jist fine," Parker ventured.

"How's that suit you, Bob?" Rutledge asked.

"It's more Charlie's decisions, Cap'n," Francher said. "It suits this chil' to go along with either one of 'em."

"Charlie?" Rutledge asked, looking at Watters.

"I reckon it won't put me out none to throw in with Will," Watters said with a nod. "He's a hard-workin' sort and quick to learn. And I sure as hell don't need ol' Bob to show me where to find beaver," he added with a laugh.

"Shit, Charlie, you couldn't find beaver if it latched itself onto your fat ass and was gnawin' away fer dear life!" Francher said, laughing, too.

Everyone else laughed—including Barlow, though he still wasn't sure how he felt about all this. He was suddenly ill at ease, feeling out of place. He didn't like that, but there was nothing he could do about it either, so he kept it to himself.

"That suit you, Will?" Rutledge asked him.

Barlow shrugged. "Makes me no never mind. I can git along with anybody here, except maybe one skunk-humper." He looked at Nottingsworth and favored him with an ingratiating smile.

Nottingsworth scowled but said nothing.

He and Watters got along all right, always had. Watters had continued to be about the friendliest man in the bunch toward him. If one could get past his offensive odor, he was not a bad fellow at all.

Barlow quickly learned that Watters was telling the truth, too, when he said he did not need anyone to help him find beaver. Barlow was astounded. To him, it seemed as if his partner could smell beaver from miles away. It was an uncanny ability to root out the thickly furred rodents. He tried often and in various ways to teach Barlow how to do it, but to no avail. Oh, Barlow got better at it as time passed, but he would never have Watter's natural talent for it, and eventually Watters quit trying to help Barlow improve his ability to find beaver, realizing he was as good at it as he was going to get.

Barlow found it easier to learn many of the other things he needed to survive and possibly prosper in this harsh, unforgiving country. He was only so-so at tracking, but he was an excellent shot, and quickly picked up on what plants and such would keep a man alive out here in starving times. He learned where he would be likely to find animals for food or warm hides in the depths of winter and ways to snare those animals, how to make snowshoes, and caring for the horses and mules in wicked weather to give them the best chance of surviving. He grew to know the signs of danger, how to use a basic fur to pack their furs into bales, how to find his way in a sometimes trackless wilderness, and much more. Within months, he was as much a mountain man as any of Rutledge's group, except that he had not fought Indians yet.

Nottingsworth was not about to let him forget that either. "Yet jist ain't a real man till you've faced some goddamn Blackfeet half froze to raise hair on ye, boy," he said with a smirk one early November night. "Or run off a pack of goddamn Crows tryin' to steal your whole cavvy of horses and mules."

"It's some surprisin' we ain't had a run-in with any Injins so far," Francher noted.

"Them is some strange doin's," Caleb Simon added. "Hell, we ain't even seed no Injins yet. Queer. Plumb queer. Wonder why that is."

Barlow, who was tired of Nottingsworth's insults and all, suddenly smiled. "It's because of me," he said firmly, grinning broadly. "Them Injins knew I was gonna be amongst you boys, and they're scared to do death of this ol' chil'. So they've been givin' us a mighty wide berth lest they provoke my wrath."

The others sat there a few moments, not sure what to think, but laughter finally bubbled up and out of Simon and Watters. Within seconds, the others—except Nottingsworth—had joined in.

"Damn, if you ain't got sand ol' coon," Simon said, still chuckling. "Ye spin a mighty fine yarn there, too, boy. Goddamn, if you don't. And who can say, maybe ye might even be right." He laughed more,

"Might be right, hell," Nottingsworth snapped. "The Injins might be givin' us plenty of room because of that dumb son of a bitch, all right, but I'd say it's more because they figure that with him along, we ain't worth their time as warriors to come agin us." He smiled without humor, glaring at Barlow.

Anger flared up in Barlow, but he batted it back down. "Least I got some hair that's fit for some Blackfoot's lodgepole," he countered.

Nottingsworth self-consciously ran a hand through his thinning hair and glowered.

"But I figure it's more that them Injins got a look at your ugly mug one time and decided ol' Scratch was ridin' with us. Reckon they figure it'd be mighty bad medicine to come agin us." He smiled again, but it was accompanied by a look that Barlow would have wore had he just spit on the other man.

Nottingsworth boiled up and charged Barlow, who rolled out of the way as Nottingsworth jumped at him. Barlow leaped up and kicked Nottingsworth in the shoulder as he was trying to get to his feet. Back down Nottingsworth went, sprawling half on his back. As Nottingsworth began to rise again, Barlow jumped toward him, stopped and landed a good solid punch to the man's jaw.

Barlow was about to move in and finish Nottingsworth off when Dan Parker and Bob Francher sprang on him, knocking him to the ground. They tried to keep him there, but Barlow was having none of it. Using his massive arms and legs, which he managed to get under him, he shoved his way to his feet, flinging his two opponents away from him like a dog shedding water. He spun, after a glance at Nottingsworth to make sure he wasn't going to rejoin the fray. But Nottingsworth was still on the ground, groaning a little.

Barlow turned back to the other two and smiled. Buffalo was between him and his two foes, growling fiercely in puppyish warning. "That's a good boy, Buffler," he said quietly. "These two skunks ain't gonna cause me no troubles."

With a last high-pitched snarl, Buffalo backed off and away, watching alertly.

"Now that I've sent the dog away, you boys can stop tremblin'," Barlow said with a sneer. "And try comin' at me whilst I'm lookin' at you, 'stead of whilst my back is turned. Or ain't you two sorry shit piles got the balls for sich doin's?"

Francher simply charged, hoping to use his longer reach and several inches in height to his advantage. But Barlow braced himself and threw his right forearm out just as Francher slammed into him. The powerful blow stopped Francher in his tracks, though not in time to keep Barlow from falling on his rear.

He got up and brushed off the seat of his pants.

Francher was on the ground, rolling back and forth a little, clutching his face. Blood seeped out from between his fingers.

"How's about you, boy?" Barlow asked Parker. He was angry but in control of himself and not even breathing hard. "You want to try your medicine against me, shit sack?"

Parker wanted to back down, but knew he couldn't in front of the others. Despite Barlow's size, he had not considered him all that strong and tough until moments ago. Now he wasn't so sure he would have any more success against the big young man than his two friends had had. But he had to try something, since he was under the watchful eyes of the others. Instead of charging recklessly as Nottingsworth and Francher had done, Parker crouched and moved forward slowly, arms in front of him, hands looking like claws seeking flesh to latch on to.

Barlow sneered and clumped forward, unconcerned, until he was just about within arm's reach, and stopped. He grabbed Parker's biceps and held on. It took Parker a second to understand, and then he did the same to Barlow. They stared at each other a few moments before Parker suddenly shifted his feet and tried to throw Barlow off balance, using his hands on Barlow's arms. Barlow didn't move as Parker strained more and more. With his feet planted, Barlow was like a deep-rooted oak.

Barlow let Parker sweat for a bit as he strained. Then suddenly he jerked his head forward and slammed his forehead into Parker's face. Parker's eyes rolled up into his head and he sank to his knees, his arms falling limply at his sides. Barlow let him fall. He looked around at the other men, a powerful challenge in his eyes. No one took him up on it.

Barlow nodded and then retook his seat. He filled his coffee cup and took a sip, still keeping his anger under control. No one spoke, and only the crackling of fires and the moans from the downed men broke the night's peaceful silence.

Finally Nottingsworth managed to lurch back toward the fire. He stopped and pointed a finger at Barlow. "You're wolf bait, you sneakin' son of a bitch," he snarled, words a little jumbled. "I'm gonna carve you up every way till Sunday, damn you."

"Any time you think you've found the balls to try sich doin's, you just have at it, boy," Barlow said easily. "But you might think to have more help than you had this night."

Nottingsworth spit, turned, and shuffled off into the

night, heading for his robes. Moments later, the others heard him bellowing and then there was the sound of a hand striking flesh. Barlow shook his head.

Before long, Francher and Parker pulled themselves up and staggered off to their robes. There was no nastiness from their areas, as both simply wanted to collapse and sleep for a month or two to get rid of the pain. They would deal with their humiliation later.

Barlow set down his tin mug. "I'm sorry about all these here doin's, Cap'n," he said quietly.

"Ain't nothin' to be sorry for, boy," Rutledge said with a shrug.

"You mean you ain't riled about this ruckus?" Barlow asked, surprised.

"What makes ye think I would be?" Rutledge seemed genuinely confused.

"You mean it don't matter none to you that I just trounced three of your men?"

Rutledge laughed a little. "Hell, boy, I'm the booshway of these here boys. I ain't their mother."

"Damn," Barlow spat sourly.

"What's ailin' ye, boy?" Rutledge asked, still perplexed.

"Well, I've kept my trap shut all this time since you took me on, figurin' that it wouldn't shine with you if I was to lay into some of these boys, what with me bein' the new hoss amongst you. So I kept my trap shut despite all the insults and sich that some of the others have tossed my way. Especially Bill."

"I reckon I could see how you might think that," Rutledge allowed, finally understanding. "But you should've asked." He smiled a little. "Or else just did what ye did tonight and seen what happened."

"I figured had I done that, you'd cut me loose out here on my own to fend for myself."

"One thing ye should learn, boy," Rutledge said sternly, "is that all men out here are on their own to some extent. Ye can't depend on nobody but yourself. I ain't here to suckle these boys. They're all men, and they been out here some years. If they can't take care of themselves by now, there ain't shit I can do to save 'em.''

"Well, I'll be damned," Barlow breathed, annoyed at himself for not having reasoned this out long ago.

"Maybe ye will, boy, but this ol' hoss thinks ye've got a ways to go before the Good Lord makes that determination." He laughed again.

Barlow nodded, not seeing the humor in it right at the moment. "Well," he finally said, "you might want to tell them others that tonight's doin's was just a taste of what I aim to do to 'em if they keep ridin' me."

Rutledge shrugged. "They'll either figure it out on their own or you'll teach 'em another lesson on it," he said. "Just one warning, boy—I don't mind some of the boys thumpin' on each other, but it'd not shine with this ol' hoss whatsoever if anybody—includin' you—was to go under from a fracas you're involved in."

"Fair enough," Barlow allowed, but then he added, "But I ain't about to be put under by one of those shit piles jist so as not to displease you."

Rutledge laughed. "I'd not expect that of ye, ol' hoss. Just don't go cuttin' one of those ol' coons down just to keep 'em from comin' at you again."

Barlow nodded. He rose and headed off to his bed.

16

RIDING OUT TOWARD their traps the next morning, Barlow asked his partner, "I reckon that Bill, Dan, and Bob are close friends. That so?"

"Close as fleas on a hound," Watters agreed.

"Anybody else here I got to concern myself about?"

"Jist maybe Johnny Clarke."

"That makes sense, what with him bein' paired up with Nottingsworth." He sighed. "How about you, Charlie?"

"Me?" Watters asked, looking at Barlow in surprise. "You think that of me?"

"Nope. Jist want to hear you affirm it."

Watters was a little annoyed, but not too much. He could see Barlow's point, and would probably have asked the same thing if he had been in Barlow's position. "You ain't got a damn thing to worry about from me, ol' hoss," Watters said earnestly. "Not a goddamn . . ." He stopped and sat stock still on his horse, listening intently.

Barlow knew better than to open his mouth. He just sat and waited, also listening, trying to hear whatever Watters was listening for. He could hear nothing beyond the wind and the sounds of birds in the cold morning air.

Then there was a gunshot, followed by a couple of others.

"Damn," Watters snapped. "Let's go, boy." He turned his horse and slapped its rump with his battered old hat.

Barlow was right behind him, though not for long, as Watters had the much faster steed. Barlow rode low down on the animal, racing back toward camp as fast as old Beelzebub would take him. Barlow's heart pounded with fear and excitement. He wondered if this was the time he would actually get to fight some real Indians. He both looked forward to it and dreaded it. He only hoped that he would acquit himself well when the battle was joined.

Nor did he give any consideration to Buffalo, who, as usual, was along with him. But there was no way the puppy could keep up even with Beelzebub, and he was soon left behind. Barlow knew the dog would make his way back to the camp. He just hoped that the animal would be safe.

Barlow didn't know why he turned off the main trail onto the barely discernible path through the woods, but he did. It was almost as if the horse had made the decision. Barlow simply didn't argue, just went along for the ride. The trees thinned in a few moments, and he could see more of the area. He spotted an Indian behind a thick bush, looking toward the camp, nocked bow in hand as he searched for a target. Gunfire popped and shouts could be heard in the camp, which was still mostly blocked from Barlow's view by the vegetation.

The Indian—Barlow had no idea what kind he was—heard Beelzebub's thumping hoofbeats and turned. He began to bring his bow around to shoot this wild white man, but was a bit too slow. Barlow thundered up, and smashed the warrior in the face with the butt of his rifle as he rode past. He hunched his shoulders, waiting for an arrow in the back, but it never came. Barlow figured he must have killed the Indian, or at least seriously wounded him.

Barlow decided he should try to regain control of Beelzebub, who was beginning to flag some. Gently the man guided the horse toward the camp, swinging in a long arc, slowing as they went. As he trotted into the camp, he spotted a warrior trying to haul a wildly battling Mountain Calf onto his pony. Barlow jerked the horse to a halt, threw his rifle to his shoulder, and put a bullet through the Indian's head.

Without hesitating, Barlow swung the horse around and kicked it into motion, heading for his group's horse herd. He knew, from what the others had impressed upon him, that the Indians—no matter what kind they were—would always look to run off the cavvyard of animals.

When he reached the herd, Barlow took in the scene in an instant. Johnny Clarke was grappling with two warriors. A couple of others lay dead in the vicinity. A mounted Indian was trying to drive the horses and mules off, but the animals were hobbled. Barlow galloped toward the mounted warrior, stuffing his rifle into a loop dangling from his saddle as he did.

The Indian sensed Barlow approaching and cast a hateful glance over his shoulder. He dropped the rope that he had looped over one horse's neck to urge it to lead the others away, and jabbed his moccasin heels into his pony's side.

Barlow knew he could not catch the Indian on his swift little pony, so when he got as close as he thought he was going to get, he pulled Beelzebub up sharply and steadied his pistol on his left arm. Then he fired. The warrior jerked as if hit, but he continued racing away.

"Damn," Barlow muttered. He shoved the pistol into his belt, and swung Beelzebub around. "C'mon, ol' horse," he muttered, he muttered, "if you got anything left in you, best show it." The horse snorted but began loping back where Clarke was still desperately battling the two Indians.

Instead of stopping, Barlow simply launched himself off the horse as he got to the three men. He landed mostly on the Indians, but knocked all of them to the ground. One warrior was faster getting to his feet than Barlow was and swung his war club at Barlow as he was rising. The stone head brushed across Barlow's ribs. It made him hiss with surprise and a little pain, but it did not damage him too much.

Before the Indian could spin back, Barlow swung his

hands up, locked together, and then brought the huge ball of muscle and bone down hard on the back of the warrior's neck. There was a slight cracking sound, and the Indian flopped onto his face, his legs twitching a bit.

Someone crashed into his back, and he went down, kicking and swinging at the unseen enemy. He got himself free, rolled away, and came to his feet. Apparently both the Indian and Clarke, in their fight, had plowed into him, and now the warrior was atop Clarke, about to bash him as soon as he could get a clear shot at the struggling trapper's head with his war club.

Barlow barreled forward, jerking out his tomahawk as he did. He skidded to a stop next to the two combatants, and fell as he slipped on the grass and dirt. "Damn," he muttered as he shoved himself up, just in time to have the Indian slam the war club against the back of his thigh. He moaned and fell again, but scrambled out of the way a bit before getting up. He gingerly tested the leg and realized that while it hurt like blazes, he could walk on it all right, so it must not be broken. He limped forward, anger burning in his eyes, fear worming its way into his stomach.

The Indian's move against Barlow had given Clarke a brief opening, and he had managed to poke a thumb into the warrior's Adam's apple, which loosened the Indian's grip on his arm a bit more. With two deft jabs and a hard-thrown elbow, he was out from under the warrior's weight. Once on his feet, Clarke scooped up his big butchering knife, which had fallen. Now he was ready to face the war-club-wielding Indian. Clarke leaped forward, bringing his left arm up to block the inevitable swing of the war club and lashing inward toward the abdomen with his knife.

But the warrior confounded him by swinging his weapon under Clarke's upraised arm. Only Clarke's momentum saved him, as the club went behind his back, and only the warrior's arm hit him in the side. But the jolt knocked Clarke's knife hand to the side, and he barely nicked the Indian's flesh with the blade.

The Indian shoved Clarke, knocking him sideways and down onto one knee. The war club went up and began coming down, ready to splatter the trapper's head.

Barlow swung his tomahawk and hooked the Indian's war club on it just under the head of it. He yanked and the stone weapon flew out of the warrior's hand. In almost the same movement, he reversed the tomahawk's direction and backhanded it across the Indian's face. At the same time, Clarke thrust his knife upward, the blade tearing through the Indian's intestines. The warrior fell.

"Goddamn," Barlow said as he sank to the ground, "that was one hard to kill ol' hoss." He was breathing heavily, and the pain in his leg was throbbing steadily.

Clarke looked at Barlow, not quite sure of what to say. Because of Barlow's feud with his partner, Nottingsworth, Clarke did not like Barlow very much. But the newcomer's actions just now put things in a different light. Barlow could have easily let the warriors kill him, saving himself in the process. But he had risked his own neck to save him. Clarke could not—would not—treat that lightly.

"Yep, that he was," Clarke offered uneasily.

"You all right?" Barlow asked.

Clarke nodded. "Just winded is all." He almost smiled. "I had my hands full there fer a spell, I can tell ye." He clapped his mouth shut, thinking he might have said too much already, acted too friendly toward a man he still somehow thought he should hate.

"I noticed that," Barlow acknowledged with no sense of derision in his voice. "I'm pleased I was able to get here before them boys put you under." He paused. "By the way, jist what kind of Injins are the critters?"

"Blackfoot," Clarke said, spitting the word out as something vile.

Barlow nodded. "You boys were tellin' true then," he commented. "They are some fierce ol' fellers." He painfully pushed himself to his feet. "I best get back there to see if the others need help," he said. "Unless you need me to help you with the remuda."

Clarke stood, too, looking weary. "I reckon we got Bug's Boys on the run now," he said, looking around. There were no more Blackfoot—living ones anyway—in the vicinity. "You get back there and things're calmed down, it might shine with this chil' to have some help then. But only if there ain't no need for everybody there."

Barlow nodded, a bit of anger growing in him. Then he turned back. "If you'd rather I jist sent someone out here, I can do that. I mayhap figure you ain't of a mind to have me helpin' you."

Clarke held his feelings in check. He was angry at having been found out. But he still didn't know what to do or think about Will Barlow. "Nope," he lied. "Jist if everyone ain't needed over there. If you're the one to come back here, that'll suit this ol' chil' jist fine." He hoped, however, that it would be someone else.

Barlow nodded again and limped off toward where Beelzebub had stopped and was cropping grass near a tree. Halfway to the horse, Buffalo bounded out of the woods and loped over toward his master. Barlow painfully knelt and greeted the puppy, which lapped his face with a slobbery tongue. "You missed all the fun there, Buffler," Barlow said with a grin as he ruffled the dog's neck fur.

He rose and hobbled the rest of the way and pulled himself into the saddle. With Buffalo trotting alongside the steed, Barlow slowly headed toward the main part of the camp. Everything looked pretty much normal, he found. Curing beaver furs hung from branches everywhere, swinging in the cold wind, just like usual. Smoke lifted out the smokeholes of the lodges, mingling with the grayness of the day. There were no bodies lying around.

Barlow stopped at his lodge. Mountain Calf was waiting for him and threw herself into his arms. She was close to tears, but would not let them come out. She could not have her man seeing her weep over something as minor as an attack by Blackfoot.

"You all right?" he asked.

She nodded. "You?" Her voice reflected only a bit of her fear for him.

"I'm fine, woman," he said gruffly. "One of those red devils got me on the leg with his war club, but the bone ain't broke, so I'll heal up in a few days." He squeezed her tight. "Now, I best go check with the others. You take care of yourself, y'hear?"

Mountain Calf nodded again and went into the lodge.

Barlow left the horse there. The animal had been hard used well beyond normal and needed rest. And Barlow didn't feel like trying to haul himself back into the saddle with his leg hurting this bad. He didn't know if walking on it would be any better, but at least it was different.

Rutledge and most of the others were having a hurried war council in front of the leader's lodge. "Where's Charlie?" Barlow asked, worried when he arrived and noticed his partner was not there.

"Makin' a paseo around the area to see if Bug's Boys are really gone or jist layin' low for the moment," Simon said. "Sit and grab some coffee, boy."

Barlow did so.

"You seen Johnny?" Rutledge asked. Clarke was the only man not accounted for.

Barlow nodded. "He's all right. Said to send him some help with the animals if you could spare someone from here."

"Why didn't you stay with him?" Simon asked.

"Ol' hoss didn't want me around," Barlow responded sourly. He glanced at Nottingsworth.

Simon saw where Barlow's gaze had gone, and he nodded.

"I reckon you left him out there at the mercy of these red savages," Nottingsworth snarled. "Goddamn you, boy, if Johnny's been put under by those goddamn Blackfoot, I'll rip your goddamn heart out and feed it to you."

Barlow calmly looked at the raging trapper and spit at him. The glob of phlegm hit his coat and oozed down. "Shut your fuckin' trap, boy, or you'll be joinin' them four goddamn Blackfoot I sent to the Happy Huntin' Ground."

Nottingsworth broke into laughter, but there was no joy or real feeling in it. "Four Blackfeet? You tryin' to tell me and the other boys here that you put *four* Blackfeet under? By yourself?"

"Well, that might not be entirely the God's truth," Barlow said slowly, deliberately.

"You're damn right it ain't," Nottingsworth snapped. "Son of a bitchin' goddamn liar."

"It might've been five," Barlow said, his smarmy grin appearing. "I got one of 'em with a pistol shot, but don't know whether I kilt him or jist wounded him."

"I ain't listenin' to this booshwa no more," Nottingsworth growled, rising. "I'm goin' to help Johnny with the cavvy." He walked away, muttering, "Lyin' goddamn bastard. Thinks he can tell me such goddamn yarns and believe 'em. Goddamn son of a bitch . . ."

"You really put that many Bug's Boys under, Will?" Simon asked.

"You callin' me a liar, too, Caleb?" Barlow countered.

"Nope. Jist askin' a question."

"Yep. I did. Well I think I kilt four. Again, it might've been five. Or it might've only been three." He explained each one.

"Damn, if you ain't some now," Simon said with a grin.

"You believe him, Caleb?" Francher asked. His face was a mess of bruises from the drubbing Barlow had given him the night before.

"No reason not to."

"He ain't got no scalps."

"Neither do you, boy," Simon said. "Jist 'cause that chil' don't shine with you don't make him a liar, boy. There's many a chil' don't get along out here, and ain't nobody askin' you to be sweet on each other. But you should have the sense to keep your trap shut until you know for sure a man's lyin'."

Watters's arrival cut off the rest of that talk, at least for the time being. "Ain't none of those critters out there now," Watters said, taking a seat on the cold ground. "We sure as hell turned their medicine bad on 'em." He laughed, happy that he—and the others—had come through another scrape unscathed.

17

WINTER'S HAND PRESSED unrelentingly on the mountain landscape where Sim Rutledge's group of free trappers had made their camp to wait out the worst of the cold months. The valley along the Bitterroot River was as pleasant as could be expected considering the altitude, latitude, and time of year. But that did not say much to recommend it. The work the men had was sporadic and as dull as dirt. With the rivers, ponds, and streams pretty well frozen over, there was no trapping worth the effort. So the men as often as not had to keep themselves busy gathering firewood, hunting on the rare chance of finding some game, making and repairing gear, and other such mundane chores.

The most important and time-consuming task, however, was keeping the animals alive. Forage had to be gathered and brought in regularly, and the horses and mules had to be protected from the worst of the weather. They also needed to be exercised regularly lest they be in too poor shape to carry riders or furs when spring arrived. Despite all their efforts, though, more than ten animals—almost all of them horses—died, which forced Rutledge to call a council of his men.

"These here are poor doin's, boys," Rutledge said. They

were all crammed into his lodge, where it was at least warm, and the howling snowstorm was kept at bay. The women were in one of the other teepees, so the men had to fend for themselves in getting coffee and meat. "Worst we've come against in a heap of time."

"We'll make out all right," Johnny Clarke said, "if we don't lose no more animals."

Rutledge shook his head. "We've had us a prime huntin' season, as you ought to know, Johnny," he said. "Which means we was gonna be hard pressed to have enough animals to carry all the plews and supplies we got now. And I reckon our spring hunt's gonna be as good as the winter one was."

"You got any suggestions, Sim?" Nottingsworth asked.

"Yep," Rutledge said sourly. "We need to git us some more animals somewhere."

"That's a hoot," Francher snapped. "Horses and mule don't exactly grow wild out here. And even if they did, we'd have a hell of a time catchin' and breakin' 'em."

"That's a fact, boy," Rutledge said.

"Why don't we go on over somewhere and steal us a bunch of ponies from the Blackfeet?" Watters suggested. "Hell, they've stole enough of our horses."

"Any of you boys ready to make a winter ride, leavin' our women and all here, whilst we go huntin' up a Blackfoot village to raid? And then havin' to fight them red bastards all the way back here?" Rutledge questioned. "Because you know they ain't about to let such a thing just go by."

When he received no affirmative answers, he nodded. "So we're back to where we started with these doin's. Any of ye have any idears that might make some sense?"

There was silence for some time, until Caleb Simon finally said, "How's about we head west and find us some Nez Perce?" he offered. "Them boys'd be willin' to sell us a heap of animals."

"Same troubles there, Caleb, almost," Rutledge said after a few moments' thought. "A forced winter march through the mountains. And we either drag all the women, supplies, and such with us or leave 'em all here whilst we make that run. And it'd take us a hell of a long time, I reckon. Such doin's don't shine with this ol' hoss no how.''

Barlow lit up his clay pipe. He had taken it up some months ago and found he liked its relaxing nature around the fire. ''It might be a heap of trouble was everyone to go,'' he said quietly, thoughtfully, ''but mayhap one or two boys could do it without much bother.''

The others thought that over for a while, and one by one, they came to realize that might be workable.

Finally Rutledge nodded. ''I reckon you're right, ol' hoss,'' he said. ''Any volunteers?'' There was no immediate rush to fill the position, so Rutledge turned to Barlow. ''How about you, Will?'' he suggested. ''After all, it were your idea.''

Barlow shrugged. ''Won't put me out too much, I reckon, to do sich.''

''I need one more man to volunteer, boys,'' Rutledge said harshly. ''Elsewise, I'll have to just pick one of ye.'' He paused. ''Well?''

''Hell, I can do it alone, Sim,'' Barlow said calmly. ''Ain't no reason to endanger anyone else.''

Rutledge looked at him in surprise, and with a little suspicion. ''You ain't ever dealt with Injins before, Will,'' he said evenly. ''Even when we traded some on the way here, ye was jist an observer.''

''That's true,'' Barlow agreed. He stretched his huge, tree-stump legs out as best he could. ''But I watched ye, and I watched Mr. Branigan when I was with him. I reckon I can handle it. Besides, a man's got to learn to do these things for himself. That's what you've said.''

''I did say that, yep,'' Rutledge acknowledged. He thought a moment. ''What about talkin' to them? You don't know no Nez Perce.''

''I know a heap more'n you think I do on that tongue, Cap'n. Mountain Calf's been teachin' it to me. Besides, I ain't leavin' her here with the likes of some of these boys around, so she can translate when the language gits beyond me.''

"You aim to take her?" Rutledge asked, eyes raised. He shouldn't have been surprised. After all, Mountain Calf was an Indian woman and could keep to the trail as well as any white man could. But, still, it caught him unawares.

"I do."

Rutledge pondered that, as the men sat in silence, listening to the snap of the wood in the fire and to the howling of a couple of wolves off in the distance. Finally he nodded. "Reckon that suits me jist fine," he said. Then he stabbed Barlow with an icy glare. "But ye best remember, hoss, that if'n ye skedaddle on us, we will hunt your ass down and carve ye into pieces so small even the buzzards ain't gonna want ye."

Barlow hated having his integrity maligned. "I ain't ever run out when I've given my word to do something. I'll be damned if I'll start now," he said with a little heat.

Rutledge nodded. "Your word's good with me, boy," he said firmly.

"Now, hold your horses here a minute, Sim," Nottingsworth said.

"Ye offerin' to go along with him?" Rutledge asked with a tight smile.

"Now I nary said I was offerin' to do such a thing, Sim, and you goddamn well know it," Nottingsworth growled. "I just can't believe you're takin' that dumb bastard's word for it. You cain't tell me you trust him."

"As much as I'd trust you or any of the other boys," Rutledge said flatly. "He's showed himself to be ever' bit as worthy as any of you. He's held up his end of workin', and done all that's asked of him without complaint. Which is more'n I can say for some of you boys," he added pointedly.

"But he's takin' his woman with him," Nottingsworth protested. "This chil' thinks he's gonna git two miles from this camp and then race for the Settlements, leavin' us out here with our thumbs up our asses."

"Jist 'cause that'd be what you'd do don't mean anybody else'd do the same thing," Simon threw in. "There's still some ol' hosses who's got some integrity."

"Go to hell, you ol' fart," Nottingsworth snapped. "I jist know that son of a bitch is gonna run like a rabbit soon's he gits away from here. If he wasn't plannin' to do that, he'd leave his woman here."

"So some piece of shit like you can git his claws into her?" Barlow snarled. "Ain't goddamn likely."

"Reckon he knows ye through and through, Bill," Rutledge said with a humorless smile. "Ye think you've hid the fact all these months that you covet little Mountain Calf? Shee-it. You're a bigger goddamn fool than I thought."

"Somethin' else you're too dumb to have thunk of," Simon said. "He's leavin' nigh onto all his plunder here, specially his plews. Only some ol' chil' dumb as you would run out on the fortune in plews he's got settin' here."

"The decision's made, Bill," Rutledge said with finality. "I trust him, and that's that. Caleb agrees with me. Unless ye want to face us both—or go along with him—jist shut your trap."

Nottingsworth was steamed, but he knew he could say nothing without looking like a bigger fool than he already did.

Soon after, Barlow headed to Simon's lodge, where the women were gathered, leaving the men to continue their discussion if they so desired. Getting Mountain Calf, they went back to their own tipi, where Barlow patiently explained the adventure on which they were about to embark. Mountain Calf was a little concerned about the dangers involved, but not overly so, and she was happy to be going with Barlow. She was even happier to be able to get to her homeland and possibly even visit her band's village.

They pulled out the next morning, Barlow riding a big, burly black mule—Beelzebub wasn't up to such an arduous trip, Barlow figured—and Mountain Calf on a sturdy Indian pony. She held a rope that led to three mules loaded with jerky, pemmican, some coffee, a bit of sugar and some flour, as well as goods for trade. Buffalo, who was a year old now and weighed more than a hundred pounds, happily bounded through the snow, tongue flapping.

Barlow was guided by a map Simon had hastily scratched out on some thin bark with a piece of charcoal. He had only been that way once, but thought he remembered the best route. Barlow wasn't sure of that, but he had no choice. It was follow the crude map or go on faith.

They headed north, roughly following the Bitterroot River, traveling more than a week to get perhaps forty miles, before swinging west. It took another four days to make it the twenty miles or so to Lolo Pass—if they were in the right spot. They rested a day and were about to attack the pass when a snowstorm swept over them, pinning them down for another three days.

When the tempest blew out, the little group started into the pass. Barlow did not want to let Mountain Calf know his concerns, but he was seriously worried about this part of the journey, mainly because of the weather. He was apprehensive, thinking that the snow might be piled treetop high and that they would have no way of getting through the Bitterroot Mountains. Or worse, they would get trapped somewhere in the pass by another storm and get caught in an avalanche. Not that he worried about himself. His fear was for Mountain Calf.

Somehow, she sensed his anxiety and mentioned it as they hit a flat spot partway up the pass that day. "Stop worryin'," she said quietly. "You're big, strong. You'll get us through anything," she told him.

He was startled, but then nodded. "I sure hope so, woman. It'd not shine with this chil' at all to have you go under because I wasn't up to these doins."

Mountain Calf smiled. "I am Nez Perce," she said proudly. "I go where you go. No danger for me. You don't worry. You need to think much about what we do. No time for worrying about me."

"That ain't as easy as you might think, woman," he protested, but he chuckled.

"I know," Mountain Calf said, grinning back at him. "But you pay attention or you'll have both us going under!"

Mostly freed of worry about the woman, Barlow pressed

ahead with more confidence. It was still an awesome undertaking for just the two of them. Every hundred yards or
so, Barlow would have to dismount and by dint of falling
and rolling, flatten the deep, sometimes ice-encrusted snow
enough so the pony and mules could make their way forward. Then they would hit a stretch of path relatively clear
of snow and Barlow would wearily haul himself into his
saddle and push forward till the next time he had to go
through the maneuvers.

It took them five days to get through the pass, and by
then even the powerful Barlow's considerable strength was
greatly sapped. Once on the western side of the pass, Barlow managed to down two deer, and he ate enormous
amounts of the meat at each sitting. He also slept as much
as possible, and two days after arriving, he was able to
continue on.

They endured more snow, some hail, and harsh, biting
winds as they worked their way southwest toward Nez
Perce country. But finally they spotted a village. They were
welcomed, fed and allowed to rest. Barlow suspected that
things went so well because Mountain Calf was with him.
The Indians in the village treated her as a long-lost sister.

Their second night there, staying in a lodge with an elderly couple, Barlow asked Mountain Calf, "You find out
where your village is?"

"Yes," she said, almost bursting from having tried to
hide her excitement. "Five, maybe six marches, by the
Boise River."

Barlow nodded, thinking. "You really want to go there,
don't you?" he finally asked.

"Much, yes." Mountain Calf held her breath, waiting
for his answer.

"Reckon we can trade for horses there as well as here,"
he allowed, trying to hide his smile. "But," he added in
mock sternness, "we got to git movin' come first light and
move fast and hard. The Cap'n and the other boys're countin' on me."

Mountain Calf nodded very happily and kissed him. She

snuggled tight against him, and he decided the extra few days of traveling was worth it.

They made Mountain Calf's village in the afternoon of the fourth day. Their reception there was even warmer and more grand than the one in the other Nez Perce village. Barlow watched with a pleased expression as Mountain Calf greeted her friends and family, her smile fairly beaming across the land. It was almost enough to melt the snow on the surrounding hills.

A feast and dance were held in their honor, and the festivities went on until long into the night. But Barlow was still up early. After eating, he went to meet with Fat Lance and some of the other warriors in the civil chief's lodge. Mountain Calf sat at his side, which perplexed the Nez Perce men.

"My grasp of your tongue is poor," Barlow said in English, which Mountain Calf translated for him. "Mountain Calf will be my translator."

The warriors talked among themselves for a few moments before Fat Lance nodded. "What can my people do for my white friend?" the civil chief asked.

"My friends and I need ponies. Plenty of ponies," Barlow said in Nez Perce. He had told Mountain Calf this morning that he would try his hand at speaking her language, but she was to jump in at any time if what he was saying was coming out wrong.

"We have many ponies. Mules, too. From the Shoshonis." Fat Lance smiled in joy.

"And my friend Fat Lance will be fair in his price for these ponies and mules, yes?" Barlow said, letting the Indian know he was not about to be taken. Rutledge had explained pretty much what he could expect to pay in trade for how many horses and mules.

Fat Lance nodded.

"Then let's go look at your animals."

18

IT TOOK BARLOW and Mountain Calf even longer to get back than it did to get to the Nez Perce villages. Trying to herd more than twenty horses and mules by himself was no easy task. Plus the weather still conspired against them. It snowed regularly, if not too heavily. But at times it was mixed with sleet or hail, making footing treacherous even on the flats.

Barlow also felt pushed by a sense of duty. He and Mountain Calf had stayed in Fat Lance's village for more than three days, and every day since they left Barlow cursed himself for having allowed it. They should have left, he knew, right after making the trade for the horses. Or, at the latest, the next morning, since they had not finished dickering until afternoon. But Barlow had seen how happy Mountain Calf was to be among her friends again, and so he had lingered, dawdling, talking to the Nez Perce men, trying to learn a little more of their ways.

Now, back on the trail and struggling with the weather, the sometimes recalcitrant animals, a somewhat melancholy Mountain Calf, a distinct lack of game, the tiredness that covered him like his skin, his annoyance with himself ate at him. Not even the knowledge that he had done well in his first opportunity to trade with Indians—and an important opportunity—could raise his spirits.

He sat there one night two weeks out of the Nez Perce village, wishing to hell he had a bottle of whiskey with him. He could use one shinin' spree now to try to forget about this abysmal journey. Not even Mountain Calf's loving ministrations were enough to improve his humor.

Barlow almost gave up when they arrived at the base of Lolo Pass. He sat there on his mule, looking up the wicked trail, which disappeared into the mist and clouds, and he began to doubt himself. Well, not doubt that he could make it, but he did question his desire to tackle this spirit-breaking way through the mountains.

If he had been in a better mood, he might have smiled a little when Nottingsworth's words floated through his mind: "This chil' thinks he's gonna git two miles from this camp and then race for the Settlements, leavin' us out here with our thumbs up our asses . . . I just know that son of a bitch is gonna run like a rabbit soon's he gits away from here."

Those words, though, gave him the strength—and desire—to do what needed to be done. He would die before he would let Nottingsworth's statements become fact, no matter how much he wanted to skedaddle. But he had enough sense left to know he needed some rest before undertaking the pass. "We'll stay here tonight, Mountain Calf," he said quietly.

"You're all right?" the woman asked, worried.

Barlow managed a weak smile. "Yeah. Jist plumb wore down is all. To tell you true, woman, I ain't got the strength to face that hellish goddamn trail right now."

Mountain Calf nodded, understanding but still a little frightened. She was not used to seeing her big, strong man seeming so frail and indecisive. She put some extra efforts into her cooking that night, and later, in the robes, she made every effort to show him that he was, indeed, still the brawny, fearless man he had always been. It didn't seem to have much effect, but Mountain Calf tried to keep her concerns to herself.

The following morning, he arose grumpy as a bear, growling and snarling, grousing about the bitter cold and the weakness of the coffee and whatever else came to mind.

Mountain Calf fought hard to hide her smiles of joy. This was her man, the way she knew him. Oh, he might be a growly old bear, but he didn't mean any of it, she knew. She also knew it meant he was feeling full of piss and vinegar; there were no more doubts.

"What the hell're you grinnin' at, goddammit?" Barlow asked at one point. "Walkin' 'round here with that goddamn silly grin on your face. Hell, someone sees you like that they'll think you've gone mad as a hatter."

"You hush and eat," Mountain Calf said, bursting with joy inside. "You need your strength to take us over the mountain."

"You keep up that grinnin', and I just might think to leave you on this side of the goddamn mountain," Barlow growled, but his own grin was beginning to peek through the tawny beard and mustache. He knew Mountain Calf didn't like his hairy face, and he generally tried to keep himself shaved reasonably close, but he was not about to worry about it on this trek.

They finished and packed up and soon headed out. As he drove the herd of animals toward the little trail that cut through the Bitterroot Mountains, he looked up, but there was no fear there today. No doubts. He would conquer this mountain and all it could throw at him. He was absolutely certain of that.

He almost lost several of the animals at various times, but through sheer strength, determination, and willpower, he prevented any of the horses and mules from falling into oblivion. When he could, he made sure Buffalo had a special treat of fresh meat, for the Newfoundland had helped keep the animals in line.

More snow had accumulated while Barlow and Mountain Calf had been west of the pass, even filling the places he had flattened on the way out there, though not to such a great depth as it had been before. Still, it meant more—almost constant—work for him to pack the snow down so that the animals could make it safely through. He cursed himself many times in the nine days it took to recross the pass for not having insisted that one of the other men come with him. By the end of the third day, he was exhausted and only his inherent strength kept him going. That and the hearty meals of meat Mountain Calf managed to come up with for him. He wondered how she had accomplished that, but realized he really didn't care. All that mattered was that she kept taking such good care of him.

Barlow wasn't even sure when they finally actually staggered out of the pass. All he knew was that he was on a flat and by looking behind him, could see the pass rising up. "Goddamn," he breathed. "We done it." Then he fell off his horse, landing in a pile in the snow.

He awoke and looked around, mind foggy. He wondered where he was and how he had gotten there. A fire was burning nearby and meat was cooking, the aroma of it mighty enticing. Buffalo came up, sniffed at him a moment and then gleefully lapped at his face.

"How're you feelin'?" Mountain Calf asked, kneeling alongside him, across from the Newfoundland.

"Ain't sure yet," he said weakly. "But I'm hungrier'n a starvin' wolf, and that meat there sure smells good."

Mountain Calf grinned, rose, and got some meat, which she carried to him on a piece of bark.

Barlow ate ravenously, gulping down the chunks of meat, then asking for more. He polished the second portion off with equal alacrity. He washed it down with two cups of hot coffee. Finally he rested his head back down, half lying against his saddle. "How long we been here?" he asked.

"A night, all day, and another night."

"You did all this by yourself, woman?" he asked, waving a hand around at their little camp. The horses and mules were roped together and tied to trees. They had enough room to graze on what little forage there was. He was lying in a makeshift lodge of tree branches and brush. It wasn't pretty, but it kept him out of the weather.

"Yes," Mountain Calf said. She was bursting with pride,

but she was a little afraid, too, wondering if she had done all right in his eyes.

"Well, I'll be damned," he said quietly. "This shines, woman. Plumb shines. I am mighty proud of you."

Mountain Calf beamed.

"We best be ready to move in the morning, though," he said. The thought was not a pleasant one. He wanted nothing more than to lie right where he was for another week or month. He still felt weak and listless.

"No," Mountain Calf said firmly. "You need rest. We stay more time. Couple days. Then we see how you're feelin'."

"But we got to get back to the others," Barlow protested. "They're expectin' us."

"They'll wait. They're not goin' anywhere."

"You know, woman," Barlow said with a small smile, "you're powerful insufferable when you're right." He allowed her to kiss him, and then he fell asleep.

Barlow allowed Mountain Calf to talk him into staying three days—not that he argued it much. She was right, his fellow trappers would not be going anywhere for a while yet. Whether he got there today or in a week would make no difference. Once he had digested that fact, he relaxed and let himself recover from his ordeal.

The rest of the trip was easy compared to what they had already done. It still snowed regularly, and snow squalls occasionally held them up for a while, but they made good progress.

Barlow had lost track of how long they had been gone from the trappers' camp, but it no longer really mattered to him when he and Mountain Calf rode back into the encampment. Not with the welcome they received.

"Told you fractious bastards I'd be back," he said with a grin as he slid off the mule.

Rutledge, Simon, Watters, even Clarke swarmed around Barlow, clapping him on the back and shaking his hand. Nottingsworth, Francher, and Parker stood back a bit, disgust contorting their features. Barlow could see the three over Simon's shoulder. He sneered at them and lifted a fist toward them, middle finger raised. The three turned away.

With the greetings over, the small group of men began to look over the animals Barlow had brought back. It didn't take long.

"Them're some prime animals, boy," Rutledge said with a nod of satisfaction. "You did well." He paused. "You bring any trade goods back?" he finally asked.

Barlow nodded. "Not much, but what's left is on the mule behind the one I rode." He watched as Rutledge and Simon checked the packs of trade goods he had brought back from the Nez Perce village.

Simon grinned. "I could've dickered them boys down even more, ol' hoss, and brought back a heap more of them trade goods. But, by God, you done right well for your first time sittin' down to trade with those sly devils. And ye done it all on your own, too."

Barlow's smile was huge. For the first time in his life he truly felt as if he had accomplished something, as if he belonged. It was a mighty good feeling, he decided.

Winter started fading a few weeks later, and the men picked up their activity, wanting to make sure everything was ready when Rutledge gave the signal to ride out. They began trapping as soon as they could, too, and were soon pulling in prime furs.

"These plews'll fetch five dollar a pound, maybe six, down to rendezvous," Simon crowed. "Goddamn, these're the shinin'est plews this ol' chil's ary seen."

Barlow wasn't sure whether to believe they would actually get so much money for their furs, but he knew they would bring in top dollar. He wondered what he would do with a possible sack full of hard cash.

Though winter refused to fully relinquish its grip on the mountain lands, Rutledge finally decided it was time to leave. The beaver in the area were nearabout trapped out anyway.

They traveled slowly, burdened as they were by so many animals bearing ninety- or hundred-pound packs of plews. They would stay for a few days wherever one of the men found good beaver sign and trap the place out before moving on in search of another likely site.

The weather gradually and almost steadily got better, though there were setbacks, of course, like the snowstorm that roared down over them one afternoon in late May. They rode it out in reasonable comfort and only lost two mules—and Beelzebub. The old horse had not been ridden since the fight with the Blackfoot, and the men would not even use him for packing anything. The steed had simply clomped along, but his age and the hard life he had lived took their toll, and this last snowstorm was too much for him. Barlow didn't think he would miss the old horse, what with his rigid gait, swayback and stubborn nature, but he did. He had been riding the big black mule that had been among Ed Brown's cavvyyard, and he decided he would continue to use that animal. But from the morning that he found Beelzebub dead, he dubbed the mule Beelzebub in honor of the old horse. The mule didn't seem to mind much.

But with the warmer weather came slimmer pickings on beaver. It wasn't that the number of beaver declined, it was that the rodents had lost their thick winter fur, so their hides were quite poor. The men pushed on a little faster now, and there were no delays for trapping, though an occasional storm still stopped them now and again.

It was with great anticipation that the group slowly neared Ham's Fork, where the rendezvous was to be held. Barlow could feel the excitement building in the other men, and allowed it to infect him, too. He wasn't sure what he would wear to enter the big doin's properly—he had no finery. But that didn't matter to him too much. He just wanted to get there, see how much money he had made for his harsh winter in the mountains, and go on a spree the likes of which he had never had before.

The group stopped a few miles from where they expected the rendezvous camp to be and stayed a day or two. While there, everyone bathed. None of them liked it much, but this was their yearly exercise in cleanliness. And they began to put on their finery—soft buckskin shirts and pants for the men, doeskin dresses for the women. All were beaded and decorated with colored porcupine quills, tin cones, and bits of shell or metal.

Barlow sat and watched as some of the others strutted around in their fancy outfits, and he vowed that by the next rendezvous he would have himself the finest outfit he could find. He felt out of place in the greasy, bloodstained, smoked-blackened buckskins that Mountain Calf had made for him back in the fall. The trousers had been patched in a dozen places, and it sometimes seemed to Barlow that the pants were held together by nothing more than the patches.

As he sat there morosely watching the others, Mountain Calf suddenly came up and knelt in front of him. She was decked out in a creamy buckskin dress and leggings. The dress clanked softly as she walked from the tin cones stitched to the bottom hem. "You are sad?" she asked.

Barlow nodded, but he smiled at her. "A little, yes," he said with a sigh. "All these others have such fine things to wear to the rendezvous, but I ain't got nothin' but this." He plucked at his soiled shirt with a couple of fingers.

Mountain Calf grinned. She shyly held out the parfleche she had carried with her.

"What's this?" Barlow asked, surprised.

"Open. You see."

Inside the leather box was the finest set of soft, tan-colored buckskins he had ever seen. "You made these for me?" he asked, stunned.

Mountain Calf nodded, still shy about it all. She hoped that he liked them.

"Damn if this ain't the shinin'est thing anybody's ever done for me, woman," he said almost in awe. "Damn, you're somethin'." He reached out a big hand, wrapped it around the back of her head and pulled her forward so he could kiss her. "You plumb shine, woman. Damn if you don't," he said heartily, meaning every word of it.

19

WITH BUFFALO—NOW weighing more than a hundred and fifty pounds—at his side, Barlow swaggered into the big tent that served as the trade room for Andrew Branigan and Company. Branigan, John Myles, and Ev Dinsmore were behind the makeshift counter.

Myles was the first to spot Barlow, and it took him several seconds to recognize the young man. His eyes widened and then he grinned. "Well, lookee here, friends," he said. "Is this a ghost or am I seein' the real Will Barlow?"

Grinning, Barlow stepped up, hand out. "It's jist me, Mr. Myles," he said quietly. He shook hands with Myles, then Branigan, and finally a tentative Dinsmore.

"You sure look plumb fanciful in that getup, Will," Branigan said.

"Why, thankee," Barlow said shyly. "My woman—Mountain Calf—made it fer me." He ignored Dinsmore's look of distaste.

"Well, she did a damn fine job, son," Branigan said. "It's good to see you."

"Same here, Mr. Branigan." He paused. "I really did want to see you and some of the others, like you, Mr. Myles, but I had another reason for comin' by."

Myles came around to the front of the counter and knelt to pet Buffalo. "This that little puppy you drug with you all that time ago?" he asked.

"Yep," Barlow grinned. "Growed a little since then, ain't he?"

"Just a tad," Myles agreed. "He sure is some handsome dog."

"I think so."

"So, what'd you want to seen me about, Will?" Branigan asked.

"I was wonderin' if you'd be willin' to buy my plews."

"Well, of course," Branigan said with a big smile. "Unless, of course, you've promised them elsewhere. I won't go against my fellow traders."

"Nah, sir, that ain't the way of it. If you'll recall, when I rode out of here, it was with a group of free trappers. We're all on our own hook as far as what we do with our plews and all."

"That's right. Well, hell, sure, we'll take 'em. Even give you a fair—more than fair—price for 'em, too. Bring 'em on in."

"Well, sir, there's a plumb heap of 'em, and I ain't jist sayin' so," Barlow said with a huge grin.

"That's good to hear, son. You need some help?"

"Nah, they're all baled up good and tight." He headed out and moments later walked in with a hundred pound pack of beaver furs on each shoulder. He made two more trips just the same way and then returned one last time with a small, partial pack. He stood and waited patiently as Branigan and Myles went through the bales without cutting them open. They could tell that the furs were the best.

"You done well for yourself," Branigan noted. He paused, doing some figuring with a pencil on a scrap of paper. "I'll go you five dollar a pound, and I'll count that partial pack as a full one. How's that suit you?"

Barlow wasn't great with numbers, but he could add that up in a hurry, and his eyes almost bugged out. It came to thirty-five hundred dollars. He had trouble even conceiving of that much money all at once. "Done," he said, afraid that if he delayed even another second that Branigan would change his mind or that he would wake up and realize this was just a dream.

"You want that in hard money or in supplies?" Branigan asked. "Maybe some of both?"

Barlow had to fight to bring himself back to the here and now. Supplies, he thought. Yes, I'd need some supplies for the next season. And a tiny kernel of reason within him told him that if he took everything in cash, he'd have nothing left for supplies by the time rendezvous was done. "I'd be obliged if you was to outfit me for next season," he said, his voice sounding strange to him. That he could have this much money at his disposal and decide on his own what to do with it was still staggering to him. "Take it out of what you owe me. I trust you to be fair with your prices on supplies." Branigan had never cheated him, and he did not think the trader would start doing so now.

"Done," Branigan said with a firm nod. "What about the rest?"

"I'll take a heap of it fer my sprees," Barlow said with a grin. Then he grew serious again. "But I'd be obliged if you'd watch over some of it for me. Dole it out to me a bit a time so's I don't piss it all away all at one time."

"Sound thinking, son." He put a metal box on the counter and unlocked it. He took out some gold coins and spread them out in a line on the counter. "Three hundred dollars do you to start?" he asked.

Barlow grinned widely. "I reckon five hundred might be better," he said with a small laugh.

Branigan smiled and put some more coins out for him. Then he reached under the counter and came up with two bottles of whiskey, which he slapped on the counter next to the money. "These ought to get you started on your spree, son," he said, grinning.

"Reckon they'll do jist that," Barlow agreed. He scooped the coins up and deposited them in a little possible sack hanging from his belt, then grabbed the whiskey bottles in one hand. "I really do value all you've done for me, Mr. Branigan," he said seriously.

"My pleasure, son," Branigan said, his face blank.

Barlow and Buffalo strolled out into the hot sunshine. Barlow went and got some meat and then found himself a quiet spot under the shade of a willow, near the creek, and sat, his back against the tree. Buffalo spun around three or four times before flopping down alongside him.

Barlow nibbled on meat and sipped whiskey. He wanted to be alone for a spell, but he didn't necessarily want to get drunk. At least not yet. He just wanted to sit and contemplate the events of the past couple of years. He had come a long way since he had volunteered to join the militia during the war against Black Hawk. And as he thought on it all, he decided he could be proud of himself. He had, he thought, comported himself well through it all. He had learned to control his temper to a great extent, had done all that had been asked of him and more, had proved himself tough enough to go up against the Blackfeet, and had made himself more money in one winter of trapping than his father had seen in his entire lifetime.

He napped a bit, and when he awoke, he decided it was about time he joined in the festivities. But first, he needed to be with Mountain Calf for a little while. He smiled at that. She was pretty special, he thought. With rapidly growing enthusiasm, he mounted his mule and rode to camp.

Barlow ducked inside his lodge, glad to be out of the sunshine and heat. It was as neat as always. Mountain Calf prided herself on keeping their home clean and orderly. She was sitting against a willow backrest, repairing a pair of her leggings. Barlow knelt beside her and ran a thick index finger down her soft cheek. She smiled at him.

"I reckon there's time for that mendin' later," he said gruffly, the lust heavy in his voice.

"You got somethin' better in mind?"

"I reckon I do," he said, trying to be light about it, but his desire could not be hidden.

"Maybe I'm too busy for that," she teased, unable to conceal her smile.

"I reckon that's a damn lie," Barlow said with a short laugh.

Mountain Calf could see the powerful need for her in Barlow's eyes, and she knew she would be wrong to tease him further. She smiled again and put her work down, then threw a small hand around the back of his head and pulled his face forward so she could kiss him, which she did with plenty of zeal.

His lips still locked on hers, Barlow scooped Mountain Calf up into his arms and rose, carrying her as if she weighed no more than a child. He placed her on the bed of soft buffalo robes and then stood to undress.

She watched him with great intensity, while at the same time slithering and wriggling out of her dress. She was ready for him, and she noted with pleasure that he, obviously, was just as ready for her. She held out her arms.

Barlow moved between her legs, and Mountain Calf wrapped her arms around his back and kissed him. Then she grabbed his erectness in a hand and placed the tip of it at the entrance to her pleasure box. "Now," she whispered into his mouth.

Barlow thrust forward and was instantly buried all the way inside her. He slid himself back until only the tip of him remained in her and then pounded back into her again. She moaned. He did it again and again, each time slamming into her womanhood with all the power he could muster. She soon was groaning steadily.

"Faster," she suddenly whispered. "Faster, more, harder, stronger."

Barlow obeyed her, hammering into her with a relentless intensity. A vein throbbed in his forehead as he fought to hold back his climax. Then Mountain Calf screeched and bucked, thrashing wildly under him. He let himself go then, and with a few more swift, powerful pokes, his juices boiled from his insides and splashed out of his pulsing manhood.

They rested in each other's arms for some time, before Barlow managed to rouse himself.

"You go?" Mountain Calf asked quietly.

Barlow nodded, not noticing that she tried to hide her disappointment. "I been waitin' a whole year for these doin's,'' he said happily as he pulled on his shirt. ''I aim to have me a spree the likes of which I ain't ever had.'' He laughed at his foolish statement.

Mountain Calf said nothing. She had known this would probably happen, but she had hoped he would be different from the others. In so many ways, he was, which had given her faith. But now she saw that he was no better than the rest. She sighed and rose, picking up her dress as she did.

Barlow kissed her quickly and then headed out, Buffalo following him. He was suddenly bursting with excitement and anticipation, thoughts on the activities in which he could take part, thoughts of Mountain Calf far from his mind already.

He rode off, still with a bottle and a half of whiskey tucked in a possible bag dangling from his saddle. He had his rifle across the saddle in front of him. He intended to use it soon. He had always been a fine shot, and had improved some since being in the mountains. It was not difficult to find a group of men shooting at playing cards stuck on a log. He pulled up and slid off the mule.

An hour later, he was half a bottle of whiskey lighter, but a couple hundred dollars, plus another rifle and two pistols heavier. He was rather proud of himself.

As the afternoon wore on, he played some euchre, losing a little; drank some whiskey; tried his hand at tomahawk throwing, losing a little more; drank some whiskey; played several rounds of the hand game with a small group of Indians and trappers; drank some whiskey; ate a little buffalo and antelope meat gotten from friendly fires; drank some whiskey; fought and beat the hell out of a fellow trapper who had knocked the whiskey bottle out of his hand; drank some whiskey from a quickly replenished supply; watched in drunken amazement as some trappers doused another with firewater and then set him afire; drank some whiskey; and . . .

He couldn't remember much after that. All he knew was that he woke up in a patch of dried grass with the sunlight pounding down on his face. He had a hangover that was so painful it would've stopped a buffalo bull. He crawled to the creek a few dozen yards away and dunked his head under the water. He might have drowned, if Buffalo, sensing that something was terribly wrong, hadn't grabbed his shirt and tugged him out of the creek.

Barlow lay there for a long time, slipping in and out of consciousness, occasionally vomiting, and frequently groaning with the agony that throbbed in his head and roiled his stomach. He thought he pissed on himself a couple of times, but he wasn't sure. He considered putting a lead ball in his head, but he wasn't all that sure he would have the strength to pull the trigger—or if he could hit himself, even with the muzzle resting against his temple.

Not until the sun had gone down did he feel any desire to even try to get up. He managed, but not without significant effort and numerous attempts. He was weaker than he had been when he had finished his trek back across Lolo Pass.

Hobbling like an old man, he found his mule after considerable searching. With a major effort, he pulled himself into the saddle and promptly leaned over and vomited again, though there was nothing left in his stomach. "C'mon, Beelzebub," he croaked, "take me home. Buffler, you show him the way, boy."

It was all he could do to hold on to the saddle horn and keep himself in the saddle on the half-mile journey. So out of touch with things was he that it took him some moments to realize the mule had stopped in front of his lodge. He slid out of the saddle and had to hold on for a few seconds because his legs would not hold him up. At last he made it inside the tipi. He stopped short when he heard some caterwauling beast raging within. His heart pounded as he wondered what it was threatening him.

Slowly his brain began to find some sort of focus, and he realized that yowling creature was actually Mountain Calf screaming at him in English and Nez Perce. He couldn't really make out any words, he just knew that she was belittling him as a worthless pile of excrement.

"Hush that wailin', woman," he said, his head roaring as if Yellowstone Falls was inside his skull.

His complaint served only to further fuel her rage and disappointment, and she increased the volume and magnitude of her verbal barrage.

Not even conscious of what he was doing, he grabbed her arm and brought his other hand up. He could see in her eyes that she knew she was going to be struck. A mixture of fear and anger washed over her face. Disgusted with himself, he let his hands drop to his sides and turned his back on her.

He staggered to the bed of robes and fell on it. He was asleep and snoring by the time Mountain Calf could stop shaking.

20

BARLOW AWOKE GROGGY but feeling considerably more alive than he had the day before. He lay there for a while, almost afraid to try to stand, but also just listening to the sounds of the day, trying to determine what time it was. He finally decided it was not long after dawn. He lifted his head and looked around the lodge. It seemed strangely empty, but he wasn't sure what made him think so.

He was hungry and wished that Mountain Calf was around to feed him. He wondered where she was, but figured she was just outside working. He finally took a deep breath in preparation of getting up. He made it to his feet with surprising ease. Once erect, he got a better look around the tipi. It was fairly empty, and the fire had burned out overnight. That surprised him. Mountain Calf was always conscious about keeping the fire going and having food and coffee on virtually all the time. He began to worry that something had happened to her.

Even worse, cold embers and pieces of partially burned firewood were scattered around. The rest of the lodge was a mess, too, despite its emptiness. The meat rack he had built recently was scattered about the lodge, though none of the meat was there. Buffalo had a satisfied look on his face, and Barlow wondered if the dog had knocked the rack over and devoured the meat.

Ignoring the growling of his stomach, he stepped outside. The sunshine was so bright it almost seared his bloodshot eyes. He closed his lids and stood there, hoping he had not permanently damaged his eyes. Moments later, he eased them open again, goaded by the strange sounds he heard. He was able to keep his eyes open this time, and he soon discovered what the sounds were—laughter. Most of his friends were sitting around laughing and hooting—at him. He looked down at himself and figured they were so full of humor because he was a frightful mess—his shirt and pants were stained by vomit, ashes, and spilled whiskey, as well as covered with dirt and some blood. In addition, both garments sported several holes. He looked like hell, but he didn't think his appearance warranted such amusement from his friends.

As he looked from one to the other, wondering what was going on, he spotted the pile of things outside his lodge just to his left. His things. His heart plunged into his sour, empty stomach. And with the heartache of realization that Mountain Calf was divorcing him, came anger, a slow, steady, consuming rage. *How dare she do this to him?*

He stood there fuming, trying to decide what to do, when the grumbling in his stomach let him know that his hunger had to be dealt with first. Once that was taken care of, he would be able to think more clearly, he hoped, and then he could plot out his next moves.

Barlow stomped angrily to where Watters was sitting by a small fire outside his lodge. "Gimme some food, goddammit," he growled, reaching for a tin mug and filling it with coffee.

"Get your own goddamn food," Watters said, still chuckling over his friend's predicament. "I ain't your servin' boy."

"Don't rile me today, boy," Barlow said angrily.

"Go to hell," Watters said gleefully. When he caught Barlow's wild look, he tried to lessen the amount of amusement he showed. "Jist eat, boy."

Barlow dug into the stew and roasted meat, wolfing down chunks of it, and gulping coffee in between mouthfuls. He cared not a whit about the coffee he splashed all over himself, or the grease or stew that dripped onto his clothes. All he cared about was filling his belly as fast as he could. It took some time, considering how empty he was, but he finally leaned back. He released a gigantic burp and finished off the coffee in the tin mug.

"So what now, ol' hoss?" Watters asked. Any enjoyment he had gotten at Barlow's predicament was gone. He had surreptitiously watched Barlow while he was eating. It was obvious that Barlow was deeply affected by what had occurred.

"Ain't sure," Barlow said, mulling over the problem. "I reckon I got to find Mountain Calf and talk to her. I cain't believe she'd throw me over jist like that 'cause I got drunker'n a lord the other night."

"You don't figure there's more to it than that?" Watters asked, a bit surprised.

Barlow shrugged. "Not that I can think of."

"Well, ol' hoss, best contemplate on it some. She wasn't quiet when she was pitchin' your things out of the lodge. Nor yesterday neither when you came stragglin' back from your little spree. Me and the rest of the boys—well, 'cept fer Bob, who was hurtin' as much as you was—kind of stood 'round listenin' in to them doins to see what the ruckus was about."

"And?" Barlow asked, his voice melding nervousness and annoyance.

"Seems you was ready to raise hair on that woman of yourn, boy," Watters said flatly.

"I did what?" Barlow asked, eyes wide.

"You heared me." Watters paused. He had lodgepoled a woman before, and while he didn't like it, she had, he thought at the time, deserved it. But he would never have thought that Barlow would do such a thing to Mountain Calf. Not the way he cared for her. And, though he apparently had not succeeded—there had been no marks on Mountain Calf that morning—it was still a surprise.

"But why . . . ? I mean, why would I . . . ?" Barlow was flabbergasted. And he was angry. He was certain his friend was making up this story. He had never even considered doing such a thing to a woman, let along one he cared about.

"Hell if I know, Will," Watters said quietly. "You was some hungover, maybe still roarin' drunk and didn't know what you was doin'."

"You ain't lyin' to me now, are you . . . ?" Barlow demanded. When Watters shook his head, Barlow sat in thought. Sweat beaded on his forehead as he concentrated, trying to dredge up from his alcohol-besotted mind what had happened last night. He was horrified at the vague images that flickered through his mind. Pictures of her taut, angry face, harsh words streaming out of her mouth, of his mindless rage, then the merciful blankness.

"Sweet God A'mighty," Barlow breathed. Once more he thought of putting a bullet in his brain, but that went against his nature. But he had to find her, had to apologize, had to make things right. "Where'd she go?" he asked.

"Best anyone could tell, she went stompin' off toward where the Nez Perce have their camps."

Barlow nodded once. Then he shoved up and trotted to his mule, Beelzebub, which was still saddled. The animal looked a little askance at him, as if worried, but caused no problems when Barlow climbed aboard. Barlow galloped out of the camp, heading to where the Nez Perce had set their camps a couple of miles away. Buffalo ran along, a little bit behind. Barlow charged into one camp, then another. Finally he found Fat Lance's camp, and he pulled to a halt and dismounted. He feared that the Indians would be angry at him, but none seemed upset at seeing him, which was a relief. It was one less thing he would have to worry about.

He stalked the camp, occasionally asking people if they had seen Mountain Calf. He figured she was trying to avoid him, but he would not give up. It took several hours, but he finally tracked her down, sitting by the creek.

She was surprised and not very pleased to see him. But

she said nothing when he sat next to her. She refused to look fully at him.

He recoiled at the hatred, anger, and disappointment that marred her beautiful face. "Mayhap you ain't gonna believe me, Mountain Calf," he said quietly. "But I never would have really hit you. I didn't hardly know where I was or who you was. Hell, I was damn near unconscious. I wouldn't really hurt you none. I jist wasn't thinkin'. And I swear I ain't ever gonna do so again. I got to have you back, woman."

Mountain Calf finally craned her neck and looked at him. Her face still showed fear and disgust, though he thought he saw some sadness in her deep, dark brown eyes. "It's not only you try to hit me," she said. "It's many things. Too much whiskey. You go off and leave me too often."

"Go off and leave you?" he asked, surprised. "Hell, I was only gone away one night. Damn, it weren't that bad."

"No," Mountain Calf said firmly. "We no good any more."

Barlow couldn't believe what he was hearing. "You want to come back to your people and not be with me no more jist 'cause I went and got into my cups one night?" he demanded.

Mountain Calf nodded, looking back toward the water again. "You no care no more," she said firmly. "And I no trust you."

"So, that *is* what's got you so riled," he said, almost with a sense of relief. If that was the true problem, he hoped he might be able to convince her to give him another chance.

"Much, yes," she agreed.

"Mountain Calf," Barlow said earnestly, meaning every word of it, "I swear I won't *ever* try to hit you again."

"Can't trust you," she countered. "It's over. We won't share a lodge no more."

Barlow was about to yell at her, try to scream some sense into her, but he could tell by something in her eyes that there was more to this than his just having made some vainglorious, liquor-induced attempt to strike her, though that was certainly an important point. But he sensed that there was some deep-seated loneliness or something in her. As he looked back at it now, he could see the beginnings of it when they had left Fat Lance's village with the horses and mules back during the winter. She wanted—maybe needed—to be back with her people. His attempted assault on her, which most Indian women simply would have accepted, was just the excuse she was using to return home with some dignity. He sighed.

"All right, Mountain Calf," he said, feeling a dull, tenacious ache begin in his chest. He sat silently for a few minutes. "Look, all those things in the lodge are yours. You should have 'em. C'mon back to the camp. You can stay in the lodge. I won't bother you none. I'll take all my plunder and stay elsewhere."

Mountain Calf considered that. She wanted that, in some ways, but in others, she was afraid to go back there and be that close to him again—without actually being with him.

Barlow forced himself to smile, nodding to the Newfoundland on her other side. "Buffler misses you already," he said.

Mountain Calf petted the dog. "I come back. Tomorrow. You stay away."

Barlow nodded. The hurt in his heart was deep and, he thought, would be long lasting. He rose. "C'mon, Buffler," he said. He walked off, found his mule, climbed on, and rode off.

Barlow stayed in the lodge that night, ignoring his friends, and letting the pain in his heart have full rein. It was not a comfortable or relaxing night, and he was up well before dawn. He stoked the fire, putting old coffee on to heat. There was no meat, so he would have to go hunting sometime that day. And probably soon, if he wanted to eat. Unless he could steal some meat from one of his friends to tide him over.

After two cups of coffee, he strolled outside, still sad, but eager to see Mountain Calf again, even if he did know she would have nothing to do with him again. There was,

he had to admit, however, a grain of hope alive in his heart.
He noted that Francher was gone. He strolled nonchalantly
over to the fire outside the man's lodge, and helped himself
to a big bowl of stew from the iron pot that dangled from
a chain, over the embers help up by a tripod of logs. Finished, he refilled the bowl and downed that, too.

Filled, he wandered back toward his own lodge and
sorted through his things. He needed very little of it right
away, so he packed it up as best he could and found a spot
to store it. He covered the stack with canvas to protect it
if the weather should take a turn for the worse.

Just as he was finishing, he spotted Mountain Calf riding
into the camp. His heart felt torn. He was very pleased to
see her, but the sorrow was still raw, powerful. She smiled
just a bit as she dismounted. Then she disappeared into the
lodge.

Barlow wanted to follow her, but he knew that would
only make things worse. With a sigh, he saddled the mule
and rode out. He took part in quite a few of the events that
roared on around him, but he passed up the alcohol.
Thoughts of the other night's doin's were still too fresh in
his mind. He grew bored after a while and rode out a few
miles, where he shot an antelope. He skinned and butchered
it there and then headed back to his camp. He figured he
would offer Mountain Calf some of it and keep some for
himself.

As he neared the lodge that had been his until yesterday,
a scream erupted from inside the tipi. Barlow dropped the
antelope skin containing the fresh meat, jumped off the
mule, and ran into the lodge.

Two figures struggled in the dimness to one side, where
the buffalo robe bed was. It took a moment for Barlow's
eyes to adjust, and he realized that Bill Nottingsworth had
Mountain Calf pinned down and her dress shoved up over
her hips. He was trying to undo the buttons on his pants
while still controlling her, and he was having a devil of a
time at it. Mountain Calf was fighting like a wildcat.

Enraged, Barlow charged forward like a wounded grizzly
and grabbed the back of Nottingsworth's shirt and jerked

him away from Mountain Calf, spun, and flung him across the tipi. Nottingsworth rolled across the fire, sending a small spray of sparks into the air.

"What the hell're you doin', boy?" Nottingsworth asked with a sneer.

"Gettin' ready to make wolf bait out of you, goddammit," Barlow responded, his anger in full bloom.

"Shit, boy, this ain't none of your concern," Nottingsworth said. He was on his feet and brushing ashes and embers off his clothes. "She cut her ties with you, boy, right in front of God and everybody else."

"That she did," Barlow acknowledged, with a fresh stab of pain in his heart. "But that don't mean's she's fair pickins for the likes of you."

"She ain't yours no more, boy. Don't matter none whether you like it or not. She's on her own string, and I aim to have her. Now go on about your business and leave me and her to ours."

"It should be apparent even to a goddamn fool like you that she ain't got no interest in you."

"Don't matter none what she wants or don't want, boy. She's jist an Injin woman, and they ain't good but for cookin' and fornicatin', and I can do without their cookin'."

"Get the hell out of here," Barlow said, his fury running over. "Or I'll raise hair on you right here and now."

"It's about time we settled our differences, Barlow," Nottingsworth said harshly.

Barlow bolted forward and slammed into Nottingsworth. They struggled in each other's grip, until Barlow flung his foe to the ground. Before Nottingsworth could rise, Barlow kicked him in the ribs, picking him up a little and rolling him. He repeated it twice more before Nottingsworth got hung up in the edge of the lodge by the entry. Barlow grabbed him by the neck and seat of his pants and tossed him outside. Then he stalked out after him.

The other men of Rutledge's small free trapping brigade had heard the commotion and were gathered outside watching. Some had been smiling, thinking it was another episode of Mountain Calf giving Barlow hell again. But when they saw Nottingsworth come flying out, followed by an enraged Barlow, they knew this was far more than a marital spat.

Barlow kicked Nottingsworth in the face, not giving him a chance to get up. Nottingsworth lay there on his back, and Barlow knelt hard on his chest. Ribs cracked, and Nottingsworth wheezed.

''I should've done this a long time ago, boy,'' Barlow said, voice hissing with rage. He clamped his hands onto Nottingsworth's throat and squeezed.

21

THE RENDEZVOUS HAD lost all of its enchantment for Barlow. With Mountain Calf having left him and having killed Bill Nottingsworth, Barlow could find no enjoyment in the festivities. Though no one—including his own group of trappers—thought less of him, Barlow was bothered by killing Nottingsworth. He had never killed before; not in such a way. Sure, he had killed warriors in battle, but he had never before taken a life with such rage-induced deliberateness. Not that he felt wrong in what he had done—Nottingsworth had deserved his fate—but he had to wonder if perhaps he was losing whatever traces of civilization he had had within him. He had heard of that happening to men out there, that they could become as savage as the Indians and animals.

Immediately after killing Nottingsworth, he had stood and looked around. The fury that still flooded through him as if it had replaced his blood prevented him from seeing the sympathy with which his friends looked at him—or the relief and renewed love in Mountain Calf's eyes. Had he been able to, he would have had her back that moment, and for all time. But the choler in him allowed him to see her only as disgusted with him for his lack of control over himself.

He had spun, climbed on the mule, and rode out of the little camp. He grabbed a bottle of whiskey from the first trader he saw and spent the rest of the evening sipping from it, though not too hard. He wanted to forget what he thought he was becoming, not get roaring drunk again and worsen the situation. He avoided everyone with a fierce determination. Curled up with the big Newfoundland, he slept that night far removed in mind, spirit, and body from the joyous celebrations going on all around him.

He spent most of the next day in much the same way—wandering, thinking, wondering. When he determined what he would do, he felt neither joy nor relief. It was just what he would do, nothing more, nothing less. He went straight to Andrew Branigan's trade tent.

Branigan stopped before opening his mouth in welcome when he saw the acrimony on Barlow's face, and waited.

"You think you can have my supplies ready come first light, Mr. Branigan?" Barlow asked without greeting or preliminary.

"Reckon so," Branigan responded, surprised. "You pullin' out?"

Barlow nodded. "I'll bring my pack animals by directly. That way you can get an early start."

"Suits," Branigan said with a nod. He wanted to ask what was vexing Barlow, but he knew that would not be wise right then. Not with Barlow as angry as he was. He hoped, though, that Barlow would loosen up on his own and spill it.

But Barlow simply turned and walked out. He rode back to his camp, and beyond, to where their horses and mules were kept. He culled out his animals and then herded them—save for two—over to Branigan's, where he left them in the care of a young man who held the job Barlow himself had left only a year ago. It seemed a lifetime ago. He returned and loaded his personal supplies on the last two animals and rode out.

Soon after, Barlow found a spot upstream where he could

have solitude. He built a small fire and cooked some meat and coffee. He ate, wiped his greasy hands on his thoroughly befouled dress buckskins, and had a pipe while he sipped another mug of coffee. Then he lay down, pulled his hat over his eyes, and went to sleep.

With heavy heart, he rode back to camp. He had considered riding out of the rendezvous without bidding his companions farewell, but then he decided that would not be right. He concluded that if he really were losing all of civilization's refinements, then he should fight to retain what little propriety he had left by doing the proper thing and letting the others know his plans.

He dismounted in front of Rutledge's lodge. Rutledge must have known he was there for he walked out just about the time Barlow's second foot hit the ground. The other men began grouping behind Barlow.

"I thought it only right that I tell you I'm pullin' out, Cap'n," Barlow said without hesitation.

"On your own?" Rutledge was not surprised.

"Yep."

"It's dangerous out there, boy, as you well know." He did not want to lose Barlow, but he knew that pleading would do no good whatsoever, so he hoped that appealing to reason might work.

"I know that, Cap'n. It don't concern me overly much. I can take care of myself."

"Against the Blackfoot and the Crow and God only knows who else?"

"Look, Cap'n, you know well's I do that any of us could go under at any time out here. Whether it's at the hands of fractious Injins or Mother Nature or any of a heap of other things. It's jist the way of things. I can't go frettin' over such doins."

Rutledge nodded. He knew now that it was hopeless to talk Barlow out of his plans. "You'll be missed, boy," he said quietly.

"I'm obliged to be well thought of, Cap'n." He stepped forward and shook Ruthledge's hand. "And I'm mighty grateful for all you done for me."

"Weren't much, boy," Ruthledge said. "Now you remember, you ever git to be longin' for some company, me and the rest of the boys'd be plumb happy to welcome you back amongst us."

"I'll keep that to mind, Cap'n." Barlow swung into the saddle. He nodded to the other men, most of whom nodded back or waved. Then Barlow was trotting toward Branigan's tent, and his pack animals. Buffalo jogged alongside.

Barlow learned very swiftly that he had taken on a much bigger task than he had supposed. He had wanted solitude and figured the only way to find it was to go his own way. But he had not thought through all the work that was involved. Not that he minded hard work, but some of it was almost beyond doing by one man. Just keeping all the pack animals under control was an awesome undertaking. Unloading and loading the horses and mules each morning and evening gobbled up tons of his time. He had to watch over the horses, gather his own firewood, build his own fires, do his own cooking. He had to maintain his own gear, hunt, skin, and butcher, and soon he would have to trap.

Eventually he grew used to his new life. The work kept him too busy to wonder too much about the loss of Mountain Calf. After several weeks, he had pretty well worked out ways to manage everything with a minimum of fuss. And only once after that did his solitary existence cause a problem.

Buffalo's low growl woke him one night. He lay there, hand on his rifle, waiting to hear or see something that would let him know what had alarmed the Newfoundland. It was just before dawn and pitch black. It was cold, too, and he was reluctant to leave the warmth of his buffalo hide sleeping robe. But he knew he had to. If there were someone out there who meant to do him harm, being in his bedroll would not be wise.

With a hushed sigh, he slid out of the warm robe, an unbidden shiver racking him as the bitter November air nipped at any exposed bit of flesh. As he edged back across the cold ground with its light covering of snow, Barlow pulled his rifle and his blanket coat with him. He squatted behind a tree trunk, leaned his rifle against it and tugged the coat on, pulling it tight around him. He blew on his hands, trying to warm them.

Within minutes, he began to wonder if anything were out there, or if Buffalo had simply growled at a rabbit in his sleep. He glanced at the ebony-furred dog, virtually invisible in the early morning darkness. The Newfoundland seemed alert and sniffed the air. Barlow decided there really was someone—or something—out there. He contemplated that for a few moments and then deduced that it had to be at least one person, judging by the way Buffalo was acting. And if that were true, they would be Indians. Continuing with that reasoning, if his assessment was correct, then those warriors would almost certainly try to steal his cavvyard.

Barlow made his way carefully toward his horse and mule herd, trying not to bump into trees or trip over brush. He half duck-walked, half crawled on hands and knees, moving blindly in the deep darkness. Several times a hand or knee landed on a stone or sharp stick, but he bit his lip to keep from cursing at the sharp pain.

He stopped and settled in behind another tree trunk, this one within a few feet of the little glade where his animals were quartered. The horses and the mules were making no unseemly noises, so Barlow figured that the Indians had not yet moved in close enough to make the animals nervous. He expected they were waiting for daybreak, which was not far off now.

He closed his eyes and leaned his head back against the tree. Buffalo would warn him if anything happened. He didn't quite fully fall asleep, and he woke at another quiet snarl from the dog. "Good boy, Buffler," he whispered. He came up on one knee, alert despite the cold.

A moment later he spotted a flicker of something to his right. Then it came again, and he got a slightly longer look. He couldn't be sure what tribe the Indian belonged to; he just knew it was an Indian, and any warrior sneaking through the woods right next to his animals could only be up to no good.

Barlow estimated how fast the Indian was moving and sighted at a spot next to a warped, twisted pine tree. His patience was rewarded when the warrior stepped between one pine and the deformed one. Barlow fired, and the warrior went down.

The all hell broke loose. Two Indians charged out of the trees, slashing ropes that hobbled the horses and mules, shouting in an attempt to get the animals moving.

"Shit," Barlow mumbled. He tossed his rifle aside and raced out through the milling knot of horses and mules, trying to make his way to one of the warriors. Buffalo, too, waded fearlessly into the swarm of hooves and tons of flesh.

Using his powerful shoulder, Barlow shoved a big mule out of the way as he neared the Indian. But he was closer than he had realized, and in the next instant, he felt the cold slice of a knife blade tearing into the side of his abdomen, right under the lowest rib. Almost instinctively, he lashed out, smashing the young warrior—a Crow, he noted—in the face.

He reached into his coat to grab his pistol from his belt. He pulled it out and cocked it with the heel of his left palm and began turning toward his left. The other warrior was almost on him in the dim grayness of the morning. He fired.

The ball thudded into the warrior's chest and dropped him right there. A couple of mules, made nervous by the gunfire, powder smoke, and all the commotion, shuffled nervously, trampling whatever life may have remained in the Crow.

Before he could turn back to the warrior he had punched, the Crow slammed into him, dumping him on the cold ground. The warrior leaped up, pulling out a war club. He raised the weapon, but never got a chance to use it, as suddenly almost two hundred pounds of snarling Newfoundland pounced on his chest, flattening him. Before the Crow could use the war club on the dog, Buffalo had clamped his jaws down on the warrior's throat and shook its great head several times. Still growling, it finally backed away.

"Damn, if you ain't something, Buffler," Barlow said, patting the dog's head, ignoring the blood on the animal's muzzle. He looked down at his side. The knife wound was bleeding heavily. It would need looking after, but that could wait. He had to make sure there were no more Crows around.

Barlow retrieved his pistol, which he had dropped when the one Crow tackled him, and reloaded it before sticking it in his belt. Then he got his rifle and reloaded that, too. He started a circuit of his camp, on foot. He wasn't too concerned. Buffalo seemed to be relatively at peace, so he suspected these three were the only ones there had been. That conclusion was bolstered when he found three Crow ponies.

Satisfied that there were no others, Barlow moved among his horses and mules, redoing rope hobbles, quietly talking to the animals to calm them. Finally he headed back to his fire and stoked it up.

He sipped some coffee and finally, reluctantly, pulled up his shirt enough to expose the wound. It did not look too bad, he decided, though it was bleeding freely. If it didn't get infected, it would be all right. All he had to do was decide whether to sew it shut or cauterize it. However, the thought of searing his skin like a fresh buffalo tongue was not appealing at all. So he got out his small sewing kit, chose a respectable-sized needle and some sinew. After a few swigs of whiskey from a bottle that was already half empty, he began.

It wasn't nearly as bad as he thought it was going to be, though he suspected the several sips of whiskey between every stitch might have accounted for some of that. But finally he was finished. He cleaned his things up a little and smoked a pipe while he finished the last of the whiskey. Feeling the cold creep into him, he wrapped himself in his buffalo robe and slept.

• • •

The wound gave him little trouble. He took two days at
that camp, which he would have done anyway to trap, before moving on. A month later, he found a place to winter
up and he put up a crude shelter for him and Buffalo, and
an even sparser one for the horses and mules.

The winter wore on him more heavily than on the land.
With the snow piled up in ten- or twelve-foot drifts, the
wind screaming around his primitive shack, his loneliness
was nearly unbearable. Many was the time he thought he
would go mad. Only the constant companionship of the
ever-growing Buffalo allowed him to retain his sanity.

Eager, almost frantic, to be away from there, and the
winter, Barlow began preparing as early as he could to
leave. Before it was safe or wise, he pulled out, needing to
be on the trail and away from the horrors his mind had
wanted to conjure up in the lean-to. Two days later he almost died in a snowstorm that seemed to come out of nowhere, pinning him in a small valley with no shelter other
than the trees. He survived it, but decided he would stay
there a while, waiting for a few better signs of spring to
arrive.

Once they did, he headed off again, quickly falling into
the routine of his solitary trail life. He trapped as he went,
pleased with the furs he brought in.

He knew he would have to decide where to go—rendezvous, back to the Settlements, or perhaps over the mountains to the west and try to sell his furs to the Hudson's
Bay Company. The latter appealed to him, as it would take
him through Nez Perce country, and there was a chance he
would see Mountain Calf. But for that reason, he was dis-
inclined to go. Seeing her again, especially if she still
wanted nothing to do with him, would be too difficult.

He finally turned his nose toward the Green River—and
rendezvous.

22

UNDER A BLAZING, fat sun, Barlow rode into rendezvous slowly and quietly, not drawing much attention until he had traversed more than a mile of white and Indian camps strung along Horse Creek. Even then, he was accorded little more than a bemused glance from the men who quickly turned back to whatever activity they were involved in. He was dressed in his plain everyday buckskins, which were well-worn, multi-patched, and black with grease, blood, and smoke. He had no fancy outfit to wear this year, nor did he care much. The last time he had sported such a fancy set of clothes, his world had gone haywire.

He gained a bit more attention when he got to trader's row. The traders watched from their tents, eyeing the four mules Barlow had loaded with packs of beaver plews, figuring in their minds what they could get away with giving for Barlow's furs and how much they could charge him for supplies. Barlow had only trader in mind—if he was around this year.

Six horses suddenly came thundering out of nowhere, being quirted by their riders, and galloped full out past him in a swirl of color, noise, and excitement. Buffalo had the sense to get out of the way and barked wildly at the interlopers. The racing horses spooked Barlow's animals and it took him a minute or two to get them back under control. "You goddamn stupid sons of . . ." He stopped himself and grinned. Hell, that was what those men—and he himself— were here for: excitement, adventure, and the release of a year's worth of frustration, anger, fear, hunger, and whatever else was pent up inside a man after a long winter.

Minutes later, he found Branigan's trading tent. The sides were rolled up, and Barlow could see Myles and Branigan inside, dickering with a man Barlow did not know. Branigan spotted him, smiled, and waved. Barlow nodded and stopped. Tying his horse to a post that had been haphazardly pounded into the ground, Barlow walked inside.

"Looks like you did right well for yourself, what with bein' alone and all," Branigan said after the three men had made their greetings. "Or did you hook on with another bunch after a spell?"

"Nope. Was on my own the whole time." Barlow grinned a little. "Damn fool thing it was for me to do, too. But, yep, I did well." He paused and then asked, "You still payin' a fair price for plews and askin' a fair amount for supplies?" he questioned. He winked to let Branigan know he was not worried about the answer.

"I think you'll find out things're even better," Branigan noted. "If your plews are as good as the ones you brung in over to Ham's Fork last year, I'll go you five dollars and thirty cents per pound."

Barlow's eyes widened in surprise, then narrowed in suspicion. "And suppose I was to take 'em to LeBarge over yonder?" he asked, a smile touching his lips.

"You might get half what I'm offerin'!" Branigan said, bursting into laughter. "Actually the best I can do is five dollars and forty cents a pound. And that's just for you. You'll get a better price with the American Fur Company, though. The bastards are payin' top dollar for plews—six dollars, sometimes more."

Barlow was shocked, and it showed.

"It's true. The bastards. They can stand heavy losses till every goddamn beaver stream in the Rocky Mountains dries up, if need be. They're aimin' to run everybody else out of the business—and the mountains. But I'll be damned if I'm gonna just let them skunk humpers think they can do so without a fight. I'll pay as much as I can afford and still make a few cents for myself.''

Barlow nodded. "Your price of supplies gone up?'' he asked.

"Some,'' Branigan acknowledged. "Not as much as most others. And The Company's undercuttin' us on them goods, too. A couple of the suppliers are gonna lose their shirts because of it.''

"You'll be all right?''

"I might, Will. My profit'll be next to nothin', but I'll have enough to pay off all the boys, still see a slight profit. Might have to delve deep into my savin's for next season, though.''

"You got enough supplies left to outfit me?''

"Hell, yes,'' Branigan said sourly. "I should amend my last statement there. I'll probably make out all right if I can sell all my supplies. Right now, that ain't goin' so well.''

Barlow nodded. "Well, here's my plews, and you can outfit me, Mr. Branigan. I'll be damned if I'd go to the American Fur Company and take their money, no matter what they're givin', if it's gonna put boys like you out of business. Such doin's don't shine with this hoss at all.''

"You're among the few here who feel that way, Will,'' Branigan said with a sad smile. "Well, let's go get your plews.''

"I'll jist leave 'em here for you, Mr. Branigan. I trust you to count 'em fair and square. Jist turn my animals out with yours at your leisure.'' He turned to leave, but then spun back. "You seen Sim Rutledge or any of his boys?''

Both Branigan and Myles shook their heads.

Barlow rode out, moving through the long string of camps that lay haphazardly along the creek. Occasionally he would stop someone, if the man appeared to be mostly sober, and ask about his former companions. Finally he found someone who pointed to the other side of the creek and said, "About a mile that way.''

Armed with that knowledge, it did not take Barlow long to find his friends' camp. Trouble was, none of the men was there. Only the women. He recognized one as the one Charlie Watters had been with the year before. Using his rusty Nez Perce, he asked, "You still with Charlie?"

"Yep. Best," the woman said with a wide grin. "He come back soon, I think, maybe."

Barlow had to smile at her imperfect English, especially since he knew his Nez Perce was probably worse. "You mind if I wait?"

"No. Sit." When he did, she served him some meat and coffee, then asked, "Whiskey?"

Barlow nodded enthusiastically at the request and thanked her profusely when it was provided. As she left, he poured a hefty helping of the whiskey into his mug of coffee. He ate heartily and sipped slowly. And two hours later, with no sign of any of his friends, he fell asleep.

He awoke when someone kicked him in the side. Roused from the depths of sleep, he came awake instantly, and with his knife in hand. Just before he could plunge the blade into the heart of a suddenly terrified Charlie Watters, Rutledge and Simon pulled him off, yelling at him.

Consciousness flooded into him and he realized where he was and who was with him. "Sorry," he said sheepishly, sliding the knife away. He reached out a hand to help Watters up. "Sorry, ol' hoss. But, damn, boy, don't ever do that again if you value your hair."

"Reckon I've learnt my lesson," Watters said, his smile returning.

The four headed toward the creek a short distance away.

"How you been, ol' hoss?" Watters asked Barlow as they walked.

"Shinin'. How about you and the other boys?"

"Same," Simon said with a grin. "We done well."

They sat by the water. As they passed a jug around, they discussed the season they had just had in the mountains, the quality of the furs they had brought in, the money being paid for them, their prospects for the next fall and spring seasons, the irascibility of the Indians they had encountered, and more.

"Where's your plews, Will?" Watters asked.

"Left 'em off at Branigan's," Barlow said with a grin. "Did better'n last year, I expect."

"Well, damn, if that don't shine with this chil'," Watters said.

"You know you could've gotten more cash money for 'em over to The Company's place?" Rutledge asked.

Barlow nodded. "I'd heard that. I also heard how they were doin' it. Such doin's don't shine with this chil'."

"What the hell do you care, boy?" Rutledge asked evenly. "Jist take as much specie as you can get for all your hard workin'. Let the suppliers and traders worry about themselves."

"Would seem the way of it for most ol' hosses, I reckon," Barlow said. "But what happens when The Company runs everybody else out? You think those cheap bastards'll still be payin' boys like us six dollars a pound for plews? In a pig's ass."

"You got a good point there, ol' hoss," Rutledge admitted. Then he grinned. "But I reckon I'll just worry about that when it happens."

"So, ol' hoss, what's your plans for the new season?" Simon asked Barlow.

It was a little more than a week after Barlow had arrived, and Rutledge's whole crew, plus Barlow, were sitting around a small fire in the middle of their camp one morning. They were universally hungover, though not too badly. Barlow had joined his old friends in their spree and showed them he could keep up with the best of them in whatever they wanted to get into—drinking, fighting, whoring, shooting, foot races, or anything else they could find to take part in.

"Ain't give much thought to it," Barlow admitted. He felt pretty good for feeling so rotten, all in all.

"Why don't you throw in with us again, boy?"

He had been hoping they would ask. He was plumb sick

of being alone, and he was sure he would go mad if he had to spend another winter up in the mountains by himself. The only other likely alternative would have been to hire on with one of the companies, and his temperament was not suited to such a life. So he did not even have to think about it. "Suits this chil'," he said with a blazing grin.

"I'm still the booshway here, in case you ain't figured that out yet," Rutledge said with a small laugh.

"Damn, I knew there was somethin' wrong in this here plan," Barlow said, joining the laughter.

"We'll set about findin' supplies today," Rutledge announced when the laughter had faded. "We'll leave out in two, three days."

"My supplies are took care of," Barlow noted. He grew serious. "I know you boys're likely to see about outfittin' with The Company, seein's how they're undercuttin' everybody else, but I'd be obliged if you'd take your business to Mr. Branigan's."

"Might cost us all a pretty penny more to do that, Will," Watters said.

"Mr. Branigan'll give you a fair enough price. Ain't gonna be as rock bottom low as what The Company'll give you, I expect, but it won't be so bad."

Rutledge pondered that for some time, and then allowed, "I'll talk to Mr. Branigan and see what he can do for us, Will. That's the best I reckon I can do. If we're gonna end up payin' some hundreds of dollars more, we jist cain't do that."

"I can't ask no more'n that. Jist make sure you tell Mr. Branigan that you're my friends."

When they pulled out a few days later, Barlow had a new woman. It was decided—mostly by Rutledge and Simon— that he could not be the only man without a woman on the journey. "I can't have a single man roamin' around out there, cooped up fer the winter without release and startin' to lust after someone's woman," Rutledge explained. "That'll be trouble for sure, and we'll have more'n enough of that without lookin' for it."

"But . . ." Barlow objected.

"No sassin' me, boy. We don't need such troubles. Besides, it'll make things a heap easier on you. Unless you enjoyed doin' all that women's work your own self last year—tannin' plews, and cookin' and tendin' fires, and such things." Rutledge grinned.

"Can't rightly say any of that was pleasurable," Barlow agreed with a chuckle. "All right, Cap'n, we'll get me a woman to go along." He felt a sudden tightness in his chest. He knew that the woman would be another Nez Perce, since all the other women were, and he hoped whatever woman they came up with for him was nothing like Mountain Calf. That would kill him, he thought.

Yellow Elk was as pretty as Mountain Calf had been, but the resemblance ended there. Oh, there were more similarities—Yellow Elk was every bit as lusty as Mountain Calf had been, as well as experienced that way. And she was as good a worker. But she did not dote on his every word, and it became obvious very quickly that while she liked him and certainly enjoyed being with him, she did not love him and probably never would. Barlow was relieved at that, though he never said anything. It became a comfortable, affectionate relationship.

The group followed pretty much the same trail that they had two years before, heading to Pierre's Hole, where they spent a couple of weeks making meat and taking buffalo hides for lodges—either new, for Barlow and Yellow Elk, or to replace worn sections of older ones. Then it was on to the eerie beauty and dread of the Colter's Hell region, and beyond, past the Three Forks area, and northwest toward the Bitterroot Mountains. But as winter neared and they began looking for a place to hole up, it became apparent that the area was trapped out—or something else had emptied the region of beaver.

"These are piss-poor times, boys," Rutledge announced one night around the fire. "And it don't look like there's nothing gonna make beaver shine 'round here."

"Why don't we try someplace else?" Cal Jones, one of the new men, suggested.

"Too late in the season, boy," Rutledge snapped. "We took our sweet time gittin' here, figurin' this place'd shine like it always has. Many other good spots'll be took up already by others. The way we heard it, the goddamn Company's got brigades followin' most of the other fur company men."

There was silence for a while before Barlow said, "Why don't we split up?"

"How do you mean, hoss?" Rutledge asked.

· Barlow had given it a little deliberation during the silence. "Couple of us head over the mountains. Now. Before it gets too late. Mayhap a couple others head east or something. Find us some other places to winter up. Mayhap you and Caleb and a couple others stay here, cache the plews we already got, keep most of the cavvy, sit things out. Once winter breaks, since there ain't no beaver here, you come get one or another of the smaller groups. Or we set a place now to where we can all meet then."

"Might work, Sim," Simon said thoughtfully. "Two boys and their women with a few horses and mules ain't gonna draw too much attention from The Company. Or anybody else, I reckon."

Rutledge grinned a little. "Two boys and their women'd sure as hell attract notice from any Blackfoot roamin' around."

"Hell, we ain't seen all that many Blackfeet. I think they're lyin' low for some reason. Besides, Will made it by his lonesome last year. Two should be jist fine."

"And," Barlow threw in, "with just a couple of us, we can move fast, get elsewhere before winter sets in full. We couldn't do that if the whole outfit moved on."

Rutledge gave it a few minutes' consideration, then asked, "Any of you boys feel a yearnin' to be elsewhere for a spell?"

"Hell, Cap'n, if Will's set on goin', I reckon I can partner up with him there, too," Watters said.

Johnny Clarke and Cal Jones also volunteered.

The next morning they pulled out, Barlow and Watters

heading north, ready to cross Lolo Pass and head toward Nez Perce and Flathead country; Clarke and Jones moving south, generally, figuring to find a wintering spot near Three Forks.

23

THE TRIP OVER Lolo Pass might have been as tough as it had been the last time Barlow had done it two years earlier, but it certainly didn't seem anywhere near as bad. Not when he had Watters to help him with the harder tasks, and two women along to keep each other company as well as tend to the horses and such. Besides, there were not as many horses as the return journey Barlow had made last time.

Still, the trek was not an easy jaunt, though they made pretty good time. Once on the western flank of the mountains, they turned southwest and pushed as hard as they could across the land. Not having to deal with many passes or peaks made the going a bit easier.

They finally settled on a wooded valley along the South Fork of the Salmon River. They raced to get some shelter for the horses and mules put up and gather up forage enough to tide them over any particularly rough times. They stockpiled firewood and they hunted. While they had plenty of jerky and pemmican from Rutledge's stores, fresh or even frozen-fresh meat was mighty welcome anytime, and it would make the preserved meat last longer.

They also managed to get in a bit of trapping and were

pleased to find that the furs they pulled in were as prime as any they had ever seen.

During their explorations of the area, they had found two Nez Perce villages within a few miles in different directions. They introduced themselves there, letting them know they were in the area. While the Nez Perce were friendly to the whites, getting to know those two bands was made easier by the presence of the two Nez Perce women, even though neither came from either of the villages.

Winter finally hit and hit hard, and the two mountain men and their women settled in to wait it out.

Not much broke the monotony of the harsh winter. The men had their chores and often played cards. They hunted when they could and spun yarns—more to prepare themselves for regaling others at rendezvous than to amuse each other. The women had plenty of work to do, making or repairing clothing, tanning the few hides of whatever kind the men brought in, and cooking. The four went to visit the Nez Perce on occasion, though not very often. They did not want to get to be an annoyance to their neighbors, nor did they want to get too friendly with the Indians, lest half of them be in their camp regularly looking for handouts or something.

Barlow and Yellow Elk spent a considerable amount of time making love, and if the sounds coming from their tipi were any indication, Watters and his woman were doing the same. It was, Barlow thought frequently, a wonderful way to pass the long, cold days and longer, colder nights. Yellow Elk never said anything, but her actions proved she agreed with that sentiment. She was a lustful young woman and was, as often as not, the aggressor in their relations. Barlow didn't mind that one bit, though he occasionally wondered if she were going to wear him down to a frazzle.

Spring seemed to take its sweet time in coming, which annoyed Barlow. He was eager to be on the move. He had had enough sitting around. But he tried to be patient. Then one morning he was out hunting when Buffalo growled. He froze, hiding behind a tree, frantically searching the area. Then he spotted a man he did not recognize. He assumed it was an Indian, though even with the poor look he had of the man, he was certain it wasn't a Nez Perce. He stayed where he was for a little while, hoping his frosty breath did not give him away. Mostly he watched the man, who was setting a beaver trap. But he also observed the area intently, looking to see if he had any companions.

He finally spotted two more men. With that, he turned and headed back to his camp. He told Watters and the two went back out. Barlow pointed the others out—they were now in their own little camp. One was chopping firewood while the other two tended to the animals.

The two men and the dog moved up slowly, carefully. Suddenly Barlow and Watters stepped out from behind trees, rifles pointing at the backs of the two men tending horses.

"You boys're trespassin'," Barlow said quietly. "Now turn 'round and let's get a look at you both. Nice and easy now."

The two men turned, irritated to be facing a duo of men with rifles pointed squarely at them.

"Tell your friend over there to set his ax down and come on over here with you boys," Barlow ordered.

The ax-wielder had heard Barlow's first command and had turned and was slowly heading toward Barlow and Watters, his ax ready. Barlow could see in the eyes of the other two men that the third was planning to attack. He whistled.

Buffalo charged out of the woods, behind the ax-wielder. The Newfoundland bit the armed man high up on the back of the thigh, tearing out a chunk of flesh along with the piece of buckskin pants. The man shrieked as he fell, his ax flying out of his hands.

Barlow glanced over and saw that Buffalo—now full grown and weighing in the vicinity of two hundred fifty pounds—was preparing to make a meal out of the man. "Buffler!" he called. When the dog trotted over to him and sat, looking quite pleased with himself, Barlow said, "Now pick yourself up, ol' hoss, and git your ass over here with your confederates. And be quick about it.''

The man pushed himself up and hobbled to stand next to his two friends.

"Where you boys from?" Barlow asked.

"We are wit'ze 'Udson's Bay Company," one said in a French accent. He sounded proud of it, as if that fact would protect him from all dangers.

"Well, I hate to tell you boys this, but you're trespassin' on American land. And this ol' hoss don't take kindly to sich doin's.''

"This is British country, ol' chap," another one said.

"That what you think?" When the three nodded, Barlow said, "Well, boys, you see them mountains way over yon to the west? Well, that be the boundary. And you're on the wrong side." He had no idea of where the boundary between British and American land was, or even if there was a boundary. But he sounded confident nonetheless. And he did not appreciate other men coming into land he had staked out for his own trapping.

The three looked at each other, surprised, confused, and angry. They had trapped here for several years and had never run into any problems. They were not used to being confronted by Americans. As far as they were concerned, men from the Hudson's Bay Company could hunt wherever they damn well felt like it. It had been that way since anyone could ever remember. But things seemed to be changing for the company. Just last year three Americans had crossed the mountains and made it as far as Fort Vancouver, arriving in poor shape. They got little help from the factor there, Dr. John McLoughlin, as he—and most others—thought the Americans were spies. Maybe these two Americans were also spies, the HBC men thought.

"What do you think, Charlie?" Barlow said. "Think these ol' boys're jist plew-stealin' bastards? Or you think maybe they're scoutin' this area out to maybe let the goddamn British make some inroads into our territory out here so they can steal all our beaver?"

Watters pondered that with great exaggeration, before allowing, "I think they're spies. They got that sneaky goddamn look about 'em. 'Course the Britishers and them damn Frenchies always got a sneaky look about 'em, so maybe they ain't spies. Think maybe we ought to torture 'em a bit, Injin style and see if they'll 'fess up?" He almost drooled at the thought—or so it seemed to the HBC men.

"Mayhap that'd do it," Barlow mused. "But, you know, ol' hoss, I jist ain't of the right humor for sich doin's today. I think mayhap I'll jist let 'em go."

"I reckon that's all right, Will. It's too cold to be standin' out here skinnin' one of these ol' boys alive."

"Go on, then git," Barlow commanded. "*Au revoir*." As the three headed for the small tent they had set up, Barlow said, "Whoa, there, fellers. Where'n the hell do you think you're goin'? Your horses are right here."

"But our t'ings," the French-Canadian said.

"You're lucky I'm lettin' you keep your damn horses, you son of a bitch. Now saddle 'em up and get the hell out of our territory."

"Our rifles, ol' chap?" another asked.

"Reckon you can keep 'em, but I'll make damn sure they ain't loaded when you leave here." As the three HBC men began saddling their horses under Watters's watchful eye, Barlow gathered up their arms and fired them into the ground. He then pulled the flints out of them and pitched them off into the woods. They would have spares in their shooting bags and would be able to fix the weapons fairly quickly and thus be able to hunt and protect themselves. But his discarding their flints would preclude them from riding fifty yards while they reloaded and charge right back here, guns ablaze.

Barlow handed the mounted men their rifles. "Sorry, boys, but your pistols stay here. Have a pleasurable journey." He stepped back and watched the three men ride out, their backs stiff with anger.

"Reckon they'll be back, Will?" Watters asked.

Barlow shrugged. "If it was me, I'd be back, but I ain't

so sure about those boys. They ain't free trappers, and I don't expect they're willin' to risk their hair comin' against a couple of mad Americans when they got nothin' personal in it.''

"Their dignity.''

"Ain't worth dyin' over. Not when we didn't abuse their honor all that much.'' He glanced at his friend. "You worried?''

Watters laughed. "Not really. Just wonderin' if we should be more alert than usual.''

"Wouldn't hurt, I reckon.'' He grinned.

They spent the next half hour or so going through the Hudson's Bay men's possessions, taking what they thought they could use and discarding what they figured was useless. There were few furs to be had, but there was a supply of dried meat, some powder and lead, several horses and mules, coffee, a small sack of sugar, some flour, and a number of traps.

Two weeks later, Barlow, Watters and their women broke camp and began heading eastward. They were to meet all the others somewhere near the Three Forks two months hence. The two men had seen nothing of the Hudson's Bay trappers in those two weeks.

The group was jubilant when they were united. The two duos that had split off had had great luck in bringing in prime furs, while the remainder of the men with Rutledge had done pretty well once they had left their wintering place. All together, they had quite a haul of plews. With enthusiasm and great anticipation, they headed for the rendezvous, which was being held in the same area as the previous year.

While there, Barlow often thought about the Hudson's Bay men and wondered what it was like out in the British area, or the region that he had heard was in dispute between Britain and the United States. What made the land so precious to the two countries? Before he left rendezvous, he had decided that he would find out.

Before making winter camp, Barlow broached the idea

of dividing the group again. Since Watters was also keen on going, once Barlow had explained it to him, Rutledge had no objections. So the two, with Yellow Elk and Watters's woman, Red Scarf, headed west, trapping as they went, but not delaying any longer than they had to at any one spot. Across the mountains that Barlow had pointed out as the border between American and Hudson's Bay areas, they ran into a desert that seemed to stretch on forever. But they persevered, relying on instincts, luck, and the occasional poor devil of a Paiute Indian to find water. They did not stay anywhere for any length of time, as they found no real sign of beavers. It being winter, the land was stark, and bitter cold, but they sometimes thought it better than being out there in the summer.

A few days later, a traveling band of Indians approached their camp. These were not the proud riders of the plains, but they were a lot better off than many of the barely surviving Paiutes they had met. Barlow and Watters warily invited the Indians in to sit and have coffee and meat.

Using a combination of English, some French, a bit of Nez Perce, and a lot of sign language, the two disparate groups managed to converse. The white men learned that the Columbia River was only two days' ride north and that perhaps a week or less of riding along the Columbia would bring them out of the desert.

They also learned that these Indians were Cayuses, and the war party was heading south toward where other Paiutes—ones better off than the scraggly ones the whites had seen so far—lived. They planned to raid for horses.

At that point, Barlow glanced at Watters, who looked back with the same concern in his eyes. Both thought they could see in the eyes of the Cayuses that the warriors were considering the long ride south compared with a short, sudden raid right there. They would get more horses and mules and better quality ones, plus two fine Nez Perce women, and plenty of other useful things.

"Reckon you boys best be on your way," Barlow said hastily, hoping they understood. "You got a long ride ahead of you."

The Cayuse war leader nodded. He rose, as did his men. They mounted up and rode out, seemingly without a care in the world.

As soon as they were out of sight, Barlow jumped up. "Charlie, git the animals tied together good and tight, and make sure they're tied to the trees." Their camp didn't have much vegetation, but there were a few stunted, wind-twisted little trees.

Watters rushed off to do so.

With the women, Barlow managed to get some small, basic dirt breastworks scraped together. The few bales of plews they had added to the protection. It wasn't much, but it was all they had.

The four humans and the Newfoundland dog were hunkered down in their pitiful defensive position when the Cayuses came galloping back. That the white men and their two Nez Perce women were not innocently breaking camp came as a shock to the Cayuses, but that did not stall their attack.

"You want first shot, Charlie?" Barlow asked.

"Nah, you take it. You're a better shot than I am." It was as if they were discussing the weather.

As the warriors charged, spreading out, Barlow calmly sighted and fired. A Cayuse was knocked off his horse, but the others continued coming. As Barlow swiftly reloaded, Watters fired. "Damn," he muttered. He had hit one, but didn't kill him.

"Last time I put my trust in you, ol' hoss," Barlow said with mock sternness as he took aim and fired again. The war leader went down, bouncing on the snowy, cold ground.

The other Cayuses decided this was not a wise idea after all and veered away from the camp, racing as hard as they could toward the northeast.

Barlow stood and watched the retreating Indians. He wondered why they had attacked them. It was such a foolish thing to do, but he never could fathom the Indian mind. Still, he had a little unease as he and the others began breaking camp. He thought this attack might bode poorly for the rest of their journey, and he hoped not all the Indians they met out there were so prone to attacking them.

24

ABOUT SEVEN WEEKS after they had split off from Rutledge's group, Barlow and Watters struggled over another mountain range and entered a whole new world. It was considerably warmer and far greener than anything Barlow had ever seen before. It seemed to rain all the time, too, the newcomers learned. Downpours were rare, though not unknown. Usually, however, there was an almost constant drizzle, often little more than a mist. For the four travelers, it was a blessing and a relief.

They continued following the wide, fast-flowing Columbia River, as they had since finding it two days after the Cayuse attack. Two days later, they spotted a fair amount of smoke off in the distance. Leaving the women, horses, and mules behind, Barlow, Watters, and Buffalo went to see what was out there. From atop a well-timbered ridge, they could see a fort across the river.

"Reckon that's Fort Vancouver?" Watters asked.

"Expect so. Don't know of any other forts out this way. And that's certainly a big enough place to be the headquarters for the Hudson's Bay Company in this area."

"Well, I got me a good idear, ol' hoss. Let's give it a wide berth," Watters said with a chuckle.

"Don't want to go pay your respects to the head man down there, eh?"

"Shit. We've had more'n enough trouble without walkin' in there and askin' for it."

The two laughed and moved back from the ridge. When they got back to the women and animals, they moved southwest, heading away from the river. Barlow didn't think finding water would be a problem. Nor did he think finding their way would be trouble. Only a few miles later, they decided to make their camp. They were tired, hungry, and worn down from the long, perilous journey, and an early night would do them all well.

It was a comfortable camp for a change, though trying to find enough dry wood to keep a fire going was a challenge. But they managed, and with the fresh meat Watters brought in, they were comfortable.

"This much water, there ought to be beaver galore out here, Matt," Watters said as they sipped coffee.

"Ought to, but I'd not count on it."

"Why not?"

"Hell, I'd wager the Hudson's Bay boys've trapped this out a heap of years ago."

"Damn, that must be." Watters shook his head in annoyance. "You think we'll find any sign 'round here?"

Barlow shrugged. He bent to pull a burning twig from the fire to light his clay pipe. "Hell if I know, boy. You're the one's so good at finding beaver sign. Keep your eyes peeled." He puffed a minute, thinking, then said, "I reckon we might find some. Since this place was trapped out a long time ago, I reckon ain't nobody traps here much anymore. Mayhap the beaver've come back in some areas. Not right near the fort, I reckon. If there was any beavers there, they would've been seen and trapped right off."

"We'll have to mosey on around the area and see if I can find some sign. If I cain't, then there ain't no beaver here."

The next day they came to a wide, powerful river. "Damn," Barlow said. "I was certain we was travelin' mostly south. From what those Cayuses told us, the Columbia heads pretty well dead west till it hits the ocean.''

"Maybe it ain't the Columbia," Watters suggested helpfully.

"Could be." He sighed.

They pressed on, following the river, and an hour later, spotted a small Indian village. "Mayhap I ought to ride on in there and ask those Injins what this river is."

"Couldn't hurt. They look peaceable enough."

"You in?" When Watters nodded, Barlow led the way down the grassy slope toward the village of small huts. The people were tall and wore poor clothing of reeds, grass, and cloth. They were friendly, though, and before long, Barlow had learned that they were Kalapuyas, and that the big river was the Willamette.

Barlow traded some beads and a bit of blue cloth for some dried salted fish and then moved on, his small group relieved for some reason to be out of the village.

A day and a half later, they found a small depression along a creek. There were plenty of trees, and the creek would offer good water. Game seemed fairly plentiful in the area, too. Barlow and Watters looked at each other and then nodded. This would be their winter home. As their lodges went up, Barlow realized that the reason he, at least, was relieved to get away from the Kalapuya village was that it seemed unnatural to him. They had wood and thatch huts instead of tipis or earth lodges. It was just too strange to see Indians living in poor imitations of white men's houses.

The camp went up quickly, in large part because it was all routine to them now. As the women put up the lodges and took care of the domestic things, Barlow and Watters gathered firewood. Again, finding dry wood was difficult, but with some searching, they found enough to keep them going for a few days. They put other wood under canvas, hoping it would dry out soon enough to be able to use.

Though it was winter, there was still grass and shoots around that the animals could feed on, so gathering forage was not important, nor was building shelter for the horses.

Hunting was in order, though, as both men were averse

to eating fish, thinking it somehow beneath them.

And as soon as their winter home was set up, Watters took off, moving up and down the small stream searching for beaver sign. He found some, but he found more on other streams in the area. With that knowledge, the two men began setting their traps. They caught enough beaver, though the fur the animals bore was not nearly the same quality as what they were used to taking in the Rockies.

Still, it was the most comfortable wintering spot they had ever found. The weather was cold, but not the bitter, bone-racking frigidity of the Rockies. Little snow fell, and what did usually melted off within a day or two, and there was not much ice, though they did get sleet on occasion and hail once in a while. The rain quickly grew tiresome, but it was, all in all, better than what they were used to, though they frequently wished for a day of sunshine.

They occasionally visited various tribes in the area or had Indians call on them in their camp, usually for a little trade. All of the local Indians seemed to be peaceful and open-hearted. The two white men didn't mind the Indians coming around, but they were annoyed at the insistence on trade, mainly because all the tribesmen had to trade was fish.

During these visits, however, Barlow and Watters learned that the ocean was only a few days ride to the west, and they were determined to get there. Deciding that their women would be all right left behind, the two men saddled up and rode out one day. Two days later, they heard the ocean's roar. Within an hour, they had found an Indian village and traded some meat for some not-very-welcome fish and information on trapping sea otters.

The two white men spent more than a week in the region, staying with the Tillamooks most of the time. When they headed back toward their camp, they had several mules laden with prime otter pelts, which they were sure would bring in good money back at rendezvous. If not from the traders, then from mountain men who would almost certainly love to have a number of such fine furs made into a good sleeping robe. It would be as warm as a buffalo robe but weigh considerably less.

For the rest of the winter, Barlow and Watters managed to avoid being seen by other white men. They were surprised by that, though they figured that most of the Hudson's Bay Company men had no reason to travel down this way. It was a while before Barlow realized that the head man at Fort Vancouver—John McLoughlin—would almost certainly know his little party was in the area. Some Indians in this vast area would have made it known. He wondered why McLoughlin had not sent men to check them out, but decided that the Hudson's Bay Company chief probably did not think them a threat. Barlow also concluded that McLoughlin knew every movement the little band made. It might even be a reason why the Kalapuyas visited so often.

Barlow and Watters kept on the alert, though they were not seriously concerned that McLoughlin or the Indians would move against them. They were just used to being wary and saw no reason to change.

It was hard to tell when spring arrived—if it every really did. Based on a crude calendar the men had begun keeping soon after arriving here, they decided in early March that it was time to leave.

They headed generally southward, deciding to try another route through the Cascades. They had learned of a route from the local Indians and decided they would rather take it than risk another encounter with the Cayuses. It might also allow them to avoid the desert they had traversed, and that was a plus for them. In that desert, there would be no beaver, or if there were a few, their skins would be so poor as to be practically worthless. But crossing the Cascades should allow them to start some trapping, and even when they came down on the east side of the range, they should still find some good beaver.

Three days after leaving their winter camp, as they were moving slowly between closely packed trees along a barely discernible trail, they were attacked. The raid by for-the-moment-unidentified Indians was startling in its suddenness and ferocity. Only the fact that there were just five warriors kept the assault from becoming an almost instant massacre.

But both Barlow, who was leading the little party and Watters, who was bringing up the rear, had been out in the wilds too long to let surprise overwhelm them. Both men rode, as they often did, with their rifles across the saddle in front of them. Barlow snatched his up and fired without aiming and without bringing the weapon to his shoulder. He hit a warrior, breaking his leg. He swung his left leg up over the mule's head and dropped to the ground on the right side of the mule—the side from which the attack had come.

A warrior rushed at him, war club raised high, knife held in his other hand. Barlow blocked the club with his rifle, held crossway in both hands, and continued the push, until the side of the rifle butt hit the Indian in the forehead. It knocked the warrior down but not before the Indian's blade tore into his side, slicing between a couple of ribs. Barlow swung the rifle around and then pounded it straight down, butt first, shattering the Indian's face.

He glanced down the long line of animals to see that Watters had downed one Indian somehow and was just creasing the head of another with his tomahawk.

Silence suddenly fell as the surviving warriors bolted off into the woods. Even the birds had stopped their chattering in the wake of the war cries, gunfire, and violence. Eyes constantly searching the rainy forest, Barlow reloaded his rifle. He neither saw nor heard anything. Finally he looked at Watters, shrugged, and mounted his mule. They pulled out, looking back only to make sure no more Indians were coming after them.

"So much for avoidin' Injins who're half froze to take our hair, ol' hoss," Watters said with a note of sarcasm that night in camp.

Barlow chuckled. He could see some humor in the irony of it all, now that it was long past.

"You know what they were?"

"Ain't sure. But from what the Kalapuyas told us, they appeared to be Umpquas, since they're the only warlike folk we've come across."

"Ya know, Matt, when the Kalapuyas first mentioned these Umpquas, I thought that name sounded familiar, but I'll be damned if I can figure out where I might know it from. I ain't ever been out here before and can't say as I know too many boys who have been out this way."

"We know one," Barlow said slowly, filling his pipe. "I felt the same as you when I first heard the name. And now I recall where. You remember Sim told us he was out here many a year ago?" Watters nodded and Barlow continued. "He was out here with some ol' chil' named Smith. Jed Smith, weren't it?"

"By damn, you're right. Now I remember. Said some Injins—Umpquas—wiped out the whole lot of them that was left behind whilst this Smith feller, Sim, and one other ol' hoss was off doin' somethin'. Took all their plunder and left 'em with nothin'. The head man over to Fort Vancouver had to help 'em out so's they had enough supplies to make it back to rendezvous." He shook his head, somewhat amazed at the coincidence. "Them damn Umpquas're some sneaky, nasty bastards, I'm sayin'."

"Won't get no arguin' from me on that."

Several days later they swung southeast, heading into the mountains. With the altitude came much colder days, but it also brought better trapping. The beaver they caught there had nice thick winter coats yet, and when cured made fine plews.

They continued in a general southeastwardly direction, working through pass after pass. When trapping started to produce a poorer quality of fur, they began moving faster, sometimes wondering if they would ever make it to their meeting with Rutledge on time. But they did, and from there it was a matter of only a couple of weeks before they were riding into the rendezvous, which was in full swing already.

Remaining loyal to Andrew Branigan, Barlow went there to sell his furs. Watters considered going with him, what with being Barlow's partner and all, but when he heard how much more the American Fur Company was offering, he gave in to his desire for money. Barlow didn't much like it, but he understood.

As usual, Branigan gave him a more than fair price, and Barlow found himself rich again. At least for the next couple of weeks. By then he would likely have blown all the money he had worked so hard to make and spent it all on frivolous foofaraw for Yellow Elk or on whiskey and gaudy doodads for himself. Not that it mattered. After the winter, a man needed a spree, and there were always plenty of beaver out there to make another fortune.

Barlow gleefully joined the festivities after taking Yellow Elk back to her people, who had a camp in the vicinity. She wanted to visit with family and friends, and Barlow felt that having her around was too restrictive anyway. This way he was free to do as he wished, including whoring if it crossed his mind.

There was, he found out soon after arriving, one big difference with this rendezvous. There were white women here. He couldn't believe it when Watters told him in wide-eyed excitement. So he had to go himself, wondering what would ever possess a white woman to come out here to this wilderness, especially to a rendezvous, where the wildest of men—white and red—congregated and joyfully violated every commandment on a regular basis.

He found the two women and was mighty disappointed when he did. Prudence Sterling and Mercy Fenwick were young, somewhat handsome, and seemed at least moderately vivacious. But they were married—to missionaries. Barlow lost all interest in them, other than a lingering curiosity at what would possess a woman to follow her man to such a place.

25

BARLOW WAS HUNGOVER again, though not frightfully so, and sitting around the camp with some of Rutledge's other men when the Reverend Josiah Sterling and the Reverend Ezekiel Fenwick showed up. Barlow watched with little interest as the two missionaries dismounted and went to Rutledge's fire. Barlow didn't know which of them was which, but the tall, thin, mostly bald one did most of the talking, and so very earnestly. Barlow almost grinned, knowing what the also hungover Sim Rutledge must be feeling listening to the pious twosome. Then Rutledge pointed to him, and Barlow cursed.

Within moments, the missionaries were standing in front of him, making him squint up into the sun if he wanted to look at them. He decided he didn't really want to. "I ain't sure what you boys want, but if you aim to talk with this ol' chil', you best sit."

The two looked at each other, shrugged, and then sat gingerly, moving the backs of their frock coats out of the way in a decidedly prissy manner. "You are Mr. Will Barlow?" one asked.

"I am. Who're you?"

"The Reverend Josiah Sterling. My colleague is the Reverend Ezekiel Fenwick."

"Can't say I'm pleased to meet you boys," Barlow said with a surly edge to his voice. "But there's coffee and you're welcome to it."

"Perhaps later," Sterling said. He was the taller of the two missionaries, bald at the top, though with a fringe of graying hair. He was quite thin, with a long, peaked nose, deep-set gray eyes, and a thin slit of a mouth.

"You boys come over here jist to set and look me over?" Barlow said in growing irritation.

"Well, no," Sterling said, a little surprised. "We . . . we have something to ask of you."

"Well it ain't gonna git asked if you're jist gonna set there on your scrawny ass bone with your mouth clamped shut."

Both religious men were appalled, though by now they should not have been. A good many of the mountain men they had dealt with here were of the same sullen, vulgar ilk.

"You have been to the Oregon country, I understand?" Sterling asked.

"Wintered there this past year. Why?"

"We have been charged by our home church council to go to the Oregon country and open a mission for the heathen Indians there so that we might civilize them and bring the Word of our Savior to them."

"Why?" Barlow asked harshly.

"Well, they must be converted to believe in our Lord Jesus Christ," Sterling responded, taken aback by the question.

"Again, I got to ask, why?"

"So they might enter the Kingdom of Heaven, of course."

"And you two, of course," Barlow commented sarcastically, "offer the one 'true' way."

"No, Mr. Barlow, not us. Our Lord. We are but His messengers."

"Them folks has their own religion, and it works jist fine for them."

"What they have is pagan idolatry, Mr. Barlow. Heathenism of the worst sort. They must be converted over to Christ's grace."

"Even if you have to kill 'em all to do it," Barlow muttered very low.

"What's that?"

"Nothin'." He could sit there and argue all day with the two missionaries. He hated their piousness, which blinded them to the realities of the world. But it would do no good. He would get only more frustrated at their hardheadedness, and they certainly would not be swayed by whatever poor arguments he could come up with.

"So, what's all this got to do with me, boys?" Barlow asked, sipping coffee laced with whiskey. It helped to settle his stomach.

"We need someone to guide us to Oregon. Someone who knows the way, who knows the Indians there, who knows the lay of the land."

"And you think that's me?" Barlow became aware that most of his friends had gathered around and were listening, most somewhat amused.

"Yes," Sterling said. He was having second thoughts about it. He had asked around most of the rendezvous already, but few were the men who would own up to having been in Oregon. The few who had refused his offer. He was getting close to desperate, and Barlow was one of the few left who had experience in that country. Even still, he was not sure Barlow was the kind of man he would want guiding him on a long, treacherous trek across vast amounts of unknown land. He was even less certain whether he could—or wanted to—entrust his life and the lives of the women to such a man.

"You're sniffin' at the wrong tree, Reverend," Barlow said politely.

"We'll pay you, of course."

"Ain't gonna be near as much as I'd git from a season's trappin'," Barlow growled.

"We . . . Well, we have no other means, Mr. Barlow," Sterling, almost pleading.

"How'd you git this far?"

"We traveled to rendezvous with Mr. Sublette's supply train. He was a very gracious host on the journey."

"I'm sure he was," Barlow said flatly. "Have you talked to Sublette? See if he'll take you the rest of the way?"

"He cannot," Sterling said regretfully. "He has a strict schedule to keep. And," he added with a sigh, "we had contracted only to be brought this far. Neither he nor I thought we'd have any trouble finding a guide for the rest of the journey."

"You know what you're facin', Reverend?" Barlow asked harshly, glaring at him.

"Well, if this part of the journey has been any indication, we are in for a rough trip," Sterling said with a sniff. "But we are not men easy to defeat."

"What about the women? You plannin' to bring them?"

"Of course."

"Are they easy to defeat?"

"I wouldn't think so. They are stout of heart and have the utmost faith in our Lord."

Barlow shook his head in irritation. They thought that God would provide them an easy way to everything. "The journey you had from the Settlements to here was a child's walk in the safe woods of home, Reverend," he said. "The rest of the way means encounters with mountains the likes of which you've never seen, I reckon. There're passes that still have snow in 'em even this time of year. There's deserts, cliffs, starvin' times. A thousand miles or more of the roughest country you'll ever see, and all of it full of griz, panther, wolves, and mean goddamn Injins."

"We are prepared to face all that and more, Mr. Barlow," Sterling said stiffly. "The Lord will provide what we need to get there and what we need when we get there. And, rest assured, Mr. Barlow, we *will* get there."

"If God will provide for you, boy, perhaps he'll provide you a guide."

The two missionaries rose and stiffly went to their horses.

Then they rode out talking animatedly with each other.

"Maybe you should've gone with them, ol' hoss," Rutledge said, as he took Sterling's place.

"What would I want to do that fer?"

Rutledge shrugged, but he smiled. "Hell, you was jist sayin' the other day that you was ponderin' goin' back to the Settlements. Maybe find yourself a woman and settle down."

"That's right," Watters said, plunking himself down next to Rutledge. "Didn't he just say he'd had himself enough adventure for one ol' hoss?"

"He did," Rutledge agreed. "Heard him myself sayin' just that."

"Since when did you two damn fools start listenin' to what I had to say?" Barlow asked, a rueful smile building.

"Always do, ol' hoss," Watters said with a laugh.

"Well, was I to guide them, I'd end up losing most of the fall and spring hunts. I don't know as if I'm willin' to give up a whole year's worth of plews just to cart a couple goddamn missionaries—and their wives!—to Oregon."

"If the trappin's all that's holdin' you back, don't go frettin' on that," Rutledge said.

"Why not?"

"You know damn well the hard times we and everybody else we've talked to has had findin' beaver these days. Beaver don't shine like it used to, even just a year ago. Sure, we brought in a heap of prime plews this time, but it took some doin's to find 'em. And you remember year before last, don't you? Where our winterin' spot had nary beaver sign to be seen."

"Hell, Cap'n, beaver'll shine again. You know that's well as I do."

"I used to always think so, Will. But I ain't so sure no more." He paused to spit some of the foulness left from the previous night's drinking out of his mouth. "I ain't given to thinkin' much about the future, but ary now and again I contemplate what that might hold for me. And wasn't nary a time that I wasn't sure I'd be out here trappin' beaver. It nary entered my head till two years ago that beaver-wouldn't shine no more. But now I ain't so sure. And I reckon it might not be another year or two afore there ain't no beaver trade no more.''

"You're jist worryin' like some ol' lady,'' Barlow scoffed.

"Like hell I am. Thing is, not too long ago I would've agreed with you. But now, things is different. Listen, boy— all of you boys—I've heard talk from Bill Sublette and some others who're in a position to know, that even if beaver does shine again, it's losin' its popularity.''

"What the hell's that mean, Cap'n?'' Clarke asked, surprised and worried.

"Over in Europe, they're makin' top hats out of some new kind of stuff, I heard. Somethin' called silk. I hear it's cheaper and a lot easier to work with. It's also a hell of a lot lighter, so they save themselves a heap of specie in shippin' it. If it holds up and they start usin' more of this here silk stuff, there ain't gonna be no more call for beaver, no matter how many we can trap.''

"You gettin' out, Cap'n?'' Barlow asked.

Rutledge shook his head. "Not yet. This ol' chil' still knows some out-of-the-way beaver streams and ponds, and I figure I can git me maybe one more good season in. I'll appraise things next year at the rendezvous. If things're lookin' as grim as I'm afeared they might be, I'll take my profits and head back east. Or maybe elsewhere, but I'll quit this here business.''

Rutledge grinned. "You boys know I ain't no better'n the rest of you. Hell, ain't a one of us put away so much as a penny in all the time we been doin' this. Nope, all we do is piss it all away here at rendezvous on whiskey and foofaraw.''

Everyone laughed. It was true, and none of them really cared. It was the life they had chosen, and if there were consequences, they would deal with them. Hell, they could die any time in any number of ways in the wild. And when they survived another year under such harsh and unforgiving conditions, they felt they had earned a spree. And, with the prices most of the suppliers charged out there, spending virtually everything they had made was easy to do.

"You tellin' me you'd be happy to see me ride on?" Barlow asked. He was not sure whether to be annoyed or not.

"To tell you true, ol' hoss, in some ways it'd be a heap easier to have one—well, two, considerin' your woman, too—less person along. Especially with beaver so hard to come by, but, hell, it might be best. I'll say this, though, I'll hate to lose you, Will. You're my best hunter. And one hell of a trapper—once your partner there finds sign for you," he added with a grin. "But . . . Well, ol' chil', if you decide to go with them missionaries, I ain't gonna stand in your way."

Barlow nodded. "I'll have to cogitate on it for a while," he said. He was sick at the thought of not being wanted in some ways, but he knew it had to be this way.

"Jist one other thing, Will," Rutledge said as he stood. "Remember, you ain't wintered with us the past two winters. Doin' so again this comin' winter ain't gonna be much different. And we can all meet back here at rendezvous next summer. If the beaver trade's lookin' brighter, you can rejoin us. We'd be mighty glad to have you. If beaver don't shine no more, for whatever reason, well, then the whole damn lot of us is gonna have to figure out somethin' else to do to fill our meatbags."

He left, heading for his own fire. Most of the others left, too, except Watters, who remained where he was. Barlow looked at his partner. "You got any thoughts on all this?"

Watters grinned. "Reckon not. The cap'n said it all, I expect. If half of what he's sayin' is true, we got some decisions to make before too long. You just got to make one a little sooner than the rest of us, maybe."

"You think he's tellin' true?"

Watters nodded. "I ain't ever knowed Sim to lie about such doin's. Now, someone might be lyin' to him, but if he's relayed that information, he likely believes it—or believes in the man who give it to him. Hell, if you're thinkin' he's just tryin' to get rid of you, put that notion out of your

head. If that's what he wanted, he would've come flat out
and said it.''

"That's what I figured." Barlow stood. "Well, this ol'
hoss is gonna get some robe time. I think I'm gittin' too
old for sich sprees," he said with a laugh.

"Like hell," Watters grinned. He, too, rose. "Just one
thing, Will. If you decide to take them missionaries, I'd
like to go along if you don't mind none.''

Barlow stared at his partner for a minute, wondering why
he even wanted to go. Then he decided he didn't care. He
would enjoy the company. He nodded, turned, and headed
into his lodge, brain already working over the problem.

Three days later, Barlow sought out the missionaries.
Without preliminaries, he asked, "You boys found your
guide yet?''

"Well, no, no we haven't," Sterling said. His long, thin
face was creased with worry.

"Reckon I can take you on out there." For some reason,
Sterling's sudden jubilation annoyed him. "My partner
aims to go along with us, if that's acceptable.''

Glad to have his guide, Sterling was ready to agree to
almost anything. "Yes, that's fine, Mr. Barlow.''

"Good. Now, there's a little matter of my pay." The
three men sat down to dicker.

26

SEVERAL DAYS LATER, the little entourage pulled out, heading roughly northwest. Barlow rode at the head of the small column, with the missionaries and their wives—in a small wagon—following. Behind them were Yellow Elk and Red Scarf, with the pack animals and some extra horses and mules, and Watters brought up the rear. Half a day or so ahead of them was Yellow Elk's band of Nez Perce. The two groups had agreed to travel sort of together for safety, and because the Nez Perce said they knew of some ways through the mountains to the northwest, that would be a little easier on the whites, especially with the two white women in a wagon.

They reached the Snake River and followed its ragged course farther northwest, and then southwest, reaching Fort Hall several weeks after leaving the rendezvous on the Green River. The place was bustling, much more active than Barlow would have thought for being so out of the way. They camped a few miles away, but Barlow rode there that afternoon. He spotted Nathaniel Wyeth, who had built the fort a couple of years earlier, and stopped near him. Barlow dismounted from Beelzebub. "What's goin' on, Mr. Wyeth?" he asked. He had seen the Bostonian around rendezvous but couldn't really say he knew him.

"New owners moving in," Wyeth said.

"You sold out?"

"That I have." Wyeth glared at Barlow. "Do I know you, sir?"

"We've come across each other on occasion down to rendezvous."

"Are you associated with the Sublettes?" Wyeth asked harshly. "Or any of the scoundrels of the Rocky Mountain Fur Company?"

"No, sir. I know many of those boys, but I'm a free trapper. I usually ride with a small band of like-minded fellers. Sim Rutledge is our cap'n. Do my tradin' with Andrew Branigan. Have done since I been in the mountains."

Wyeth's harshness eased somewhat. "Sorry to have been rude, sir, but I cannot abide the way the Sublettes and their cronies do business."

Barlow shrugged. "So who're the new owners?"

"The Hudson's Bay Company."

It was Barlow's turn to look sour. Seeing that Wyeth had noticed, he said, "I feel about the Hudson's Bay Company as poorly as you feel about the Rocky Mountain Fur Company." He grinned a little off-kilter.

"Well, you'll have to deal with them now, if you plan to stay around here, my good man." He did not seem the least bit concerned whether that was good or bad to Barlow.

"Ain't plannin' to hang my hat here. Got me a couple of missionaries I'm taking to Oregon country."

Wyeth nodded. "Ah, yes, I took the Reverend Lee out there a couple years back. He's set up a mission in the Willamette Valley."

"Saw it when I was in the area last year. Reckon he'll have some competition now."

"I expect they're all the same, those missionaries," Wyeth said with a sigh.

"Mayhap, but these two I got along are a wee bit different."

"Oh? How so?"

"Brung their wives with 'em."

Wyeth's eyes grew large. "The truth, sir?"

"Yep."

"I might have to stop by and pay my respects. It would be nice to have a conversation with someone civilized for a change. I . . ." He stopped and grinned ruefully. "I meant no offense, Mr. . . . ?"

"Will Barlow." He shrugged. "No offense taken, Mr. Wyeth. I don't expect boys like me are much good at conversin' with educated fellers like you."

"Well, there's a many of your mountaineers who can spin a hell of a tale and certainly keep it interesting," Wyeth admitted. "But, still, there's something about conversing with another educated man."

"Or woman?" Barlow suggested.

Wyeth looked aghast and then chuckled uncomfortably. "Yes, that, too, I would say. I imagine these ladies are not about to converse with a strange man out here in the wilds."

"Reckon not." Barlow leaned on his rifle and grinned. "And to tell you true, Mr. Wyeth, I expect them women ain't much to talk with at the best of times. I'd wager they're as damned pious as their husbands." He straightened up. "But they got sand in 'em, though, them two. First white women to ever chance comin' out here, and plannin' to stay at a mission for Injins. Sure are uncommon females, this chil's sayin'."

"I would say you're right, Mr. Barlow."

"I just hope we can get that damn wagon over the Cascades, as well as some of those damn mountains before we git that far."

"They brought a wagon?"

"Yep."

"Damn fools, even if they are missionaries," Wyeth said. "Mr. Barlow, I suggest you leave that wagon behind. You'll never make it."

Barlow stood there, rubbing his jaw. "I was afeared of that, but it weren't worth arguin' over back there. I figured we'd have to abandon it sooner or later. Reckon I was just puttin' it off."

"I urge you not to put it off any longer. Those women must become broken to saddle riding. You can't expect to just abandon the wagon and have them take to horses."

"Oh, they'd manage, this ol' hoss thinks," Barlow said with a laugh. "But I reckon you're right. Best get 'em used to it now before it becomes necessary. Well, thankee, Mr. Wyeth."

"My pleasure."

Barlow pulled himself onto the mule. "Well, if you aim to pay your respects, you best do it soon. We'll be pullin' out first thing in the mornin'. We've set our camp two miles down yonder." He pointed.

Wyeth never did show up at his camp. Barlow didn't care one way or the other. He moved them out when they were ready, just as he planned to. The two male missionaries were far more put out by Barlow's order to leave the wagon behind than the women were.

"Mercy and I are fair horsewomen, Mr. Barlow," Prudence said. "We will get along fine, I assure you." When her husband tried to continue his protest, she placed a hand on his arm. "Now, now, Josiah," she said quietly, "it would be unseemly to argue with our guide. He does, after all, know this territory better than we do. And if he is sure the wagon will not make it, then the quicker we dispose of it, the better off we shall be."

Sterling did not like it, but he and Fenwick went off to saddle the two horses that Barlow had chosen for the women.

Barlow was surprised to see that the women had brought sidesaddles with them. He shook his head, certain that they would never make the entire journey riding like that. But there was nothing he could do about it now.

They rode out soon after, the women sitting merrily on their sidesaddles, their long flowing dresses and their bonnets—tied on with long ribbons—looking incredibly out of place.

The going got rougher as they continued to follow the Snake River southwest, until it made its long, slow loop toward the northwest. They hit some desert finally, though it was not nearly as bad as the one Barlow and Watters had encountered the year before. And, with the Snake River so close by, they were not usually without water.

Soon after, though, they met up with the Nez Perce, who had waited for them that day. During a council with the Indians, Lame Dog, one of the chiefs, said in his own language, "We're heading north now. You continue following the Snake, then head west, the way we talked about before we left the Seeds-ke-dee."

Barlow nodded. "Thank you, Lame Dog, for helping us on this journey. I will not forget my red brother for all his help."

That evening Barlow got news he was not prepared for. "I'm going with my people tomorrow," Yellow Elk told him.

"Why?" he asked, surprised and unhappy.

"I don't want to go to Oregon again," Yellow Elk said flatly.

"That the only reason?" Barlow felt sadness bite into him. He had known all along that Yellow Elk didn't love him, but they had grown close and so comfortable together that the thought of being without her was not a pleasant one.

Her hesitation in answering let him know she had other reasons but was apparently reluctant to talk about them. He decided he didn't have the heart or the energy to try to dig the reasons out. They would not matter anyway. It was obvious she had made up her mind, and that was that. At least she had had the decency to tell him to his face. She very easily could have pitched all his things out of their lodge as Mountain Calf had done, divorcing him without explanation.

"All right," he said quietly. "You want me to move my things out tonight?"

"No," she said quietly. Her frown suddenly shifted to a wide, playful grin. "We play tonight," she said in English.

Barlow had to laugh. She had, in some ways, broken his heart, but was still fun and wanted him. He was not foolish enough to turn her down. "That shines with this chil'!"

She reached for him and pulled him close. He came along willingly. In moments they were tearing each other's clothes off, and he was entering her as she squealed in delight. He couldn't help but pound into her hot and furiously and filled her with his juices much sooner than he would have liked.

Yellow Elk was ready for him before he entered her, and reached a small climax moments later, and then a bigger one just before she felt his powerful release into her. She cried out with passion, fulfilled.

As he caught his breath, he tried to apologize for not lasting nearly as long as usual.

"Hush," she said, placing a finger on his lips. "It was wonderful."

"Too fast," he argued.

"Sometimes fast is good," she said in English. "Later we do slow. It be good, too."

"You think so, eh?" he asked with a grin.

"Know so."

An hour later, he found out that she was right.

It was with a sad heart that Barlow watched as Yellow Elk rode off in the morning with the band of Nez Perce. But he was not as bothered by the departure as Watters was. Barlow had found out that morning that Yellow Elk and Red Scarf had decided together to go back to their people. Watters had been with Red Scarf for three, maybe four years, and had loved her. He couldn't understand why she was leaving him if she cared as much for him as she said she did. But he was incapable of understanding the yearning of the young woman to be among her own people again, to not be an outsider all the time. She had been pulled in two by the opposite desires, but had finally succumbed to the call of blood, rather than love, because of Yellow Elk's influence.

Barlow walked over and clapped a hand on Watters's shoulder. "You'll find yourself another woman." He knew even as he said them that the words were useless.

"Not like Red Scarf," Watters said bitterly. "Damn,

Matt, why'd she have to go and do that to this ol' chil'?''

"Ain't no man knows the ways of a woman's mind, ol' hoss. Nor all the ways of an Injin's mind. Put the two of them together, and we ain't ever gonna grasp what their thinkin' is.''

"You're both better off without those heathens sharing your tents,'' the Reverend Josiah Sterling said from somewhere behind the two mountain men. "Maybe someday when they have been brought around to the ways of our Savior, they might be worth your cares and efforts.''

"Your pious buffler shit don't shine with this ol' hoss,'' Barlow snapped, spinning to face the missionary. "You jist keep your distance from me and keep your flappin' hole shut and we'll get on jist fine.''

Sterling looked as if he had swallowed a skunk.

"Now,'' Barlow continued, unforgivingly, "if you're done with your goddamn preachin' for this mornin', we best get movin'.''

Sterling turned and stalked off to where his wife and the other couple waited on their horses.

" 'Bout time you put an end to that goddamn noise,'' Watters said softly, almost managing a chuckle.

Barlow nodded. He had tried to stay away from the missionaries since they had left rendezvous. He just could never understand how someone could be so full of himself as to think he was the Almighty's personal messenger. He hated their proselytizing even more. He thought them fools for not realizing early on that they would never be able to convert him.

The rest of the trip was as uneventful as the earlier part had been. Not that it was easy. There were some places where the going was incredibly tough, and more than once they had to walk the horses and mules down some particularly steep mountain slope.

With the Indian women gone, the white women took over the cooking chores, if none of the other work. They proved to be thoughtful and creative and often directed their husbands to dismount and pick some herb or root or berry.

The stews they made were hearty, tasty, and a big surprise
to the two mountain men. And they always made sure that
Buffalo had a good portion, despite the fact that the huge
Newfoundland was quite capable of running down his own
food.

The women had been rather afraid of the pitch black dog
for some time, particularly after they saw him tear into a
small deer one time. But the dog had an innate charm that
began to win them over. And they soon realized that the
dog would, in all likelihood, protect them from just about
anything that might consider attacking them.

For his part, Buffalo loved the attention.

Barlow and Watters, with enough to do as it was, pressed
the two missionary men into some tasks, such as caring for
their wives' horses, gathering firewood, and such. The two
mountaineers loaded and unloaded the supplies, tended to
those animals, as well as their riding mounts. They would
put up the small tent the women used, as often as not start
the fires, since the others seemed incapable of it half the
time. They hunted, scouted the trail, hacked away at vegetation to clear a path when necessary, generally bucketed
up water, and more.

Finally, though, after more than two months on the trail,
they made it across the Cascades, and within days were in
the Willamette Valley.

27

"WHERE AWAY YOU want to go, Reverend?" Barlow asked Sterling.

"I suppose it would be proper to report in to the head man at Fort Vancouver," the missionary said thoughtfully. "What did you say his name was?"

"Doctor John McLoughlin."

"He's a physician?"

"I believe so."

"What do you know about him, Mr. Barlow?"

"Not much. Jist what the Injins 'round here told me when I was here last. And a few things I've heard from time to time."

"And . . . ?"

"I hear he's a big critter, maybe six and a half feet tall and weighty, too. The Injins says he's a fierce lookin' devil. I gather he scares the hell out of 'em. But I hear he's fair, usually, if you play fair with him."

"Sounds like a man who can be reasoned with."

"Reckon so. But . . . Well, he's a Scotsman, which means he's likely open to your idea of startin' a Methodist mission."

"That's encouraging, but you seem doubtful. Is this Doctor McLoughlin a . . . well, a man without religion as so many men out here seem to be?''

"I don't rightly know where he stands on such things, Reverend. My doubt comes from the fact that many of the men in his employ are French-Canadian.''

"And what would that—''

"They're Catholic, Mr. Sterling. And they have been here for quite some time. I hear tell they have Mass regularly, and I believe they've been workin' to convert many of the Injins hereabouts.''

"And Doctor McLoughlin allows such a thing to occur right under his nose?'' Sterling asked indignantly.

Barlow shrugged. "I don't know much more'n I jist told you. I expect if what I heard was true, then McLoughlin does allow it. Why? Probably to keep his employees happy. He is, after all, a businessman first.''

"This is disturbing news, disturbing news,'' Sterling muttered.

"Hell, look at it this way, Reverend. He might be happy to have another Catholic-hatin' minister in the area to work not only with the Injins, to counter the Catholic presence, but also to minister to his men who aren't Catholic, and there're a heap of those, too, I expect.''

"Well, yes, yes, that sounds right. He will welcome us with open arms so that we may tend to his soul and those of others.''

Barlow shook his head, thinking that Sterling was quite crazy. "You want to mosey on over there now? Or wait till tomorrow?''

"Now,'' Sterling said firmly. "We are here after a long journey, and to delay even another instant would be wasteful.''

The small group worked down the hill onto the flat alongside the mighty Columbia River. It was almost an hour before they managed to get a ferry across, but within minutes of hitting the northern shore, they were entering Fort Vancouver. Barlow felt a little funny about it all, considering the treatment he and Watters had given those three Hudson's Bay Company men a couple of years before. Not that he worried about it. If those men were here, and if they spotted him, and if they wanted to cause trouble, he would deal with it then.

McLoughlin's house/office was an imposing structure, and they all walked up the wide steps with a touch of trepidation. At the entry, a clerk asked their business and then went inside. He returned seconds later and invited everyone in. Barlow and Watters declined.

"There someplace here where we can fill our meat-bags?" Barlow asked.

"What's that, sir?" the clerk asked.

"There someplace where me and my friend can git something to eat?"

"Oh, of course. Down the stairs here and around toward the back to the house is the cook's area. Joseph is there, and he will fix you something."

"Much obliged."

The two hurried down the stairs and around the corner. Joseph turned out to be Joseph Beaubien. He was willing, if not overly eager, to fix them a meal. And he was almost petrified of Buffalo.

The two men sat at a table and drank some coffee while Beaubien cooked. Buffalo lay on the floor alongside his master. Barlow and Watters soon engaged Beaubien in conversation, and he grew friendlier. By the time the young French-Canadian served them a meal, it had grown from some plain meat to a succulent melange full of deer meat and a wide variety of vegetables, herbs, and spices "from ze garden out back," Beaubien said proudly.

"And for you, *Monsieur le grand chien*," he said to the dog, his voice quivering, "a big bone with plenty meat on it, eh?" He tentatively held out a deer thighbone, which indeed did have a fair amount of meat attached to it.

"Take it nice, Buffler," Barlow said quietly.

The dog reached out its huge head, the big jaws opened, and he gently plucked the bone out of Beaubien's fingers, much to the French-Canadian's surprise. "May I pet 'im?" he asked.

Barlow nodded, and Beaubien patted the Newfoundland's broad head, and began to smile.

The two Americans dug into the tasty stew—and hunks of freshly baked bread—with gusto, complimenting Beaubien with every other mouthful. So proud was Beaubien that he gladly served them a second helping, and then a third.

They finally sat back, sipping coffee into which Beaubien had poured a decent dollop of whiskey.

"Damn, a chil' could git used to sich doin's," a thoroughly satisfied Barlow noted.

"Hell, I'm settin' here wonderin' if ol' Joseph over there will let us move in here. We can sleep in back there where they do the cleanin' and such."

"*Vous êtes tres fou, monsieurs,*" Beaubien said with a laugh.

"Eh, what's that?" Barlow asked.

"How you say . . . ?" Beaubien started. Then an index finger drew circles in the air near one temple. ". . . Mad?"

Barlow and Watters roared with laughter. "That's a fact, ol' hoss," Barlow said.

Soon after, the two Americans rose. As they headed toward the door Barlow stopped and placed a couple of coins in Beaubien's hands.

"No, no, monsieur," Beaubien said, shocked. "Zis 'as been paid for by ze fort. Zere is no charge."

"I know that, boy. This is for you."

"But Monsieur *le docteur* pays me."

"I reckon he does, boy," Barlow said with a grin. "But I reckon he don't pay you near enough for what you do. Now you take this here specie and you put it aside for you to spend on somethin' for yourself, understand?"

Beaubien's headed bobbed. "*Mais oui! Mais oui!*" He grabbed the coins and stuck them in a pouch he had hanging inside his shirt. "*Merci beaucoup*, gentlemen!"

Barlow and Watters wandered outside and found a quiet spot along the stockade wall across the fort from McLoughlin's house, where they could watch for the missionaries. They sat, leaning against the log wall. Barlow absentmindedly petted Buffalo. He had almost dozed off when a flash of something bright against the misty green of the landscape caught his attention. His eyes popped fully open, and he watched, mouth agape, until the young woman had gone around the side of the nearby building out of sight.

"Damn, did I jist see what I thought I saw?" Barlow muttered.

"Hmmm, what's that, ol' hoss?" Watters asked sleepily. He had dozed off and was still basically asleep.

"Jist the most strikin' woman I ever saw," Barlow muttered.

But Watters was snoring and paid him no heed.

So Barlow sat and thought about the vision he had just seen. She was fairly tall and robustly womanish. He was sure of that despite the blanket coat she wore. Her hair was sort of black, but it had seemed to be tinged with red, making it shine, even through the drizzle. Her face was broad and strong, but still retained a delicacy that would have seemed out of place on anyone but her. Everything else about her was a blur to Barlow, but the impression of her as a whole was incredibly powerful. He leaned his head back against the wall again and just let the vision of the woman play over and over in his head.

The two missionaries and their wives eventually came out. Barlow whacked Watters on the arm. "Time to go, ol' hoss," he announced.

They rose and walked across the fort. Sterling nodded, and they got their mounts and headed for the ferry.

"Well, Reverend?" Barlow asked as they moved into the ferry. "How'd your palaver with ol' McLoughlin go?"

"He's a wonderful man," Sterling enthused. "Absolutely top notch. He's glad to see us and is behind us in all we would like to do. Indeed, he even promised us every help."

Barlow was skeptical, but said nothing about it. "So where away now?" he asked instead.

"Doctor McLoughlin suggested we stay the night right here along the Columbia. He mentioned a place up the . . .

Willamette River, I think he called it . . . for the mission.''

"Willamette is right. How far?''

"Fifteen, perhaps twenty miles. He said there's a small waterfalls there. We might be able to use that as a source of power for a mill or other such endeavor.''

Barlow nodded. "We can make it in one good long day of ridin' tomorrow, if you're of a mind to. Though I reckon that might be hard on the ladies.''

"That is a difficult choice, Mr. Barlow. I am most anxious to begin work on the mission. There is so much to be done. But, yet, we must think of the womenfolk. After all, while women are here to serve us, we are here to protect them.''

"Well, don't fret on it, Reverend. We'll see how it goes. If we make it, or if we don't, I expect it'll be God's will.''

"Most certainly,'' Sterling said, surprised, and more than a little pleased. Perhaps, he thought, he was getting through to the gruff mountain man.

With the rain much heavier than usual, making for slippery footing for the animals, the small party took two days to make the journey. They spent the first night near the Reverend Jason Lee's mission. Lee was hospitable enough but seemed a bit irked that he would soon have competition for his Indian converts.

The group moved on the next day, and by early afternoon, Barlow was riding out ahead of the others, searching for a likely spot to put the mission. When he found one, near the small falls as McLoughlin had suggested, he rode quickly back to the group and led them to what Sterling immediately declared the Promised Land.

Over the next couple of days, they set up a more permanent camp, one that would be in use for some time. Plenty of firewood was gathered and put under cover to keep it dry, meat was laid by, preserved by jerking over slow fires. While Barlow and Watters did most of the work, the Reverends Sterling and Fenwick spent most of their time planning their mission, sketching it in ink on papers brought all the way from the East Coast.

Finally the camp was done, and Barlow approached Sterling. "Me and Charlie'll be headin' out come mornin'," he said.

"What?" Sterling asked, startled.

Barlow repeated his statement.

"But you can't do that," Sterling sputtered.

"Ain't many men've told me I cain't do somethin' when I've set my mind to it and lived, ol' hoss. Best watch your words."

"No, no, I'm not *telling* you that you can't. I'm . . . Well, I don't know. I'm just taken aback by it is all."

"You shouldn't be." He nodded thanks as Prudence Sterling handed him a mug of coffee. She was really a pleasant-looking woman, Barlow thought for the hundredth time. Graceful yet strong, quick to smile, rarely complained no matter how tough things got. And, while she was correct in everything she did, Barlow thought he could detect a note of mischievousness in her dark brown eyes. But he had decided long ago that it would not be right to test whether that was true or not.

"Why shouldn't I be?" Sterling asked.

"Me'n Charlie have fulfilled our contract to you, Reverend. We was to bring you from the rendezvous on the Green River to the Willamette Valley. When you think on it, we completed our duties to you the minute we come over that hill and saw Fort Vancouver down below. But we spent a few extra days with you, guided you to here, hell, even found this spot for you. And we helped you get this place set up so's you and Reverend Fenwick can set to work on building your mission right away. There wasn't no call for us to do that. Not that we expect anything extra for it. We jist figured you and the ladies could use a little extra help. Now that's done, our duties've been fulfilled, and we'll be movin' on."

"But what will you do?"

Barlow shrugged. "Ain't given it much thought, really. I expect I'll head back over the mountains, see if I can find the boys before winter sets in."

"That won't be long, you know."

"I know. Don't know what else I could do. I suppose I could jist head over the Cascades and trap there for a while before winterin' up somewhere in the Sierra country."

"What about Mr. Watters?"

Barlow laughed. "Funny thing about ol' Charlie," he said, still chuckling. "He cain't keep that Nez Perce gal out of his head."

"Red Scarf?" Sterling was aghast.

"Yep. He's got a hankerin' for her somethin' awful." He looked at the two women. "Beggin' your pardon, ladies. I don't mean that in a sinful way, of course. It's jist that they was together mayhap four years or so, and he grew mighty fond of her. Anyway, he's figurin' on ridin' like the devil for the Nez Perce country and see if he can hunt up ol' Lame Dog's village before winter sets in."

Sterling forced himself not to say anything about that situation. It would do him no good to provoke an argument now with such a volatile man as Will Barlow. "Why don't you stay with us, Mr. Barlow?" he asked instead.

"And do what?" Barlow was surprised at the question. He was the last person he figured the missionaries would want to spend time with.

"Help me and Reverend Fenwick build the mission." He could hardly believe he was saying it. But, as much as he disliked the wild, pagan ways of this man, he also knew Barlow was hard-working, strong, and would be an asset in the construction of the buildings.

"You're funnin' with me, right?"

"I most certainly am not. I need the help, Mr. Barlow. Reverend Fenwick and I cannot do it alone."

The thought was absolutely ludicrous to Barlow. Why would he stay there? The trapping was poor. And he was not comfortable with the Hudson's Bay Company's Fort Vancouver so close by. Then a picture entered his mind— the vision of a young woman with red-tinted black hair and a full figure. He smiled at that thought. If he stayed in the vicinity, he could look for that woman. True, he disliked the missionaries, but on the other hand, if they got to be too troublesome, he could just pick up and ride off.

"I'll do it," he announced, not sure whether he or Sterling was the more surprised.

28

IT DIDN'T TAKE all that long for Barlow to find the woman he sought. He spotted her minutes after arriving the very next time he visited Fort Vancouver. He saw her across the fort's grounds and knew it was her, even at a distance. With Buffalo at his side, he headed in her direction and managed to get close enough to her for a good look—without seeming too obvious about it. He was relieved in a way to see that his first impression had been accurate.

Now his problem was getting to know her. He considered just introducing himself and trying to attract her interest. But she moved around the fort with a decided comfort, which indicated that she was just not any Indian woman. She had Indian in her, that was certain, but she was not a full blood. Because of that, and because of her mien, he figured she was the daughter of one of the white fort workers, not a trapper, and so was a station or two above the common folk around there. And she was certain to see him as common, considering his look and his profession.

He figured his best choice would be to find out who she was and then decide how to proceed from there. With that in mind, he wandered into the trade room and asked for a twist of tobacco. When he got it and paid for it, he asked the man behind the counter, "You know who that young woman is?" He pointed out the door.

"Aye, I do," the man answered warily. "Why d'ye want to know that, laddie?"

Barlow bit back the flippant remark that had bubbled up. He had caught the wariness in the man's tone, and he suspected this man either knew the woman or knew her parents and was protective of her. So, he simply said, "She looks a bit familiar is all. Like mayhap I knew her when she was just a chil'."

"I dunna think ye'd have known her then," the man said, seeming to relax a little. "I'm her pa, Duncan Stewart."

"Pleased to meet you, Mr. Stewart," Barlow said without the slightest hint of the shock he was suffering. "I'm Will Barlow."

"Aye, another Scotsman," Stewart said with a grin. He appeared to relax considerably.

"Well, I reckon so. But I've never been to the old country. My pa was born near Inverness, but he come over here when he was quite young."

"Ah, like so many others." He smiled a little. "But we have our ancestors in common, of course."

"Of course."

"My daughter's name is Sarah, Mr. Barlow." He paused, staring intently at his customer. "But did ye really think ye knew her?"

Barlow stared right back. "Nope," he said evenly. "But I was hopin' to git to know her. I think she's the most strikin' young woman I've ever seen."

Stewart was a little taken aback by Barlow's sincerity. He was, however, impressed with it, and by Barlow's forthrightness. He was uncertain, though, whether he would want this man courting his daughter. Barlow was an American, first off, and a mountain man besides. That meant he likely had rough-hewn ways. And poor prospects. On the other hand, Stewart had heard that this man had brought those new missionaries out here a few weeks ago. That might indicate that Barlow was ready to settle down. When it came down to it, Stewart decided that he'd sooner have this man court his daughter than any of the eligible young man in and around the fort.

"Are you askin' to court her, Mr. Barlow?" Stewart asked.

Barlow, who had been leaning on the counter, straightened. "Well, sir, I reckon I am," he said firmly.

"I have some misgivings aboot allowing that, Mr. Barlow. One of them is that I dunna know how long you're planning to stay in this area. Or what you'll do to support my daughter."

"Understandable qualms, Mr. Stewart. I aim to stay at least the winter here. I've pledged my word to Reverend Sterling and Reverend Fenwick to help them build their mission. Beyond that, I ain't so sure. But I can tell you this, Mr. Stewart, if I'm still courtin' your daughter by then, I'll find some way to make sure she's took care of properly."

Stewart thought about it for a bit, then nodded. "My house is almost half a mile upriver. Stop by tonight in time for supper. You don't mind Indian cooking, I assume?"

Barlow laughed. "This ol' hoss can eat nearabout anything, 'cept mayhap clams."

"I'll tell the missus to keep them out of supper," Stewart said with a smile. "And just one other thing."

"What's that?"

Stewart grinned again. "Just make sure your canine there behaves himself, eh?"

"Hear that, Buffler," Barlow said, patting the big dog's head, "you been invited to supper, too. But you best be on your best behavior."

Buffalo released a short, deep bark and wagged his tail.

"Hell of a dog you have there, Mr. Barlow,"

"That he is." Barlow turned and with Buffalo at his side, strolled out. He was a bit dazed at what had just happened. Not only had he seen the woman almost immediately, barely minutes later he was given approval to court her. It was startling in its speed and effortlessness.

Outside, he stopped, wondering what he should do. His

buckskins were filthy and rank, but Stewart had no cloth garments Barlow could buy. He figured that whenever a shipment came in that included clothes, they were sold off almost immediately. He wondered if he could borrow some more respectable clothes, but then he laughed at that. There were not very many men built like he was—average height, but twice that in broadness. He finally decided he would just clean himself up as best he could and not worry about his clothing too much. Stewart knew what he was like, and had no qualms about him that way.

Barlow found the Stewart home with no trouble. It was a simple wood structure, somewhat larger than he had expected, though it was not a very large place. Inside, it was comfortable, with plain, but sturdy and serviceable furniture. The walls had several drawings of what Barlow could only assume was Scotland.

His biggest shock came, however, when he met Mrs. Stewart—called Julia by her husband. He hoped he did not reveal his surprise when she turned, smiled brightly, and curtsied, giving him his first clear look at her. She would have been an almost plainly pleasant looking woman— were it not for the greatly sloping forehead. He smiled, still trying not to reveal his astonishment.

When he glanced at Stewart, the Scotsman was smiling. "Aye, 'tis a surprise to most who meet her for the first time. Unless you have come across Chinooks before."

"Cain't say as I have." Barlow nodded at Julia again, and the woman, not in the least embarrassed by her flattened head, turned back to her work.

" 'Tis a pity, really, but most of the Chinooks have disappeared. Diseases have dwindled their numbers almost to extinction."

"Ain't the only tribe that's happened to."

Stewart poured himself and Barlow a mug of whiskey and they sat in the small sitting room. Sarah was already there. She tried to ignore Barlow, and he pretended she was not there.

"To your health, sir," Stewart said, raising his glass.

"And to yours."

After a sip, Barlow asked, "So the Chinooks are the real Flatheads?"

"Real Flatheads?"

"There's a tribe back in the Rocky Mountains called the Flatheads, but they sure as hell don't have that attribute, as your wife does."

"Misnomers," Stewart chuckled. "So many Indians have suffered from that. But, yes, the Chinooks would be the real Flatheads. They strap their infants in their cradleboards and tie a board across their foreheads. That is how they get that look. A most barbarous practice."

"I don't mean to pry, Mr. Stewart, but does your wife lookin' that way bother you any?"

"Nae. It did at first, aye. But she was such a good woman that I soon overlooked it."

"That's sensible." He paused, then asked, "And I notice that you've not allowed your daughter to undergo such treatment."

"Nae, laddie. Oh, Julia wanted to, but I had to put my foot doon on that one." He chuckled.

"Also mighty sound, I'm thinkin'."

Soon they were sitting at the dining table and passing around dishes and platters of various foods, many of which Barlow had no idea of what they were. But everything was tasty enough, and Barlow wolfed it down, trying to be at least a little reserved in asking for extra helpings.

Afterward, Barlow and Stewart returned to the living room, while Sarah helped her mother. Then Sarah joined the men. Soon after, Stewart excused himself. Barlow was relieved to finally have a little time alone with Sarah, though he knew her father was only a few feet away in the kitchen.

Despite his relief, he was a little worried. He had no idea of what to say to this woman. "Your name is beautiful," he said hesitantly, feeling like a fool. "It fits you well."

"Thank you." She was shy, but not overly so.

"My name's Will. Will Barlow."

"Pleased to meet ye, Mr. Barlow."

"There's no need to be so formal, Sarah."

"Yes, sir."

Damn, Barlow thought. "Do you object to me courtin' you?" he suddenly asked.

"I dunna know if I can answer that, Mr. Barlow. I dunna know ye a'tall."

"Fair enough. Do you mind if I continue to come callin' on you? So we can get to know each other slowly."

"I think that'd be nice."

He suddenly felt much better.

Over the next few months, they saw more and more of each other. While Barlow spent a considerable amount of time helping the two missionaries build their mission, he also managed to get to Fort Vancouver—and a small cabin half a mile upriver from it—quite often.

Eventually, Sarah began riding out to where Barlow was staying. He had made a camp of his own a mile or so from where the mission was being built. She never stayed long, as she was expected back by her parents. Plus there was the fact that Barlow's shelter consisted of a rickety lean-to. Once she began visiting with some regularity, though, Barlow set about building a somewhat more substantial shelter. He built a framework of small logs over which he stretched a number of buffalo hides he had had from his journey there. It didn't take long to finish, and it certainly wasn't very pleasant to look at, but it was warm and, most important, dry. What it resembled was a buffalo-hide wickiup.

Sarah was genuinely impressed when she saw it for the first time. That he had managed to accomplish it with few tools and less time was a sign to her that the affection he was showing her was real.

"I want to see the inside," she said coyly.

"You sure?" Barlow asked, his groin tightening. He hoped it meant what he thought it meant.

"Very sure." Sarah reached up a slim finger and brushed it down his cheek. Inside, she turned to face him and kissed him hard. "It's about time we had a place to be alone."

"You want to be alone with this ol' chil' do you, woman?"

"Aye. Very much."

"You could be askin' for trouble."

She smiled and pecked him on the chin. "I dunna think so, Will."

He peeled her cloth dress off her and then fumbled with some undergarments that were new to him. She gladly helped. Then she was naked and she coyly posed for him.

"Oh, Lord A'mighty," he breathed. He had not felt like this about a woman since Plenty Robes, the Pawnee woman. Not even Mountain Calf had made him feel this way with just one look.

Sarah was fairly tall, a trait she had gotten from her father. She had the wide, womanly hips of her mother's people, full, substantial breasts with large areola, a slim, rising belly with a deep-set navel, and long, shapely legs.

Barlow practically tore off his clothes as Sarah lay on Barlow's two still fairly new otter-skin sleeping robes and watched. She gasped in delight when she saw that he was fully erect.

Barlow smiled and knelt on the sleeping robes near her feet. He kissed her toes and then trailed wet kisses and licks up one leg and then down the other. Heading northward again, he stopped at her sparse patch of red-tinged pubic hair, which surprised but excited him. Kneeling on his shins, he lifted her bottom, and she instinctively placed one leg on each of his shoulders. His mouth gently touched her womanhood, his tongue probing inside the delicious wetness. As his lips and tongue worked patiently on her labia and her pleasure bud, Sarah's buttocks began to wriggle in Barlow's hands. He became more insistent in his ministrations and she grew more and more frantic in her movements. Suddenly she shrieked loudly and stiffened for a second before intense shudders racked her.

When she had calmed down some, Barlow gently set her ass down and then slid up to kiss her, hard. Then he mouthed her nipples, while a hand stroked her womanhood with loving persistence. Before long, she climaxed again, her love tunnel clenching and unclenching on his fingers.

Unwilling to stop, Barlow continued what he was doing, and Sarah soon began a series of small peaks, each building on the previous ones, until a great shuddering climax shook her whole body.

When she had stopped quivering, he entered her, gently, slowly, firmly, his erectness stretching her soft, velvet walls. She gasped again, pleasure oozing through her, and he groaned with passion. He began sliding in and out of her, his strokes strong, resolute. His pace gradually increased and Sarah's pelvis rose and fell in perfect timing with his powerful thrust.

Barlow could feel his release building, and he began driving into her with a furious passion. Moments later, he roared as his climax tore through him and shot straight into Sarah, who bucked and clutched and grasped as her own passions peaked.

Wheezing a little, Barlow pushed himself over until he was lying next to her, not wanting to lie on her with his bulk. "Gooddamn," he gasped.

"Yes," Sarah panted in agreement.

29

BARLOW AND SARAH were married in the spring at the mission he had helped build. The Reverend Josiah Sterling performed the ceremony with mixed feelings. While he saw this as an opportunity to bring the young half-breed woman into the fold of his church, he was almost certain that Sarah was pregnant even as he read the solemn words. Then there was the fact that he was virtually certain by then that there was no hope that Barlow would ever change his sinful ways and embrace the church's teachings. He had been surprised—well, shocked, really—when Barlow had approached him about officiating over his marriage to Sarah, but soon realized that the mountain man had done it solely because Sarah and her family wanted it. Still, Sterling felt it his duty to perform the ceremony, and, being the pious, God-fearing man that he was, he harbored yet a kernel of hope that eventually Barlow would see the light, especially if Sarah took part in church services regularly.

The minister also looked on the post-wedding revelry as a time to proselytize to the multitude of whites who took part. While his main task was to convert Indians, he saw no reason to forget about the whites in the area, most of whom could use some considerable sermonizing judging by the behavior he had seen.

Because Duncan Stewart was a longtime employee of the Hudson's Bay Company, many of the British firm's employees attended the wedding and party afterward. Among them was Dr. John McLoughlin himself, whom Barlow had met on several occasions while conducting business at Fort Vancouver. Barlow hired Joseph Beaubien to supply the food for the party, paying him a decent sum on the side, because McLoughlin had offered the young man's services for free.

The day after the ceremony, Barlow began building a house for his new bride atop the little ridge at the spot where he and Watters had wintered the first time they had come to the Willamette Valley. Barlow had shown Sarah the site, and she had loved it as much as he did. With the creek right there, they had plenty of water. There was enough land without trees to do a little farming, yet the heavily wooded areas all around would provide plenty of fuel for their fires and would be teeming with game. The beaver trapping was not great, but there were some to be taken, as well as otter and other fur-bearing animals. The site was secluded, but there was little risk of Indian attack, as all the tribes in the area were rather peaceable. The couples' new home was only a few miles southwest of the mission. That kept the newlyweds far enough from the mission to not be disturbed too often, yet close enough that one could be of help to the other should the need arise. It was a little farther from her parents' home than Sarah might have liked, but she knew that Barlow wanted a little distance between him and Fort Vancouver, seeing as he was an American and this had always been thought of as British country. Not that he was afraid of anyone at the fort nor that he worried about McLoughlin sending men over to harm them, but he figured if he kept to himself, the British company would have no reason to think ill of him, and he did have to rely on the fort for supplies of all kinds.

Indeed, he got along fairly well with McLoughlin, as

well as some of the other men from the fort. Enough so,
that a group of the Hudson's Bay Company men came to
assist him in building his house. With their help, the
cabin was up in less than a week, and the newlyweds
moved in. Barlow and Sarah settled into a fairly comfortable lifestyle. He planted a garden but he also continued
to trap. And to hunt, often selling meat to Sterling's mission, other area missions, and at Fort Vancouver. Beaubien was always looking for fresh meat for the meals he
served to the Hudson's Bay Company officials, and was
willing to pay well for it, at least when Barlow brought it
in. The hunting and trapping kept Barlow out in the
countryside. He was a little too footloose to tie himself
down to a single patch of land and just sit there. Still,
there were times when he was alone in a little camp on
some overnight hunting trip when he would look wist-
fully at the Cascades and could envision the days when
he was wild and unfettered far east of those mountains.
More than once he considered just saddling up old Beelzebub and riding out. But he never did. He loved Sarah,
for one thing. And, for another, he knew those days were
gone forever. There was just no reclaiming the past.

Things were, for the most part, pretty quiet, and he was
generally quite content with his new life. He grew tired of
the rain more often than he would have liked, but there was
nothing he could do about that. And the only real trouble
he had was an occasional altercation with some of the Hudson's Bay men, generally over his being an American. And
those scuffles mattered little to him.

Right after the house was finished, Barlow gathered up
his furs and baled them. "You want to go to the fort with
me while I trade these plews in?" he asked his new bride.

"No. There's much for me to do here." She smiled,
happy. "Gotta make a good home for my husband."

"Jist you bein' in it makes it a good home, Sarah,"
Barlow said earnestly. He kissed her and finished saddling
Beelzebub. He pulled himself onto the mule. With Buffalo
trotting alongside and a string of pack mules behind him,
Barlow rode off. He took his time, and spent a night out

in the open on the way. He could not see pushing the mules hard enough to make the twenty-five miles or so to the fort in one day.

As he pulled into the fort, he was feeling good about things. Marriage to Sarah was setting well with him, and he figured that any minor troubles he had with the Hudson's Bay Company men would lessen even more now that he had married one of their daughters. He couldn't help but wish that his father-in-law was one of the traders for the fort, since he figured that would assure him of getting the best price possible for his furs. He wasn't sure he could trust the company's traders being entirely fair with him because he was an American. He had found out just after beginning to court Sarah, though, that her father had only been running the trade room temporarily the day they met while the other traders were off doing some tasks. Stewart, instead, was one of McLoughlin's top clerks, a position of considerable responsibility.

Barlow stopped at the trade room and dismounted. Inside, Peter MacDougal was behind the counter. He greeted Barlow politely if not overly warmly.

"I brung in my plews, Mr. MacDougal."

"Aye. Let's look them over."

They went outside and MacDougal spent some time checking the collection of beaver, otter, bear, and ferret hides. Then they returned inside, where MacDougal did some figuring with pencil and paper. "Six hundred thirty-two dollars is what I owe ye, Mr. Barlow," MacDougal said in his thick Scottish burr.

Barlow stood there speechless for a few moments, stunned by the announcement. Then the shock gave way to a rapidly rising anger. "You goddamn thief, you," he snapped. He ignored the group of men who had entered the room. "You think that I'm gonna accept such a paltry goddamn amount for all them plews, you skunk-humpin' piece of shit? Such miserable doin's don't shine with this chil'."

" 'Tis all they're worth, Mr. Barlow," MacDougal said evenly. He shrugged. "I canna' change that."

"Like hell that's all them plews're worth. You goddamn parsimonious son of a bitch."

"That's enough of such talk, Mr. Barlow," MacDougal said, anger building. "I've given ye the best price I can, sir. And only because ye're a relative of my friend Duncan Stewart."

"And I say you're a lyin' sack of buffler shit," Barlow snarled. "You closefisted bastard, I'll—"

"That'll be enough of such talk, mate," someone said from a few feet to Barlow's left side.

The American turned and for the first time noticed the six Hudson's Bay Company men who had come into the small trade room. "One of you fractious sacks of shit have somethin' to say?"

"Aye, mate," a big Englishman said, bulling forward to stand in front of Barlow. "Mr. MacDougal has told you what your furs are worth here, mate. Either accept his offer or take your furs elsewhere."

"This ain't no concern of yours, ol' hoss," Barlow said tightly.

"We're makin' it our concern, mate. Mr. MacDougal is a fellow employee of the Hudson's Bay Company. Besides, we've got business here, and you're delayin' us in that business."

"Et vous etes l'Americane," another man said, his accent and clothing identifying him as a French-Canadian.

"You bet your froggie little ass I'm an American, boy," Barlow growled. "And I'm goddamn proud of it, too." He looked back at the Englishman. "Now, you jist stand here quietlike till me and Mr. MacDougal're done with our business. Or you and me're gonna tangle."

"Your business with the trader is done, mate." The Englishman aimed a punch at Barlow's face.

Barlow dodged the blow and kneed the Englishman in the stomach. As he stepped to the side, Barlow grabbed his foe by the back of the head and slammed his face onto the counter, then released him. The Englishman slumped to the floor.

The other HBC men tried to charge Barlow, but the

confines of the small area, as well as the Englishman lying on the floor, prevented it. Barlow managed to club one man in the face, sending him reeling back into his fellows, slowing the entire assault. Buffalo growled and barked.

"C'mon, Buffler," Barlow said, as he plunged forward, stepping on the Englishman to give himself some impetus. He and the huge dog plowed into the knot of men almost as one, driving the whole throng back and out the small door, where the entire passel of them tumbled down the two steps and fell into a loose pile.

Everyone scrambled up and watched each other warily—Barlow and a snarling two hundred fifty pound Newfoundland against five HBC men. "Well, boys, don't jist stand there," Barlow snapped after some moments of inaction. "I ain't got all day to watch you scratch yourselves."

The five charged. With a wild-animal howl that blended with Buffalo's growls, Barlow waded into the rushing horde of men. Amid the flailing fists, wild kicks, the screeches and yells and snarls, men went flying this way and that. Barlow was in his element now, feeling a little rush of pleasure each time his knuckles hit flesh or a foot connected with bone. He hardly felt any of the blows that fell on him.

Barlow had the impression that other men had joined the fray, but he couldn't be sure. He just knew it seemed as if there were an unending army of men coming at him and the dog as the two kept knocking enemies down, or sent them scurrying. Many of those who stumbled out of the circle of fighting came away with chunks of flesh missing to the Newfoundland's teeth or with bones fractured from the wild man in the midst of the cyclone.

Then someone was able to get close enough to crack Barlow on the back of the head with a big piece of wood grabbed from the firewood pile near the bakery. He staggered but did not go down. Still, it slowed him enough that his other enemies were able to swarm all over him and bring him down. Not that it was easy keeping him there. His strength was prodigious, but they managed.

"Lock him up, mates," someone ordered.

Someone hit Barlow on the head with the small log again, dazing him and knocking most of the remaining fight out of him. He was jerked roughly to his feet. Despite his dizziness, he noted with satisfaction that at least seven men were sitting or lying around clutching at various injuries.

Buffalo had backed off a little and was growling and barking in fury. One man raised a pistol and began to aim it at the dog. Barlow had enough energy left to kick it out of his hand, while yelling, "Go, Buffler. Git!"

The Newfoundland hesitated only a moment before turning and racing away.

Barlow looked at the man who was in charge. He didn't know the man's position in the company, but he knew Ian Wordsworth was something of a sergeant-at-arms around the fort. "Anybody tries to shoot Buffler, and I'll rip his goddamn heart out from him. Wordsworth, you understand me?"

"Your dog'll not be hurt—unless he attacks someone," Wordsworth said in a way that let the others know that he meant it. Wordsworth was a fair man, and Barlow believed him. "Now lock Mr. Barlow up."

Barlow was dragged away and confined in a small storeroom, where he languished for more than a day. The only one he saw during that time was Joseph Beaubien, who brought him two meals, both excellent.

"I feed you good, eh, *mon ami*?" Beaubien asked.

"You've treated me right well, Joseph," Barlow responded with a nod.

McLoughlin and MacDougal gave Barlow a day and a half to calm down before paying him a visit. The Hudson's Bay Company's chief for the entire Oregon region was a wild-maned giant of a man—six-foot-four or so, weighing two hundred and fifty pounds or a bit more. With the shock of white hair and a stern visage, he was enough to put the fear of God into just about any man. Despite his own bulk and tenacity, Barlow did not want to tangle with McLoughlin unless absolutely necessary, though he was not really afraid of him.

"So, lad," McLoughlin said, his voice sounding like thunder rolling over the mountains, "I understand ye do nae agree wi' the amount ye were offered for your furs. Is that right?"

Barlow nodded. "That's right. Hell, I knew I wouldn't get nearly what I'm used to, since I ain't devoted most of my time to trappin', but goddamn, that paltry offer MacDougal made was a goddamn insult to this ol' chil'. I figure he was tryin' to underpay me 'cause I'm an American and not one of your employees, even though I'm married to the daughter of a man who's been in your employ for many a year. That don't shine with this chil' at all neither.''

"Can ye read?"

"Some."

"And do sums?" McLoughlin asked.

Barlow nodded.

McLoughlin turned to his clerk. "Show Mr. Barlow the books, Mr. MacDougal," he said.

Barlow looked over the books, face growing grim as he did. He still found it hard to believe, but he had been paid the same rate as most of the HBC men and free British trappers, getting a bit more than some, a bit less than others, based on the quality of the furs that had been brought in.

Barlow finally handed the book back. "It's that bad?" he asked, knowing in his heart the truth of it.

"Aye."

Barlow nodded, accepting it, though he was sick in the pit of his stomach. He had known beaver would never shine again like it did a few years ago, but it was far worse than he had expected. "So what happens now?" he asked, his spirits low.

"Depends on ye, sir," McLoughlin said as softly as his thunderous voice would allow. "If ye promise to nae attack any of my men again, I'll set ye free and we'll forget all about this little ruckus ye caused."

''I'll still git what Mr. MacDougal offered for my plews?''

''Aye.''

With a nod, Barlow agreed.

30

IT WAS A night they would not soon forget. In all the time he had been in this part of the Oregon country, Barlow had never seen such a storm. While it might rain damn near all the time here, rarely was there lightning or thunder, and even rarer were the times when the thunder, lightning, and howling, screeching winds ripped through the countryside.

It was, by all accounts, a hellacious night on which baby Anna Barlow chose to make her appearance. Barlow and Sarah had planned to have Sarah's mother here, and possibly some of the other women married to Fort Vancouver employees. They knew what to do and would make Sarah as comfortable as possible under the circumstances, and they would keep Barlow out of the area. This was not for men to deal with.

But the storm had blown up so hard and so swiftly, and Sarah's labor began much too suddenly to allow Barlow to get out and bring back the women. He would have to take care of her. And that thought scared the hell out of him. He had no clue of what to do, which worried him no end.

They had been taking their ease when the first hint of the storm made itself known. Its sudden fury startled Barlow, and he sprang out of his chair and pulled on his thick,

Hudson's Bay blanket-coat. With Buffalo at his side, he hurried outdoors and quickly battened down whatever he could, making sure the mules were as safe and comfortable as they could be. He tied down oiled canvas over the wood-pile to both keep it dry and prevent any of the wood from being blown about. Loose gear was put inside the makeshift stable or lashed to trees.

Before he could finish these endeavors, the rain came with a rush and a fury that Barlow had seldom seen any-where. Even with his thick blanket-coat, he was soon wet through and shivering. He worked a little longer, growing more irritable by the moment. Finally, he snarled at the downpour and then grinned at Buffalo. "Come on, boy," he said, "it's time we was inside out of this fractious storm."

Buffalo, who did not look at all concerned at this strange weather, was nonetheless happy to head for the warm, dry cabin.

The house wasn't the best one Barlow had ever seen, but he had worked hard on it in the months since he and Sarah had married, and it was quite comfortable. It leaked only a little, and the fireplace was well-suited to keeping the small dwelling warm in the relatively mild winters of the area.

Sarah grinned when the dripping dog came in and shook himself, flinging water all over the place. She was more sympathetic to Barlow, and she waddled over to help him remove his coat. "Go," she said, "sit by the fire. It'll take the chill off you."

Barlow nodded. He needed no encouragement to do as she suggested, and he sat in the rocking chair he had bought at Fort Vancouver when it had arrived by ship from En-gland. It was his prized possession in the house, mostly because he planned to make it Sarah's once the baby was born.

Minutes later, Sarah served him a cup of hot tea.

Barlow sipped a little as Sarah awkwardly eased herself down to the floor, where she sat between Barlow's legs. He held his tin mug in one hand and used his other hand to stroke his wife's glossy, red-tinted black hair. "I sure hope that chil' don't pick this night to come out," he said jokingly.

Sarah grabbed his hand and held it to her cheek for a moment. "If it happens, it happens," she said calmly.

"Easy for you to say, woman," he joshed. "You don't have to do anything but squat there and shoot that young'n out! I'd have to handle all the hard doin's."

"Oh, hush," Sarah said with a small laugh. "If the baby comes, you will do whatever you need to. And you will do it well." She sighed with happiness, still holding his hand to her soft cheek.

Barlow smiled into the dimness of the lantern light. He was happy here with Sarah. He had never thought he could come to love a woman as he did her. But he had found that over the past year, since he began seeing her, he had come to love her greatly. It still startled him in some ways. But he did not question it. He just accepted the fact and appreciated that she seemed to feel just as deeply about him.

An hour later, Barlow jerked awake when Sarah gasped in pain and clenched the underside of his thigh. "What?" he mumbled, still groggy.

"It is time," Sarah said, her voice slightly strangled.

Barlow was afraid of very little in this world, but for a few moments, a fear like he had never experienced wormed into his stomach. *What was he to do about this?* he wondered. *This was woman's business.* He had no idea of what to do for her, or even if there was anything he could do.

"You sure?" he asked.

"Aye," Sara grimaced as another contraction bit into her.

"What can I do?" he asked.

"First, help me up and to the other room. The rest you will know when it's needed."

Barlow had his doubts, but he pushed himself up, careful to get over Sarah, who was still sitting on the floor. He knelt and then stood, bringing her up with him. Even as close to term as she was, she was no effort for him to lift and set on her feet. She waddled off to the small room, partitioned off with blankets that they used for sleeping. As she pushed aside one of the blankets, she turned. "Eat something," she said with a smile. "You might need your strength soon." She laughed a little.

"What about you?" Barlow asked.

"I'm nae hungry, Will," Sarah said with another small laugh.

"I didn't mean that." He was becoming a little exasperated.

"I know. I'll call you when I need you."

Barlow nodded and turned toward the fire. He squatted in front of it, carving strips of meat off the deer haunch dangling near the flames, nicely roasted a while ago, and now there just to keep it warm. He chewed quietly, feeding pieces to Buffalo. The occasional noise from Sarah inside the bedroom area startled him each time, but gradually the surprise eased. Or else it was drowned out by the storm, which seemed to have increased in fury within the last half-hour or so.

Finally Barlow took a seat in the chair again and was soon dozing, lulled to sleep by the steady rumble of thunder, the pounding hiss of the rain, and the howling of the wind. None of it frightened him. He'd heard far worse in some places up in the mountains. In his snug little cabin, he was safe, dry, and warm.

The next thing he knew, Sarah was calling him. As he jerked out of the chair, he noticed that the fire had burned low. Several hours had passed. He almost tore down a blanket as he charged into the bedroom. Sarah was squatting, holding on to a bedpost as she grunted in the throes of labor.

Not knowing what to do, really, Barlow knelt beside her and wrapped a large arm around her. "Decided to go about it the old way, did ye, woman?" he asked, trying to hide the return of fear that had bitten into him. "Like your ma?"

Sarah nodded and released a grunt of assent, though she did not look at him. Her face coated with sweat, was a mass of furrows and contorted muscles.

Time and place seemed to fade for Barlow. He was unaware of what he was doing or of time passing. He blanked out for a spell, while not really losing consciousness, noting only a few moments here and there—like suddenly finding himself making a sort of basket with his hands, into which the baby dropped. He dimly remembered a knife appearing in Sarah's hand, and she did something with it under her stained skirt.

Then Sarah was taking the wrinkled bundle of new baby from him and was cleaning it. He started to wake from the fog somewhat when Sarah handed the infant back to him.

Sarah smiled despite her fatigue, and then lay on the big four-poster bed. It, too, had come from England, but Barlow had gotten a good deal on it when the original buyers couldn't come up with the cash. Sarah reached out her arms, smiling through the sweat and tiredness on her face. Barlow gingerly handed her the squirming bundle of child— a girl, he noted dumbly.

"Anna," Sarah said as she took her new daughter. "We call her Anna."

Barlow nodded. The name was fine by him. He stood there and watched as Anna hungrily fed at Sarah's breast. He had never been so close to a birth before, and it was both thrilling as well as unfathomable to him. But he suddenly knew that he would always have a special bond with Anna—a bond born of his physical proximity to her birth and of the rare and hellacious storm that still roared around the isolated cabin.

Barlow found himself quite comfortable in his new role as father. He adored his little girl and spent as much time with her as he could. He found a deep fulfillment in playing with her, especially when he was rewarded by her frequent giggles.

Sarah was almost startled at the change in her husband. She loved just sitting there and watching the two of them, often joined by the giant dog, enjoying their little games. She was even more surprised at the gentleness shown by Buffalo. The great, shaggy dog was as gentle as a lamb with the girl. He would, though, turn into a snarling, two-hundred-fifty-pound terror if he thought the infant was in danger.

Oh, Barlow still had a bad case of itchy feet and as often as not would be out wandering around the rainy woods, hunting and trapping. But the knowledge that he had a warm, wonderful wife and a darling, adored daughter to return to had a powerful draw on him, and his excursions frequently were shorter and closer to home.

That became even more true when Will Jr. was born a little more than two years later. With the birth of his son, Barlow realized that his truly free days were over, and it surprised him that he didn't care. He was content with what he had. He would be absolutely lost, he sometimes thought, if something were to happen to his family, but he did not really worry about it much when he was home, only when he was away from them.

Barlow found it a little hard at times to believe he had become so settled. He wasn't that old and he still had a little bit of a wild streak about him, but he was considerably domesticated and didn't mind. He occasionally chuckled when wondering what his father would think of him now. Not that he really cared what the old man thought; it was just humorous to him that he had turned out pretty much the way the family had wanted him to be—and a way he had fought against since he was a child.

The change in Barlow was even more evident in the fact that he would do whatever he thought necessary to provide as well as he could for his family. He wasn't much of a farmer, but the amount of rainfall in the area, plus the mostly mild temperatures, made up for a lot of his agricultural deficiencies. He also continued trapping, though he put less and less time into it because of the diminishing returns, though he could always make some extra money bringing in wolf, fox, bear, and other hides. And he hunted, both for food as well as cash. He still helped out at the mission on occasion, though he was no more fond of the Sterlings and Fenwicks. Occasionally he even went into horse trading with the Cayuses over the Cascades. The first time he did so, in the company of a man from Fort Vancouver, he was a little nervous, remembering the battle he and Watters had had with those Indians several years earlier. But either the Cayuses didn't remember or no longer cared, and he was readily accepted.

He took Sarah to services at Sterling's mission each Sunday. She had insisted on going, though she knew better than to try to make him take part. Barlow would fish in the Willamette River or just nap under some trees while Sarah was there. Usually afterward, they would ride somewhere perhaps halfway to the Columbia, where they would meet Sarah's parents for a picnic lunch.

Barlow regularly rode into Fort Vancouver, often bringing meat and sometimes his furs. Sarah accompanied him at times, but he usually went alone, at least at first. The men who worked at the fort were still wary about him for some time because of the fight he had had with their friends that time, but within a few months of his marriage, that was forgotten, and while they would never accept him as one of them fully, they at least began to treat him with respect.

At that point, and especially after Anna was born, he would take the family to the fort with him more often than not. Sarah and Anna enjoyed the excursions. They got to see Sarah's parents and her friends, and Anna soon had friends among the children who lived in and around the fort. Barlow knew they were safe there, and as long as they were with him, he would not have to worry about them. Even if they were alone at the fort while he was conducting business, others would watch over them.

That was proved one day when one of the fort workers, a young Englishman named Harry Stiltoe, found Barlow enjoying a meal in Joseph Beaubien's domain under the factor's house.

"Not to anger ye, Mister Barlow," Stiltoe said, taking off his ragged cap and holding it nervously in his hands, "but one of the clerks told me to fine ye and let ye know that your woman and child were accosted by a couple of men."

Barlow's face hardened and he set his fork down. "Boys from the fort here?" he asked tightly.

"Nah. Was Yanks." Stiltoe sounded almost proud. Or at least relieved.

Barlow's eyes widened. "You certain, boy?"

"Aye." Stiltoe made his face mostly blank again. "But the clerk said ye shouldn't worry. Some of our lads sent them Yanks packing."

"Where's my family now?" Barlow asked harshly.

"At the trade room, with Mister Stewart."

Barlow nodded. He gobbled down a few more mouthfuls of food. "Where's them boys who accosted my family?"

"In the fort's pub." Stiltoe thought he knew what was coming next, so he added, "Their names are Cochrane and Beecham."

Barlow nodded once more and shoveled the last of the food into his mouth. He stood. "Thankee kindly, Joseph," he said to the cook, his words garbled by the food.

"De rien," Beaubien said shyly. He enjoyed the company of the bulky American.

"C'mon, Buffler," Barlow said, as he stalked out, clapping his hat on as he did. He strode quickly across the compound and slammed into the cabin in the far corner that served as a saloon for the fort's workers and visitors. He and the dog stopped just inside the door and surveyed the place. It took him but a few seconds to spot the two Americans, who seemed to stand out among the French-Canadians, Scotsmen, Englishmen, and other assorted men who were longtime inhabitants in this country.

Barlow stalked straight up to where they leaned on the bar, grabbed each one with a big hand and jerked them halfway around, splashing whiskey from their cups all over them and the bar.

"What the hell . . . ?" One of the two sputtered. He was tall, with big round shoulders, a mean face, and a long, scraggly beard.

"You two shit piles the ones who waylaid my family a bit ago?" Barlow demanded.

"What? That ol' squaw and her brat?" the other one questioned. He was of medium height, but looked hard and tough—until one powerful blow from Barlow's right fist turned him into a crumpled heap on the floor.

Barlow looked at the other. "You're one lucky ol' cuss, boy," he said through gritted teeth.

"Oh? Why's that?" the man asked casually, despite his partner lying with a broken jawbone at his feet.

"Because if you had harmed my wife or chil', you'd have been gutted and hided already, boy."

"Sheee-it, son. Jist 'cause you snuck a punch in on ol' Cochrane there don't mean you'll have the same luck with this ol' hoss."

"Ain't no luck needed, boy," Barlow said, voice even but deeply threatening. "When someone aims to molest my family, I don't need no goddamn luck."

"Got the hair of the bear on ya, do ya, boy?" But he kept a wary eye on both Barlow and the Newfoundland. Truth be told, the dog scared him a lot more than the man did. "Hell, it was jist a squaw. I ain't ever seen a man git so ruffled over someone looking to sport a little with a squaw."

"Listen to me good, you walkin' pile of buffler shit," Barlow snapped. "You ever cross my path again and I'll carve you a new asshole just before I cut your heart out and feed it to Buffler here."

The dog growled just a little, as if eager to have such a treat.

"Keep that damn dog away from me, boy," Beecham snapped. "And keep yourself away from me, too, if you know what's best."

Without hesitation or warning, Barlow slammed a powerful fist into Beecham's midsection. The blow cracked several ribs and knocked the wind out of Beecham, who doubled over, wheezing, his face red. Barlow took the man's greasy hair in hand and pulled his face up a little bit. "That squaw is my wife, you goddamn oaf. And that little gal is my young'n. I don't take kindly to folks molestin' 'em. Now I could easy slit your throat here, boy, nice as you please, were I of a mind to do so. But doin' so don't suit this chil' right now. But I'll tell you again, ol' hoss, but this one last time only—git your ass out of this territory and stay the hell out. You don't, and I'll make wolf bait of you as sure as I'm standin' here holdin' your life in my hands right now. You understand me, boy?''

Beecham gargled out an affirmative, looking pained.

''Good. Now let's jist send you on your way.'' He spun, still holding Beecham's hair. He now grabbed the back of the bent-over man's belt and began duck-walking him toward the door of the saloon. A few feet from it, he launched Beecham, whose head ran smack into the log wall of the building, to the left of the door. He sank like a stone.

''Well, damn,'' Barlow said easily, ''I've never known my aim to be that far off.'' He did not seem very concerned. He strolled over, grabbed the back of Beecham's shirt in one hand and dragged him outside. Moments later, he performed the same service for Cochrane, who was still unconscious. After a quick swallow of whiskey, Barlow walked out, followed by a bounding Buffalo.

Barlow thought hard for some time after that, wondering what he should do. If his wife and child could not be safe even here at the fort, where would they be safe? Any harm to Sarah or Anna would destroy him. He was in a quandary about it, but within days, Sarah had talked some sense into him. But every now and again, a twinge of fear at the possible loss of his family ate at him. Sarah and Anna—and Will Jr., when he came along—were all he had. Or wanted.

31

BUFFALO WAS ACTING mighty strange, Barlow thought, as he watched the big Newfoundland. The dog would stop and start, then wander in front of Barlow's mule, most of the time whining softly. Barlow finally pulled to a stop and sat there atop Beelzebub, trying to determine what was making the dog so jittery. But there was nothing that he could tell. He dismounted and tied the mule—and the two pack mules laden with fresh meat—to a tree and walked a little off before stopping again. He stood stock still, a hand lightly brushing Buffalo's head.

He wasn't sure, but he thought he smelled smoke, which wasn't all that unusual around those parts. They were only about half a mile from home. There were probably Indian villages nearby, he thought.

Looking at the Newfoundland, Barlow said, "Calm down, Buffler. It's likely jist a camp somewhere nearby." He turned, got his mule, mounted up and rode out slowly, as he had been. The remnants of a cold rain dripped from the needles of pine trees. It had stopped raining, and, indeed, the clouds had split, allowing the weak sun to poke through, though it brought little heat. It wouldn't last long, but it was a pleasant break from the usual grayness and gloom.

Buffalo was still nervous and acting strangely, but Barlow could not figure out what it was. But the closer they got to home, the more irritable the dog became.

"This don't shine with me one goddamn bit," Barlow muttered. Buffalo was so well-behaved around him that the man knew something serious must be bothering the dog, and it did not appear to be something wrong with the dog himself. He tried to put it out of his mind and think of his family instead.

Barlow thought of how glad he would be to get back to his home and family. It was fall, and the rain that so often fell was chilling. He looked forward to being in his warm cabin, the sounds of his children around him, the comfort of feeling his wife's naked flesh next to him as he slept. A man couldn't ask for more than that.

His pleasant thoughts were disrupted by Buffalo's increasing jitteriness, and it annoyed him. That worried him. Something was definitely wrong here.

Barlow jerked the mule to a halt, slid out of the saddle, and knelt. "C'mere, Buffler. C'mon, boy." When the dog came over and licked his face, Barlow said, with worry creeping into his voice, "There somethin' wrong at home, boy? That what you're tryin' to tell me?"

Buffalo's tail wagged so hard his whole rump shook from it as he backed away and barked. He came forward, nudged Barlow several times on the chest, and then backed away again, barking some more.

Barlow nodded. With fear wrapped around his heart like an icy blanket, he mounted the mule and rode off, slapping the animal with his hat until he was galloping. He didn't worry about the pack animals behind him. They would keep up or he would leave them behind. This was no time to dawdle.

Once he saw that his master was moving, Buffalo turned and raced ahead, going pretty much full out, keeping several yards ahead of Beelzebub, leading the way, tongue lolling out as his big body heated up from the exertion.

• • •

The cabin was still smoldering when Barlow thundered up the little rise and jerked his blowing mule to a halt. It was eerily silent—with no sound of birds or insects; just the hiss of an occasional drop of old rain as it hit hot wood and evaporated. The cabin was still mostly standing, its front door agape. A portion of it had collapsed, but the fire had not fully taken hold.

Rifle in hand, Barlow dismounted slowly. Buffalo stood there, panting from the run, but looking eager to get to the bottom of this strange mystery. Barlow was wary, though he was certain no one else was around. Leaving the mule where it was, he edged toward the cabin, fear and sickness twisting his stomach into a painful knot. He stopped, leaning against the door jamb and peeked inside. Bile rushed up into his throat, and he had to swallow hard to keep it from spewing out.

"Goddamn son of a bitch," he hissed quietly. He eased away from the door and cautiously but quickly searched the area, making sure there was no one around. Then, with heavy heart and the frigid clutch of loss eating at him, he slowly made his way back to the cabin.

He stopped at the doorway, trying to steady himself, steel himself for what he was about to see. But it did no good. With an annoyed growl at himself, he stepped inside and lit a lantern. And almost immediately wished he hadn't done so.

The light splashing across the room showed two bodies lying a few feet apart in puddles of fairly fresh blood. Barlow knelt beside Sarah, who was facedown. He gingerly rolled her over, and had to turn his head away. He had seen worse, but never to the woman he loved. She was almost naked, her white-woman's dress cut and torn away from her front. He assumed she had been raped, repeatedly, before they had carved her up. Her face was frozen in a rictus of agony and shame.

Barlow closed his eyes against the horror, but it did no good. He could still clearly see in his mind's eye the gaping, jagged wounds in Sarah's fragile body. He groaned with the pain of his loss, unable to move, unwilling to do anything right then.

Still, he had to check on Little Will and Anna. He finally opened his eyes, rose, and went the few steps to the other corpse that was in plain sight. Buffalo was nuzzling the small form, whimpering some more, as if trying to wake the little one. The dog looked up at Barlow with sad eyes, as if asking, "Why won't the baby wake up?"

Barlow gagged when he saw that they had dashed Little Will's brains out on the floor before slitting his throat so deeply that he had almost been decapitated.

In a low, pain-ravaged voice, Barlow moaned a string of curses that would have scorched the cabin walls had they not already been charred. The often unintelligible words poured forth like a fount of venom, an unending stream of vulgar vitriol.

Buffalo whined some more, nuzzling first Sarah and then Little Will, wanting them to get up and feed him or play with him. This was not right, the Newfoundland knew, and he just wanted his people to stop being this way.

Barlow's oaths stopped in midstream, and he sat a moment, mouth hanging open. "Anna!" he whispered finally. "Where are you, darlin'?" He jumped up, eyes frantically searching the main room of the two-room cabin. Not seeing another body, he ran into the other room. No one was there either.

"Anna!" he yelled, racing out of the house. *"Anna!"* He stopped, waiting to hear the almost three-year-old's voice. But only the wind came to him. He knelt. "All right, Buffler," he said urgently, "we've got to find Anna. Understand me, dog? We got to find our little girl. Can you find her for me? Can you?"

Barlow didn't know whether the dog understood or not, but the Newfoundland suddenly trotted off into the woods, with Barlow close behind.

An hour's search ended fruitlessly. Barlow and Buffalo had searched all around the cabin. A couple of times, Barlow thought the Newfoundland had picked up a scent, but it never seemed to go anywhere. He even went across the stream with the dog and checked there, figuring that the Indians who had committed these heinous acts had probably used the stream to cover their tracks. Thinking they might have ridden or walked in the water for some distance before coming out, Barlow had Buffalo work both banks for more than a mile in each direction.

But after all of that, he found nothing. With a heart as heavy as one of the steamboats that plied the Willamette and Columbia Rivers, he turned back toward the cabin. As he trudged along, sick, sad, enraged, he realized that if there was any ray of light in all this horror it was the fact that he hadn't found Anna. That meant she was alive! And, unless she caused too much trouble, she would stay alive. She was too young to molest and kill. She would be given to some family in the perpetrators' band to be raised as one of their own. He stopped, confusing the dog for a moment, as the vow formed in his head: I will not let them keep her. And then came out in words: "I'll find you, Anna, and bring you back!" he bellowed to the sky.

"C'mon, Buffler," he said, a sense of urgency clutching him, "we got work to do." He began trotting toward the cabin.

He set his rifle down against the rickety log fence he used as a corral, and climbed inside. A minute later, he had two more mules tied to Beelzebub and the two pack mules, which had showed up while he had been looking for Anna. He went inside, after taking some moments to steel himself, and found a couple of the thick Hudson's Bay blankets both he and his wife favored for sleeping as well as for making into warm winter coats. He carefully wrapped Sarah's body in one, heedless of the sticky, coagulating blood he got on himself. He carried the blanket-wrapped corpse outside and tied it to one of the mules. Then he went back and did the same with Little Will's body, fighting back sobs all the while.

Just before leaving, he pulled an arrow out of an outside cabin wall. He wasn't sure what tribe it was from, but he was certain someone at Fort Vancouver would know and tell him who perpetrated this abominable outrage. He wrapped it in buckskin and slipped it down the back of his shirt. Barlow pulled himself onto the mule and got moving, his face grim, hard as hate and rage and sorrow fought for dominance.

Just after darkness had fallen, he rode into the small compound of Sterling's mission. He dismounted and pounded on the door until Prudence Sterling—looking mighty annoyed at the disturbance—answered it.

Prudence was startled to see him. ''Mr. Barlow!'' she said in surprise. ''Whatever are you doing here at this hour?''

''Your husband inside?'' Barlow demanded.

''Well, yes. Come in.'' She was frightened by the positively savage look of the former mountain man.

''Send him out here, please, ma'am,'' Barlow said, making an effort to be civil.

''But . . .''

''Now, ma'am!''

Wide-eyed with shock and fear, Prudence spun and ran down the hallway, calling to her husband.

Sterling came out of a room at the end of the hall, wondering what the commotion was about. Prudence stopped and mumbled a few words to him, and pointed toward the door. Sterling hurried that way. ''What can I do for you, Mr. Barlow?'' he asked. He was agitated at the disturbance, but also concerned. While he and Barlow had never really gotten along all that well, he grudgingly respected Barlow as a man of honor. He knew that the mountain man would not have come here and been so rude to Prudence, if he didn't have a good reason.

''Get a lantern,'' Barlow ordered.

As his wife had been, Sterling was taken aback by Barlow's frightful look. He grabbed a lantern from the wall and hurried outside, following Barlow toward the string of mules. A light rain, typical of the area, hissed down on them.

Barlow stopped by the two mules carrying the bodies. ''Sarah and Little Will,'' he said, his voice cracking with grief.

"Dead?" Sterling mumbled stupidly, shocked.

Barlow nodded, not caring whether Sterling could see it or not. He knew the question had been asked out of surprise and did not really need an answer. "Injins," he said.

"Anna?" Sterling was afraid to ask but had to know.

"Gone. Took by the savages."

"Thank the Lord."

Barlow ignored the response.

"Who did it?"

"Don't know," Barlow growled, voice eerie and haunting as if rising from a grave. "But I'll sure as goddamn hell will find out, and when I catch those murderous pieces of shit, I will wreak vengeance on them like they never goddamn ever saw before."

Sterling was almost appalled by Barlow's raw vehemence, but on the other hand, he could understand it, and he could even forgive his blasphemies at the moment. "What can I do for you?" the missionary asked quietly.

"I want you to lay Sarah and Little Will to rest, Reverend," Barlow said in that hollow voice that spoke of death already felt and death to come.

"Of course, Mr. Barlow. Of course." He paused, grief etching his face now, too. "First thing in the morning. Now, come inside, have some warm food. In the morning we will do what is necessary for your loved ones. In the meantime, I'll have some of the converts prepare the bodies."

"No," Barlow snapped. "Just take 'em off the mules for now. Don't unwrap the blankets." His voice was colder than a Montana winter's night. "Those festering skunk humpers butchered 'em up real well." He pushed back the bile that rushed up his esophagus.

"I understand," Sterling said, shaken.

"Do 'em good, Reverend. They deserve a right proper sendoff to heaven."

"What about you?"

"I'm headin' to Fort Vancouver. I'll say farewell to Sarah and Little Will in my own way and in my own time.

But right now I gotta get out after those bastards."

"For revenge?" Sterling asked. "That's not the way, Will."

"Not for revenge. For Anna. Revenge can wait."

32

GRIEVING AND FULL of rage, Barlow rode through the night to Fort Vancouver. He kept the pace slow, considering it was night and the trail dangerous, but he rode steadily, Beelzebub never protesting. In addition to the mules carrying the bodies of Sarah and Little Will, he had left the two other animals packing the meat with Sterling. He had let Sterling talk him into delaying long enough to get some hot food and coffee in him, though.

"Without proper food in you, Mr. Barlow," Sterling had said, "you'll not be in top form to take on those savages, even if you do catch them."

That had gone a long way to convince Barlow. It also helped that Prudence had a place set out for him already and came out to talk him into staying for a short while to eat. So he had wolfed down three bowls of meat-filled stew, along with a plate of biscuits and three cups of hot, black coffee thick with sugar. While Barlow ate, Prudence made sure Buffalo and Beelzebub were well fed and watered.

"Thankee, Mrs. Sterling, for the meal and all the other care and considerations," Barlow said, as he slapped on his hat, grabbed his rifle, and headed outside.

Despite the slight delay in leaving the mission, Barlow

arrived at the Columbia River well before dawn, so he was forced to wait. He was too furious and sorrowful to really sleep, so he paced for a good long while. He finally sat, however, with his back against a tree trunk, his rifle across his lap, his legs crossed. He dozed fitfully, jerking awake every few minutes as dreams of Indian attacks tore through his mind. And all were basically the same—he was helpless to prevent or fend off the attack for whatever reason.

Finally he gave up trying to get any real rest. He paced some more, waiting. But finally he knew that light would be cracking the sky over the Cascades any minute. With that, he rode down to the small cabin that the main ferry-man called home, and he pounded on the door.

"Hold your horses, goddammit," someone shouted from inside. "Who the hell is it?"

"Will Barlow!"

Hamish Everett yanked open the door. "What in the hell do you want at this goddamn ungodly hour?" he demanded. He was pulling his suspenders up over his shoulders.

"I need to get across the river," Barlow snarled. "Now!"

"You'll wait till it's light out, dammit." Everett was not happy with having been woken early. Nor did he appreciate Barlow's tone.

"It'll be light by the time you drag your fat ass out of there and get to doin' your job, you worthless sack of shit."

"I'll not be spoken to in such a manner, dammit," Everett said as he began to shut the door.

Barlow slapped a palm on the door and shoved, putting his broad shoulder behind it. Everett staggered back a little ways as the door slammed open. Barlow stomped in, grabbed the chubby, slack-faced ferryman's throat in one hand and smashed his back up against the wall.

"You'll take me across the river right goddamn now, or I'll carve your fat ass into pieces so goddamn small even the coyotes won't be willin' to feed on 'em," Barlow said, his fury and sorrow chilling his voice.

"What the hell's got into you, Barlow?" Everett asked,

voice quavering nervously. He knew Barlow fairly well and had always liked the man, Barlow had never been pushy or arrogant, as many of the other men around here were. Barlow had always treated him well, never condescendingly. He realized something must be terribly wrong. At first he thought Barlow might be drunk, but that was obviously not the case.

"None of your goddamn business. Jist believe me when I say I got to get across that river, and I ain't got the time to parley about it with you."

"All right," Everett said, still nervous but not as much. Now that he had realized something must be very wrong with Barlow, he knew that if he did what he was told, things would be all right. "Can I get my shirt first?"

"Long's you be quick about it. You ain't outside in about one goddamn minute, I'm comin' in to git you, and this time I won't be so considerate in my actions."

"Yessir." Everett scurried away toward the back of the house while Barlow clomped outside. It was cold, and the eternal drizzle was present. In the bare beginnings of the dawn, mist could be seen thickening along the river and wrapping itself around branches of pine trees back away from the riverbank.

Everett rushed out, pulling on an old, work-stained, time-worn osnaberg shirt. He buttoned it as he half trotted toward the ferry. Barlow was right behind him, towing Beelzebub, while Buffalo strolled along beside him.

The trip was cold, extremely damp, and seemed to take hours, but it was finally over. As Barlow walked off the boat, he said, "Don't go nowhere. I expect to be back directly and will need to get back across."

"Yessir." Everett gulped. "But what if somebody . . . ?"

"Tell 'em they'll have to wait, or I'll make wolf bait out of 'em." Barlow mounted the mule and rode off toward the fort's gate, which was in the north wall, away from the river.

Inside, he stomped up the stairs of McLoughlin's impressive structure and went in, shoving past a startled junior clerk. Straight down the short hallway was the dining room where the officers of the Hudson's Bay Company took their meals. Breakfast was just beginning. Barlow didn't care. He stomped into the room and, trying to be at least modestly civil, removed his hat. The men seated at the table were dressed well, in frilled white shirts, swallowtail coats, and fine wool pants. Most of them looked disdainfully at Barlow, whose buckskin trousers and homespun cotton shirt were bloodstained and greasy. He hadn't shaved in a couple of days, and he was thoroughly disheveled.

"My apologies, Dr. McLoughlin, for interrupting your mornin' meal like this," he said quietly. "But I have a most urgent matter that I must discuss with you."

"Can it wait?" McLoughlin asked in the growl of his voice.

"I don't figure so."

McLoughlin shoved his chair back and rose. "Gentlemen, continue with your repast," he said. "Excuse me." He led the way into his small office area, right off the front foyer. There he could overlook the workings of the fort. He sat and indicated another chair for Barlow, who took it. "Now, Mr. Barlow, just what is so urgent and pressing?"

Though his stern visage and wild mane of white hair made him look angry all the time, McLoughlin was, Barlow had found, a decent man. He was not to be taken lightly, and he was not a man to put up with those who willfully stirred up trouble, to be sure. But he generally would help when and where he could.

Barlow told McLoughlin what happened, saying it straight out, in a monotone voice.

While Barlow spoke, a servant entered the room with coffee for each of them. Barlow was grateful for it and sipped some before continuing his saga.

McLoughlin's great, white head shook sadly when Barlow had finished. "I extend my sympathies to ye, Mr. Barlow," he said quietly, and sincerely. "But what would ye like me to do aboot it?"

Barlow was a bit shocked. He had expected McLoughlin to jump up and begin shouting orders for a party of men to be formed immediately and head out to look for Anna.

"Help me try'n get my child back," Barlow said angrily. "And, goddammit, mayhap punish the dirty savages what took her."

"I canna do that, Mr. Barlow." McLoughlin actually seemed melancholy about having to make such a rejection. "I have no men to send with ye on your quest."

"You got have hundreds of employees at your beck and call, McLoughlin," Barlow snapped.

"Aye. But all the trappers are gone, as are most of the hunters. Ye know that."

"But what about the . . . ?"

"Aye, there are a few hunters left here at the post, but they're untrustworthy, and I would nae inflict them on ye. The rest of the men employed here are unused to tracking and fighting Indians. They're tradesmen or simple laborers. E'en most of the hunters who work here have nae experience in such things." He shook his head again in regret. "'Tis a terrible thing that's happened, Mr. Barlow. I've nae heard of the Indians in this lands perpetrating such a despicable thing."

"You won't help even for the daughter of one of your own longtime employees?" Barlow asked. He simply could not believe that McLoughlin would be this hard-hearted. He had never seen him be that way with anyone before.

"My hands are tied, Mr. Barlow," McLoughlin answered flatly, with finality. "I'm sorry. Now, if you'll excuse me . . ."

"Just one more thing, Dr. McLoughlin," Barlow said, biting back the retort and the curses he wanted to fling at the fort factor. When McLoughlin sat back down, Barlow pulled out the arrow he had taken from the wall of his cabin. He had wrapped it in buckskin and stored it down the back of his shirt. He unwrapped it and handed the arrow to McLoughlin. "Do you know what tribe that's from?" he asked.

McLoughlin looked at it, but then shook his head. "I canna say. I dunna know much about such things." He paused, thinking. "But there's a half-breed Clackamas named Black Sky who does some hunting for the fort. Let me see if he's around.'' He called for one of his junior clerks, told him what he wanted, and sat back to wait, sipping the last of his coffee.

Within minutes, the clerk was back. ''Aye, sir, he's here. I understand he's at the blacksmith shop having some traps repaired.'' When McLoughlin nodded, the clerk spun and left.

McLoughlin handed the arrow back to Barlow. ''Go see Black Sky. He should know what tribe that's from.'' He rose. ''I truly am sorry, Mr. Barlow, that I canna be of more help to ye in this matter. But I will say this to ye, I hope ye run those scoundrels to ground and make them pay for their infamies. Aye, and I hope ye find your wee daughter alive and well.''

Barlow nodded. He was not appeased at all, so not given to kindly accepting such platitudes. On the other hand, he didn't have the time nor inclination to argue about it. He had asked for help, which in a way was terribly difficult for him. He was rejected. Asking again would be too much like begging, especially since he knew McLoughlin well enough to know that once the man had made up his mind, there would be no changing it.

McLoughlin turned and picked up a pen, dipped it in ink, and scratched out some words on paper, which he then blotted and gave to Barlow. ''If ye need supplies or anything of that nature, give that to Mr. MacDougal at the trade room. If I canna help ye with men, then, by God, I can help ye with such necessities.''

Barlow nodded again. ''Thankee, Dr. McLoughlin,'' he said without much emotion. He rose and rolled the arrow back up in the buckskin. Then he left. He hurried to the blacksmith's shop, in one corner of the fort. Seeing an Indian man dressed like a white hunter, he went up to him and asked bluntly, ''Are you Black Sky?''

The Indian nodded. ''Who're you?''

''Name's Will Barlow.''

Black Sky shrugged. ''Don't mean shit to me.'' He turned away.

Barlow grabbed him and jerked him roughly around to

face him again. "I ain't in no goddamn humor for foolin' with you, boy. I got a question. You give me an answer and I'll not bother you no more."

"I got an answer for you, boy," Black Sky snapped. "No. Whatever the hell you want from me, it's no."

Enraged, Barlow suddenly slammed a meaty fist into the Indian's stomach, knocking the breath out of him and doubling him over. Letting Black Sky stay there trying to catch his breath. Barlow pulled out the arrow and unwrapped it. Then he grabbed the Indian by the hair and jerked him upright. He shoved the arrow in front of Black Sky's face. "What tribe did this come from, boy?" he asked harshly.

The Indian was almost breathing properly now. He blinked several times, and then reached up and took the arrow, studying it. He grunted quietly a few times as he turned it in his hands. "Need more light," he said and stepped outside. Barlow followed him. At that point, it took him only a few seconds before he held the shaft out toward Barlow. "Umpqua," he pronounced.

"Umpqua?" Barlow muttered, shaking his head as he took the arrow and began to rewrap it. "You sure?"

"I don't like bein' called a liar," Black Sky responded.

"Right now, boy, I don't give a duck's pecker what you like or don't like. Are you sure this is from the Umpquas?"

Outside, where it was much lighter despite the overcast, Black Sky got his first good look at Barlow. He did not like what he saw in the man's hard eyes. There was death in those two glittering orbs. His death if he didn't answer the man's questions. He nodded. "I'm sure." He waited for Barlow to say something, but when nothing came, he asked cautiously, "Where'd you find that?"

"Wall of my cabin. Down on Chehalem Creek."

"They attacked?"

Barlow nodded.

"Damn, that's unusual."

"Why?" Barlow asked, looking sharply at Black Sky.

"For one thing, even the Umpquas don't do much raidin' anymore. Not enough of 'em left to go makin' war on others too often. For another, they're a far piece from home.

Their land's a hundred miles, maybe a little more, down the coast.''

Could it be that they were getting back for the failed raid they had made on him and Watters three or four years ago? Barlow wondered. He couldn't see why they would. They had set an ambush that was turned back at the loss of several of their warriors, but it was unlike the tribes out here— at least the ones he knew a little about—that they would hold a grudge like that. But he could think of no other reason why they would have attacked his cabin—and no one else's. It was just too unlikely that the Umpquas would attack him twice, both times miles from their homeland.

Not that it mattered to Barlow now. But Black Sky had given him a direction to go and put a name to the miscreants. ''Thankee for the information, Black Sky,'' he said, suddenly wanting—needing—to be on the move. ''C'mon, Buffler.'' He trotted to the trade room and gave MacDougal the note from McLoughlin. Hastily he ordered supplies and had them loaded on a couple of mules he also got from MacDougal. He rode over to the ferry. Everett was there, being harassed by several men who wanted to go across the river. Everett looked mighty relieved to see him.

As the ferry moved slowly across the water, Barlow let his rage build, now that he had someone to focus it on. As soon as the boat was tied on the south bank, Barlow trotted off with Buffalo—all two-hundred-fifty pounds of him— trotting beside.

33

BARLOW HEADED SOUTH and a little east. He rode steadily, keeping a good but not harmful pace. Not wanting to deal with the anguish of going through the burial of his wife and infant son, he skirted Sterling's mission and pushed on. He also avoided his homestead. He had no reason to stop there.

So he swung around it by a mile or so and then worked back toward where he thought he might cut the trail of the Umpquas as they headed back to their homeland. Only a couple of miles beyond, he called it quits for the night.

In the morning, Barlow pressed on after a hurried breakfast of bacon and coffee. He traveled mostly by instinct. He had never been the best tracker anyway, and with all the rain in the area so often, there would likely be no tracks to follow anyway. At least not ones he would be able to find. Since he did not really know where to find the Umpquas, he started to travel in a long series of arcs, from the Willamette almost to the coast and then back east to the Willamette, always moving further southward.

Barlow pushed as hard as he could, rising before dawn and getting on the trail, such as it was, as light was just breaking. He would not stop until dark was almost com-

plete, trying to arrange it so there was just enough time—
and thus light—to unload and tend to the mules and gather
some firewood. He traveled faster than he normally would,
but kept the pace slow enough to not harm the animals.
When he tracked the demons down, he did not want to fail
in getting Anna back or making the Umpquas pay for their
evil acts because his animals were too worn to keep up the
chase.

The days dragged on one after the other, passing a week,
then edging up on two weeks. He had seen nothing of the
Umpquas he sought, or any other Indians. He began to
wonder if he was wasting his time or if perhaps he had
been sent in the wrong direction by Black Sky. But his rage
and anguish pushed him on, kept him strong of purpose.

One day almost two weeks after the horrible event, Barlow came across a Kalapuya village. He had seen no other
villages during his travels, so he now decided he'd stop and
see if he could pick up any information.

The Kalapuyas welcomed him politely but warily. When
they learned he had nothing to trade and no presents for
them, they became taciturn. Sweating from the pressure and
the annoyance of their silence, Barlow struggled to get them
to understand his desperation. Using a combination of English, sign language, and the version of pidgin English
known as Chinook, he tried to explain to the Kalapuyas
what had happened, what he was trying to do and who he
was looking for.

The Indians were in no mood to be giving out information to a white man, even one they had become somewhat
friendly with over the past several years. Not when he had
nothing to offer in return, not even some poor trade goods.
Barlow suspected there was more to their refusal to talk
than they were indicating. Aggravated, he finally rode out
of the village and made himself a little camp a half-mile or
so away from them.

Barlow didn't know at first what woke him that night,
so he lay there quietly. Buffalo, lying beside him, occasionally offered a faint growl, so Barlow knew someone
was out there. After some minutes, Barlow slid out of his

warm otter sleeping robe and into the chill, misty night. It reminded him of that night so long ago when the small Crow war party tried to steal his horse herd. He moved a bit away from his robe and with Buffalo at his side, squatted there, waiting.

Suddenly a shadow moved swiftly toward the sleeping robe. Barlow held a hand over Buffalo's short, stubby snout for a second, letting the dog know he should be quiet. The shadow stopped at Barlow's "bed," and resolved into the form of a man. In the dim glow of the fire's embers, Barlow saw that it was a Kalapuya. Barlow raised his rifle. The Indian reached out, and Barlow almost squeezed the trigger. Then he realized that the Kalapuya had no weapon in hand, but was, apparently, just going to wake him.

The Indian froze when he realized there was no one in the sleeping robe. He looked around nervously.

"What do you want, boy?" Barlow called out.

"Talk to you."

"Why?"

"Have things to tell."

"Build up the fire," Barlow said, buying time. "And put coffee on to heat."

The Kalapuya did what he was told and then sat cross-legged by the fire. Barlow had watched, and as the flames crept higher, he got a good look at the Indian. It was then that he decided that the Kalapuya was likely no danger to him. He rose and stepped out of the trees and squatted at the fire across from the Indian. Buffalo lay down at Barlow's side, but kept his eyes on the visitor.

"You got a name, boy?" Barlow asked.

"Two Otters."

"Pour yourself some coffee, Two Otters, and then tell me what's on your mind."

Two Otters took his time to fill a tin mug with hot, thick coffee, had a sip, then said in passable English, "The Upper Umpquas have several villages southeast of here. Three days' travel, maybe."

"You know which one I'm lookin' for?" Barlow asked tightly.

Two Otters shook his head. "But I think the ones you want are the Lower Umpquas. They're called Kuitsh. They're much more warlike than the Upper Umpquas."

"Where are those devils?"

"Couple days' ride south of the Umpqua River. About same from Fort Umpqua."

"Fort Umpqua?" Barlow asked, surprised.

"Trade post put up by the Hudson's Bay Company many winters ago."

Barlow nodded. He sat there for a while, sipping coffee and thinking. Then he asked, "Why're you tellin' me this when the rest of your people wouldn't?"

"Kuitsh attacked our village several moons ago. Again less than a moon ago."

Barlow nodded again. He figured the second raid must have been during the Umpquas—Kuitshes—journey north on the way to attacking his cabin. "Why wouldn't the others talk?"

"Afraid. They think the Kuitshes come back again if they hear we talked."

"Makes sense, I reckon," Barlow said flatly. He was of the opinion that the Kalapuya should be prepared to fight back harder if the Kuitshes returned.

He spent another hour talking with Two Otters, milking him for information about where the Kuitshes called home, what they looked like and anything else he thought might help him, including information about other tribes he might encounter.

The next morning, Barlow pulled out, moving almost straight south for the time being. Two days later, he headed west, having estimated that Fort Umpqua was only a few miles ahead, and he had no desire to encounter anyone from the fort. As he entered the Umpqua River to cross it, two Indians burst out of the brush, charging him, one from each side.

He had no time to get his rifle up and fire before one of the Indians leaped in full run and crashed into him, both tumbling off Beelzebub to the water. Barlow managed to get both hands on the Indian's right wrist, preventing him from using the knife he held in that hand. He squeezed as hard as he could, pressing his thumbs into the warrior's skin, cutting off the circulation and digging for nerves. Finally the Indian dropped the knife. With relief, Barlow smashed the warrior in the side of the face with a fist, knocking him into the water on his right side.

Barlow scrambled up, yanking out his tomahawk as he did. As the warrior tried to rise, Barlow hacked him on the side of the neck with the tomahawk. A fount of blood shot out of the Indian's severed carotid, and the warrior fell.

Barlow spun, looking for the other warrior. But Buffalo had intercepted him and tore out the warrior's throat. The Newfoundland was still standing nearby, half growling, looking as if he were making sure the Indian would not get up again.

"Good boy," Barlow said, petting Buffalo. He was sore, but grateful that he had fallen in the water, which had made his landing a little easier than it would have been on dirt or rocks. Otherwise, he was uninjured. He checked on the two warriors, making sure they were dead. He decided they were Umpquas, based on the way they were dressed. But Upper Umpquas.

Uneasily, he moved off, crossing the river, and then turning southwest, wondering when the next attack would come. He didn't have long to wait. Five Upper Umpquas charged into his camp the next morning. His only warning was Buffalo's startled growl.

Barlow came up out of his sleeping robe with rifle in hand. He fired, not sure if he hit anyone. He ducked out of the way of a war club, got his shoulder into the warrior's midsection, and threw him up and over his shoulder as he straightened. The Indian's back snapped when he landed on a rock.

Another warrior slammed Barlow to the ground and came close to braining him with a war club made of an old rifle stock with several iron knife blades jutting out of it. Barlow smashed him in the throat with a fist. The warrior dropped his war club and clasped both hands to his shattered larynx, gargling in pain.

Barlow rose, rage boiling through him. He heard Buffalo yelp, and he jerked around to see the other three warriors surrounding Buffalo, who was bleeding from a wound. The Newfoundland was still snarling and barking, willing to take on the world, but he would have had a hard time with three war-club–wielding warriors.

With fury, Barlow bellowed and stormed ahead, crashing into two of the warriors before they could attack the dog. Buffalo spun and lunged at the third Umpqua. Barlow fought like a wild man and soon had dispatched the two warriors, though not before being hit once on the shoulder with a war club and being stabbed twice, in the leg and in one arm.

Left on his own, facing only one enemy, Buffalo took care of the third Umpqua without much trouble.

Wheezing a little, Barlow hurried to the dog and patted his head quickly, praising him. Then he checked the dog's wound. He breathed a sigh of relief when he saw that it was just a superficial knife wound. "You'll be fine in no time, Buffler," he said almost happily.

He got coffee going and some meat cooking before he checked his own wounds. The two stab wounds were minor. His shoulder hurt like hell but would not slow him too much, as there were no broken bones. But he was enraged at the attacks, and though these Umpquas were probably not responsible for the assault on his cabin, he began to hate all Umpquas and anyone who would have anything to do with them.

After a quick meal, a still furious Barlow loaded up the mules with his dwindling supplies, saddled Beelzebub, and rode out. Near midday, he spotted an Umpqua village in the distance. Working his way through the trees, he got to within a hundred yards or so of the place. He watched over the rickety wood and thatch houses for a bit, his anger rebuilding. Then he brought his rifle up. Picking a suitable target, he fired, and dropped a warrior, causing panic in the village.

Barlow patiently waited, until the people in the village began appearing again. With deadly rage, he shot down another warrior and smiled grimly as the tribe panicked again. In moments the village looked deserted, as everyone had scurried into the houses.

He pondered waiting for another target, but then decided not to press his luck. Besides, he was getting bored with just sitting here waiting. He rode off then. But in the next week and a half, as he searched for Kuitsh villages, he played his deadly little game several more times. None of it slaked his thirst for revenge, however, and he knew that it would not help him find little Anna. Of course, if he terrified the Indians throughout the area enough, that might help him rescue his daughter.

Discouragement did begin to grow inside him, however, as he pressed on and on, with no luck in finding the warriors who had perpetrated the atrocities against his family. But he was not about to give up. Not now, not ever.

Nearly a month after it happened, he knew he was in Kuitsh land, and he became much more cautious in traveling. The extra wariness could not overcome strong odds against him, however, when he was attacked by eight warriors who were not only mounted, but rode almost as well as the Plains Indians he had encountered.

Barlow raced for the safety of the trees and made it, barely. He slid off his mule and let the animals go, swatting Beelzebub on the rump. The animal trotted off a ways, with the two pack mules following. Barlow swung around and fired his rifle, taking down one of the attacking Indians.

As he reloaded, he kept an eye on the warriors. They were not Umpquas nor Kuitsh. He thought for a moment that they might be Cayuses, but that didn't seem right either. He fired again, wounding an Indian, and began to reload once more. He decided these warriors were Klickitats. He had heard a fair amount about them. Most of them were north of the Columbia River, but some had moved down here to the Umpqua Valley, where they raised Cain among other Indians and whites alike.

The Klickitats had split, swerving toward each side of

Barlow. By the time he was ready to fire again, he could
not find a decent target. He cursed considerably, worried
now that the Klickitats were in the woods, too.

"Ah, shit," he roared when he heard Beelzebub's wild
braying. "C'mon, Buffler." He charged off through the
rain-wet forest, but it was too late. He heard hooves slapping on damp leaves and pine needles. He reached a small
clearing just in time to see the Klickitats, with his animals,
ride into the trees across the glade.

"Goddamn son of a bitch bastard, dammit!" Barlow bellowed. He stood there, shaking with anger. He felt hollow
inside. He had failed, and there was nothing he could do
about it. He was now afoot, with no supplies, and miles
from any settlement. The nearest place was Fort Umpqua,
and he'd as soon be dead as go there. He could not face
those Hudson's Bay Company men in that remote outpost,
especially if he appeared to be begging for help.

Making matters worse, winter was rapidly approaching.
Though winter here was much milder than it was in the
Rocky Mountains, it would be bad enough for a man with
few resources. Sighing with self-loathing, he turned and
began walking north, heading toward the Willamette
Valley, hoping he could make it before winter hit him. He
had no idea of what he would do there; only that he had
to get there. Then he would decide what to do.

Marching at a good pace, and moving in as straight a
line as he could, he made it with no real trouble, the journey
taking him just over three weeks. As he neared his homestead, however, he realized that he could not go there.
Could never even look at the place again, let alone live
there. So he skirted it, realizing that it had been a mistake
to come back here. There was nothing for him now here.

He pressed on, reaching Sterling's mission. In a voice
that allowed no arguments and no questions, he got a horse,
a pack animal, and some supplies from the missionary and
then he headed east into the Cascade Mountains. In a couple of weeks, he had found a place to winter up. There he
sat, with only Buffalo for company, and he let his self-
loathing eat at him.

With the arrival of spring, he headed down out of the mountains and went to Fort Vancouver. There he traded in his furs, getting hardly anything for them from the unsympathetic Peter MacDougal. From there, he went to what passed for a saloon at the fort, figuring that a good dose of whiskey—something he hadn't had in a long time—might let him know what he should do with himself.

Inside he was invited to sit by Sam Thorne, an HBC man he knew fairly well. As he was sipping at his sixth whiskey, Thorne asked, "You ever find the devils who killed off your family?"

"No," Barlow spat out, bile rising.

Thorne could not see the pain or the self-hatred that boiled inside Barlow. "Well, it's about time you found yourself another half breed or even a squaw to bring to your robes," he said with a grin. "You been without a woman too long, and it don't do a man well to brood over what's lost, especially a half—"

Without thought or hesitation, Barlow clubbed the man down, and seconds later, found himself fighting a passel of Hudson's Bay men. They seemed to come out of nowhere, and there seemed to be a never-ending supply of them. But Barlow was not himself. He was a raging, wounded buffalo bull being set upon by a pack of wolves, and he was not about to go down lightly. He fought with a ferocity and strength that stunned the other men. And with Buffalo's fanged, clawed help, he beat back the onslaught of men, until he was the only one standing.

Suddenly John McLoughlin and two clerks appeared before him. "What's this all aboot, Mr. Barlow?" McLoughlin asked, his voice even rougher than usual.

"Couple of these skunk humpers made light of my late Sarah and Little Will," Barlow snarled. He downed a large mug of whiskey in one gulp.

"What will ye do now?" McLoughlin demanded. He did not want this wild man spending any more time in the fort than necessary.

And it came to Barlow in just that second. He knew now what he would do. It was so simple—and so obvious.

"Well, Dr. McLoughlin," he said evenly, "I aim to find my daughter, Anna, if it's the last goddamn thing I ever do." Once he did that, he knew he would be able to settle down again.

McLoughlin nodded. "I canna' think of a better quest for ye," he said, not showing the relief he felt that Barlow would not be a pest around the fort.

Barlow shrugged. He walked out of the building and mounted the horse he had gotten from Sterling. With his back straight, he called to Buffalo as he rode out of the fort, looking for his destiny.

JAKE LOGAN
TODAY'S HOTTEST ACTION WESTERN!

LONGARM

Explore the exciting Old West with one of the men who made it wild!